SUMMER'S SHADOW

The Hunters Trilogy: Book 2

SARA J. BERNHARDT

Lavish Publishing LLC

First Edition

The Hunters Trilogy - Book 2

All Rights Reserved

Published in the United States by Lavish Publishing, LLC, Midland, TX

Paperback edition

ISBN:9781944985516

Cover Design by: WYCKED INK

Cover Images: ADOBE STOCK

www.LavishPublishing.com

Contents

For my Adam

Prologue

IT STARTED the night my parents were murdered. Before that, everything was normal, and even more than normal, it was good. My mother was the kindest, warmest woman anyone was sure to meet. Unfortunately, she suffered some minor lunacy. Not to say she was completely mad, but she often had completely irrational ideas seeded in her head. Nobody was sure where they came from. For example, she was convinced I was photosensitive, so much so that the sunlight would destroy me, burn me up like a fledging vampire.

My father, on the other hand, was a businessman—a banker. He was intelligent and hardworking. Even through my mother's "episodes," as he called them, he loved her completely. He stood by her through everything. Her ravings sometimes drove him to such annoyance it would border rage, but he never struck her, never shouted at her, never even so much as spoke to her harshly.

As for me, I often wondered if I was really their son. After all, I clearly didn't inherit my looks from either my mother or my father nor was I crazy or have any aspirations of being a businessman of any kind. I wasn't sure what I wanted to be, but I did know it involved something beautiful, something artistic. My father always told me I was too smart for my own good and that business was where I belonged. Perhaps he was right. "Genius" I wouldn't say was the right word to describe me, but when he used it, it sounded right. For years I dealt with my mother's beliefs of my photosensitivity and even began to believe her. She never let me outside during the daylight, and when my father argued over it, she simply started sobbing uncontrollably, saying that he was trying to kill her baby. It would usually take him hours to soothe her when she got like that.

1

Caring for my mother was my job growing up, as my father worked all the time. Outside of school, it was all I ever did. Of course, I was homeschooled during the day—private tutors so I could stay indoors to appease my mother. I never complained about his work nor did my mother. He made a lot of money to take care of us and provide for us. I guess in a way, I was proud of him. I hoped someday to make him proud of me, no matter what I chose to do or to be.

His providing for us lasted only so long. His business partner, Matthias Castlebar, turned out to be a crook. He destroyed my father almost effortlessly by simply accusing him of embezzlement. I was young, so at the time, I didn't understand exactly what was happening, but I *did* know my father was an honest man and that Castlebar's accusations were completely false. My father lost everything, and the money would only last us so long. It was then that I took up my father's place as provider. We needed money, so I went out one evening to find a job. Is it possible that one event can forever change the course of destiny? Or is it all preordained in some elaborate design of the world? Whatever the answer, I would soon find myself at the crossroads of such an event. This one small change in my daily routine would shape everything I was…and *everything* I was to become.

Chapter One

IT WASN'T QUITE dark yet, just dim enough for my mother to let me out. I walked into the café, early for my shift. My manager, Richard, seemed to be in a good mood. He was wiping down the counters and whistling.

"You're early," he said.

I nodded. "What do you need?"

"Ah, just refill the coffee. That's usually all folks come in for during the night."

I did as he instructed with my mind set elsewhere—set at home with my crazy, beautiful mother and my now unemployed father. Richard was right; only about three people had come in, and all of them ordered coffee.

Time passed quickly, and by the time I was finished wiping down the counters again, it was already midnight. There was still a man there, sipping his coffee. He was older, white hair and white stubble of a forming beard. There was something about him that seemed very sad. He was all by himself, staring into his coffee before he'd take another sip. I was about to tell him we were closing, but he beat me to it.

"I see you're getting ready to close up," he said. "I'm sorry to keep you. I needed a place to seclude myself for the night. I've found my caffeine limit." He broke into a dry, sputtered laugh. "Redline," he continued. "Walter Redline. You are?"

I didn't respond. I tried to think of something—anything but my own name. "Clem."

"Clem?"

I nodded.

"Nice to meet you, Clem."

Something about him intrigued me deeply, and for some reason, my curiosity got the better of me. Moments later, I found myself sitting beside him, staring into his eyes as he spoke.

"I recently lost someone who meant everything to me."

I stared at him for a moment. "How?"

He smiled synthetically. "I'm a researcher. I found something that I feel I need to protect him from. My grandson."

"Something...bad?"

He nodded. "Something dangerous."

I pulled my eyebrows together.

"Oh, don't be worried," he sputtered in laughter again. "It's nothing *you* need to worry about."

We talked about a number of different subjects and somehow came to the topic of literature; he seemed to absolutely love it.

"Frankenstein," he said. "One of my favorites. Inspired me, you know."

"Inspired you how?" I asked.

"Well...I'm a scientist, a professor."

"Professor."

"Yes. There is something about that book that brought me to believe in the miracle that was Victor Frankenstein's discoveries."

"What you're saying is that you believe in creating a monster from lifeless matter?"

He chuckled huskily. "Ever read the book, Clem?"

I shook my head. "Can't say that I have."

"That's what I thought."

"I know the story."

"Yes, but the creation you speak of was very different than what modern culture assumes."

"Is it?"

He raised his eyebrows. "Victor was simply a genius. A genius who unlocked the secrets of nature and set into motion a long and tragic chain of events that show that maybe *he* was the true villain."

I was instantly mesmerized by Mr. Redline's passion. "So, he wasn't mad?"

"Oh no!" he answered. "He was simply brilliant."

"Mr. Redline—"

"Walter. Please...Walter."

"Walter. Are you teaching any classes at this time?"

He shook his head. "I am not. I'm retired, but I would never turn down a young person willing to learn."

We talked for hours, and Walter seemed completely interested in everything I had to say. He listened to me the way I dreamed of being listened to. He understood how I wanted to do amazing things in life and how I wanted to be someone who could change the world.

"If you wouldn't mind," he started, "I would love nothing more than a young man with your mind to help me with my research."

"My…mind?"

He smiled. "Someone as brilliant as you are, Clem. If anyone can solve this mystery, it is you."

"What…mystery, Mr.—Walter?"

"The mystery of immortality. If we can somehow discover how life becomes death, we can discover how to stop it…can't we?"

Not knowing what to say, I stayed silent. I was so fascinated and engrossed I couldn't turn away. Immortality! Incredible.

"Perhaps we could cure my mother," I said.

"If we can, I would trust no one more than you."

"So you will teach me?"

He shook my hand. "I would love to."

Walter met me at the café the next night, and we talked. We discussed what he would teach me and how. He handed me a book.

"Read this," he said.

I looked at the cover and almost laughed. "Are you…serious?"

"Of course I'm serious. Just trust me, and read the book, please."

I looked at him strangely and glanced at the book—Mary Shelley's Frankenstein.

"It's a story, Walter."

He laughed. "So is your life. So read the book so you someday can have a story that people want to read about."

I laughed and nodded. "Okay. I understand."

I studied for months with Walter. I studied forensics and anatomy. I studied every subject about the human body, about sickness and death. I could feel something in my blood and my bones, telling me I was close, that something miraculous was approaching, just about to kindle that light in my brain. Obsession set in, making it nearly impossible to sleep or eat. At work, I was like a zombie, only waiting to meet Walter again.

"You're gifted," he had told me.

An incredible friendship had developed between Walter and me. He believed in me and supported me more than anyone in my life ever had before. I knew he would believe me about that approaching discovery just around the corner. I had all of my notes jotted down in a small red notebook—every thought, every feeling, and every insignificant idea that made a significant difference in the direction my studies were leading me. I was so close. Nobel Prize was on the tip of my tongue.

Chapter Two

THE SOBS of my mother wouldn't stop. For hours, my father tried asking her what was wrong, but all she did was hide her face and continue to ignore him.

"What is it?" I asked. "Why are you crying?"

She stood up from the chair and pulled me into an uncomfortably tight hug, weeping in my ear. "I love you, Clem."

"All right, all right. I love you too, so why are you crying?"

"Because you're going to leave me!" she yelled. "Because you aren't a baby anymore."

I smiled. "I'm not leaving you, Mom. I'm going to stay here for as long as you need me."

"I need you forever."

"Then I will stay here forever. Okay?"

She frowned. "Don't you have to leave tonight?"

"Yes," I said. "To go to work, Mom, but I'll be back, okay?"

My father sat beside her and continued to soothe her while I left for work. Dealing with my mother's episode had made me late again. I decided I should cut through the alleyway, save me about ten minutes. On my way, I was aware of every movement in the darkness of the alley. It was strange that I felt nervous. I knew something wasn't right. I had never been afraid of the dark. I grew up in the dark, lived in the nighttime, but this time…something was not in order; something was misplaced. I could feel so much more since my studies with Walter. I had become in tune with everything around me. Unlocking the secrets of nature had put something in my mind that was able to tell me when danger was near. I was frightened. For the first time in my life, I was *truly* frightened. That's when I saw him—a man about six feet tall with an unkempt, shaggy beard, his hair messy and tousled. The dark stranger stared at me solidly, unmoving. His face was rock hard, and he walked toward me, staring at me. My instincts told me to run, to take off in the other direction, but my legs wouldn't move. My mind was screaming at me to unhinge my limbs and get away, but I still stayed completely still—paralyzed. I tried continuously to unfreeze until I was able to take a few steps back, but at that point, the stranger was already only inches from my face. He shoved me against the wall and held a knife to my throat. My teeth were chattering, and the sweat broke out in beads down my face. I offered him anything I could think of.

"Take my wallet," I said. "I don't have much money, but I swear that's all I have."

He didn't answer; in fact, he only pressed the blade harder against my skin and smiled at me. He turned me over harshly, and the last thing I saw was a brick wall against my face.

When I awoke, I felt this sense of heat. It was like nothing I had ever felt before. It was as if the sun had engulfed the Earth and I was being suffocated by it. It was so intense that it was painful. I couldn't open my eyes; it was like they were glued shut. I kept trying for minutes at a time with no luck. Sweat dripped down my face. That's when I felt that I wasn't alone. I could feel the presence of another. I tried to open my eyes again but still couldn't.

"Are you all right?" I heard. It was the voice of a woman.

Finally, my eyes opened, and I was instantly horror stricken by the sight—of the sun. I covered my head with my arms and started screaming, "The sun! Good Lord, get me out of the sun!" I continued to cry out and wail "the sun, the sun" over and over again.

"My God," I heard the voice say. "You're ill."

I began sobbing into my hands, and again, I lost consciousness.

When I came to, the first thing my eyes met was a beautiful face, the face of a woman. She had very small features and clear, fair skin. Her eyes were large and round and shone amber in the light. Her hair was dark and rested in waves past her shoulders. She was stunning.

"Where am I?" I asked. "And why am I here?"

"You were screaming," she said. "You were screaming at me to get you out of the sun."

I was terrified then of how I must look. I knew from what my mother had told me that my skin was black and shriveled, and I must have been covered in blisters. Why, then, didn't I feel pain?

"My God," she said. "What happened to you?"

She would surely turn away in fear, now wouldn't she? She would run from me in disgust. She touched my neck, and I felt a sting in my skin.

"What?"

"You're cut. You're cut badly. What happened?"

I looked down at my hands and body, realizing I wasn't burned at all. What luck.

"I...don't know what happened," I said. "I was mugged last night. I don't even remember how I got away."

"I'm surprised you're alive. You're lucky your throat isn't slit."

I felt the cut where the mugger's knife had begun to rush through me before I lost consciousness. That's when I remembered Professor Redline and how I had to get home to him. My discovery was mere months away, and I had to get home to finish working.

"I have to go!" I yelled out.

"You're sick," she said.

"No," I tried to shout. My voice was throttled. "You don't understand. That doesn't matter. Sickness will mean nothing. That is why I have to get home."

"Listen to me, please," she pleaded. "You have a fever, an intense fever. You need to get to a doctor."

"No!" I insisted. "I have to get to Professor Redline. I have to discover it!"

"Discover what?"

"The secret to immortality. I'm so close."

I tried again to lift myself but kept falling back down. That light I was waiting for was finally kindled, and now along with that light were other lights —other remarkable thoughts and ideas I was finally understanding. I was sick, and the things I was saying must have sounded like the ravings of a madman.

"Please stay here," she begged. "If you won't let me take you to a doctor, at least let me take care of you."

I couldn't answer her.

"My name is Vivian Black."

"Clement Thortan." My voice was faint, and I wasn't interested in saying anything.

She took me to her home and laid me gently on a bed with a wrought iron frame. I couldn't leave even though I urgently needed to. I was too sick and weak. Vivian was kind; she patched the wound on my neck and insisted on caring for me. It rained that night, and I took pleasure in the feeling of the fire she had lit in the hearth across from the bed. I reached into my pocket and pulled out the tiny red notebook I had used to write down my notes. All of the recordings in the months I had studied with Walter were written down in perfect clarity. I thought I was wrong in my beliefs, that something in the patterns I was finding had been miscalculated. None of my notes made any sense. None of the recordings or sketches meant anything to me. I read through them over and over until I began to feel so enraged that I squeezed the notepad in the palm of my hand until it started to hurt. I cried out in rage and threw the notebook into the fire. I started crying uncontrollably into my hands. Vivian came in shortly after.

"Why are you crying?'"

I tried to say a million things. "The notes," I started, "they… I…"

She only stared at me with a puzzled look on her face. I sighed and hid my face in my hands. "You wouldn't believe me." I looked up into her eyes. "You wouldn't believe me if I told you."

"You're still sick," she said softly. "Just rest."

"I need to get home. I need to tell Walter of my discovery. If I don't, I am going to die."

"Who is this Walter you rave about? You call his name in your sleep, and you talk about…well…about death."

"You wouldn't believe me," I said. "I wish I could explain everything to you. I do."

"Just rest."

"I'm not crazy. Really I am not."

"Oh, Clem, I do not think you're crazy."

"You do. You do think I'm insane."

She smiled. "I don't think that. But you *are* sick, and the things you are thinking, I believe are because of that."

"These things I have been saying about scientific discovery and the things I had said about reversing the curse of mortality, I know it all must sound like meaningless raving, but it is all quite true."

She smiled and left the room.

"I'm not crazy!" I screamed.

Before I slept that night, Vivian prepared a bath for me. She helped me out of bed and almost carried me to the bathroom. She shut the door but insisted on staying close by in case I needed something. It made me uncomfortable that I was so helpless. I must have looked so pathetic to her. It took me a long time to realize why it even mattered to me. Why did I care so much that I wasn't charming and strong to her? I had never felt anything for a woman before, but with her, it was different. There was something about her that aroused a strange curiosity in me. Something made me feel a strong, maddening desire for her. I wanted her more than I had ever wanted anything before. I knew it couldn't happen that way even though I wanted it to desperately.

This woman was as kindhearted as she was beautiful. She was warm and tender, taking care of me almost like a lover. She washed my clothes for me and set some different clothes outside the door. She mentioned that her brother was close to my size.

"He left a few things here last time he came to visit. You could probably fit comfortably."

I smiled, but there was only one thing I was able to say. "You don't need to do this."

"I know."

The next morning, it was the sun that awoke me. The curtains were open, and sun was shining into the room. With a groan and all the strength I could muster, I rolled myself out of the bed. Hitting the floor with a thud, I groaned again and crawled toward the window to open it. I felt no pain. There was no burning, no blistering flesh. What Redline had said about my mother being 'just a crazy old woman' replayed in my head. The professor was right; she was just a crazy old woman after all.

The sun was beautiful. It was as if the Earth was engulfed in a ball of radiant light and warmth, like the universe was wrapped in this beauty that had never been known before now. I was overwhelmed with joy. All my life, I had been deprived of something so simple yet so amazing as the ordinary, everyday light of the sun. It must have been a miracle!

I was on my knees now, yelling and screaming. "Oh!" I cried out. "Oh, it's a miracle! Miracle!"

Vivian came in as I expected.

"Clem?"

"Look!" I screamed. "Vivian, look. It's the sun, the sun, my darling!"

"Clement, you're sick. Go back to bed."

"No, look!" I began clapping my hands and screaming nonsensical things to her. I was yelling out things like that I was a genius and had created a miracle. I was laughing uncontrollably, which could have easily led to a perfect fit of hysteria. I was mad with joy but, undeniably, I was mad.

I yelled for Walter, telling him that I had discovered the secret. I believed I had discovered everything. The genius of Victor's was now mine as well. I didn't understand then how delirious I was. I didn't realize that these secrets consisted of intricate patterns, and all of my months of studying and all of my recordings were ashes in Vivian's fireplace. How could I have been such a fool?

I felt ridiculous around her, trying to tell her things, and all she said was, "Rest, Clem."

She cared for me still, even when my raving would wake her in the middle of the night. I remember wanting to get home. Some nights, I would even awake screaming, begging her to tell me who she was and why she had kidnapped me. It would take her hours to control my weeping and silence me back to sleep. She never raised her voice at me, but sometimes, she would cry. I never knew why she cried.

It was early morning one day when she came in to bring me breakfast.

"I need to get home," I told her. "I need to get to Walter."

"Clem, I am fond of you. I promise you that. But you need to stay here if only for a while longer."

"No," I argued. "If I do not get home, I am going to die."

Vivian's cheeks flushed as slow, silent tears rolled down to her chin. She turned away, trying to hide it from me. She looked beautiful even when she was sad. My caretaker had her brown hair piled upon her head, and her long legs were hidden beneath a black nightgown, which I despised with every fiber of my being. I loathed that horrific fabric covering her beauty. She sat beside me on the bed.

"Why do you cry?" I asked her. "You cry often even when I can see it."

"I'm sorry," she whispered, her voice cracking with each word.

"No." I touched her face and gave her a puzzled look. "No...I'm sorry. I don't understand."

She put her hand over mine still touching her cheek and stroked my fingers.

"It's not that I'm sad," she said. "I am only scared for you."

I removed my hand from her soft skin and leaned back on my pillow. I sighed heavily and covered my face with my hands.

"Please don't be angry with me," she retorted. "Please. It isn't that I don't believe you. I have told you this before."

"You believe I am crazy."

"I believe you are sick."

"Vivian..." It was the first time I had said her name. I wasn't sure what I was going to say as *those* familiar thoughts came again. "Vivian, I love you." The words were soft and meaningful.

She smiled at me and almost laughed. "I love you as well, Clem."

"No, I mean it. I mean...I really... I want you...for myself." I couldn't describe my desire, the longing I felt, which I sometimes believed was trying to consume me, to swallow me alive.

"Clem, can you do one thing for me?"

I didn't answer.

"Tell me that again. I mean, when you are well."

"I don't understand."

"Just do that for me. Please."

She didn't believe me. I was resistant but nodded. She brought me breakfast in silence, and after that, I slept most of the day. It must have been a relief for her. She sometimes even slept on the floor beside me in case I awoke screaming. She had such an amazing heart.

I was sick for days, and still, Vivian never yelled at me. By the time I was finally well again, I knew I owed her my life.

"There was something I was supposed to say to you," I told her one afternoon. "When I was well. To prove to you I meant it."

"Do you still?"

"I do," I answered softly.

She sat beside me on the bed, and I touched her cheek. "I want you for myself," I whispered.

She leaned toward me, and when our lips met, it was like nothing I had felt before. It was like the world spun, and for that moment she was with me, everything was right in the world; everything was in order. I didn't care about getting home to Walter. I knew then that I was in love. She hardly knew me, and yet she was still tender toward me. She moved closer, deepening the kiss. The passion raged inside me, but she pulled away from me before I had time to wrap my arms around her.

"What's wrong?" I asked. My heart plunged into my stomach.

"There is this frightening admiration I feel for you, Clem, that I don't understand."

I didn't understand it either, but I didn't care.

"Do you need to understand it?" I asked. "Does it matter?"

"I know nothing about you. I just...I want you to be safe, and I want you to be well. But that's all I can give you."

My body began to shake, and my insides felt like they were being torn from my body.

"I'm sorry," I muttered.

"Why?"

"I'm clearly an idiot."

She chuckled. "Why would you say that?" She pulled her hair over one shoulder, and I couldn't look at her. She was too irresistible.

"I'm a kid," I whispered.

She exhaled. "I know."

"You do?"

"Of course. You never had to tell me your name. Your wallet had always been in the pocket of your jeans."

"Oh," I mumbled. "Right. Obviously."

I thought the mugger had taken it.

She smiled. "I'm sorry then. I shouldn't have encouraged it."

"I'm glad that you did."

She just bowed her head.

"I mean it." I laughed. "Rightly or wrongly, it was something I will never forget. Please don't feel bad over it."

"I could never. I barely know you, and yet…I find that I feel close to you somehow."

"I know I owe you something. If you will let me tell you my story, I can be sure it will be a payment you will never forget."

"You should never feel as though you owe me anything, Clem, but if you want to tell me what happened to you to cause your brain fever, I am more than willing to listen."

I told her everything, starting with Walter Redline and his teachings. I tried to explain to her that I had unlocked the secrets of nature and discovered things I was never intended to and then destroyed those discoveries in her fireplace. Everything I had worked toward was now ashes. I would have to start from the beginning again. My love was silent the entire time I spoke; she never took her eyes off me. She listened to me the way people dream of being listened to. But the look in her eyes told me what she was thinking.

"You don't believe me, do you?"

"Of course I do," she answered, sounding surprised. "Of course I believe you, but I also believe that your illness is what causes you to believe it."

I huffed. "You don't understand. I tried to tell you before I had gone mad. I tried to tell you that I don't have to be this way."

"Clem—"

"You don't need to say anything. I am sorry for taking up your time. I am truly grateful for what you have given me, and one of these days, I swear I will find a way to repay you."

"Please don't leave."

"It's a dream, Vivian. I cannot stay."

She nodded and smiled, but I could still see that she was holding back tears. I kissed her softly on her forehead.

"I'll see you again. I have to get home to Walter and my father and mother. I'm leaving now. Thank you again."

"Don't you need me to take you home?"

"Don't be silly," I said, laughing. "I know my way around. I'll walk. It'll be good for me to build my strength back up."

She didn't argue, but I could tell it hurt her feelings. I left it at that. I'd make it up to her someday.

It was still sunny out, and it was miraculous. It seemed to flood over the world like a massive tsunami—an unstoppable tidal wave. I watched the people as I walked, watched them crowding the streets and supermarkets, watched as they entered restaurants. I was intrigued by it. It was new to me. But I hated those people, those insects who had taken for granted what I had lived so long without. They didn't know what they had, did they? I hated them for other reasons too—hated them because they showed me what I was. I wasn't anything special, was I? I was one of them now; I was weak—and mortal. I would never discover Frankenstein's secret. My dream was dead.

I spent the entire walk contemplating how I would tell this to Walter and how I would explain to my parents where I had been. I promised my mother I would be back, didn't I? I had also missed countless days of work. I really didn't know how long I had been sick. I was afraid to know. It had to have been a long time. Hadn't my father called the police? He probably thought I ran away. In which case, he would have let me go. Maybe that's why nobody came looking for me.

I got home close to evening and took a deep breath before unlocking the door. The house was dark and silent. Nobody came rushing to the door to rejoice my return. I couldn't hear my mother's meaningless rambling or my father coaxing her. My mother didn't race to the door and pull me into a gut-wrenching hug, and my father didn't come running to yell at me for not coming home and leaving him alone with my mother. Something wasn't right.

I saw a shadow in the dark, a figure. I instantly flipped the light switch, begging for it to be my mother having another crazy episode—but she had never been silent before, not even in her sleep.

I realized when the light illuminated the face that I didn't know her. It was a woman I had never seen before. She stared at me, looking as frightened and confused as I was. I found myself pressed against the wall, feeling a strange energy radiating from the woman. She continued to walk toward me, and I pressed my back harder against the wall, unaware of what I was frightened of. She certainly didn't look threatening; her beauty was mesmerizing. Her hips moved gracefully like an angel. Her white silken gown slid across her hands at her sides. I could almost imagine flowers woven intricately through the lengths of her blood-red locks. She reached out a delicate poreless hand. I shut my eyes, prepared for pain, but I felt a gentle coolness on my cheek. I opened my eyes, and the angel was staring at me, smiling.

"Ah," she whispered, her voice unnaturally soft and sweet, "an intruder. How lucky that he must be so beautiful."

I tried to speak, but it came out in a pleading whisper. "This is my house."

She froze for a moment. "You're Clement?" It didn't sound like a question.

I nodded.

"William Thortan is your father?"

I nodded again.

"Are you familiar with the name Matthias Castlebar?"

I couldn't respond at first. I was instantly infuriated simply by the sound of his name. I wanted to hit her, to beat her senseless. I tore her hand away from my face. "Thief," I growled. "He destroyed my father."

"Yes," she said, but she was calm, composed.

My voice was still venomous. "What's going on?"

"I found him here," she said, ignoring my question. "Your father and your sick mother were here by themselves, and Castlebar was here as well. I followed him."

I stared, still shaking.

She paused only briefly then continued. "I tried to stop him—to *kill* him." Her voice dropped.

Oh, dear God. What's happened?

"I approached him," she continued, "and…well, I did kill him. But I was too late."

"What do you mean 'too late?'" I spat. "What do you mean 'too late!'" I was yelling now and realized I was inches away from her, pointing an angry finger toward her face. My voice became choked, and I growled between clenched teeth, "Who the *hell* are you?"

"I killed him," she said. "I promise you I killed him, but I was too late."

I shoved past her and walked quickly to the living room.

"CLEM!" she screamed. I could hear her racing after me. She grabbed the back of my shirt and pulled me back until I fell.

"Don't!" she pleaded. "You don't need to see that, Clem."

Oh God! I started screaming, struggling from her, trying to get to my parents, trying to see what she didn't want me to see. I felt like I was making sense, but I knew I wasn't saying any words out loud. I was only crying, and the tears saturated my face. I was numb with grief. I knew it then. I didn't need to see it for it to be confirmed. They were dead, and it was my fault.

Oh God. If only I would have gotten here sooner. If only I had given Walter my recordings, I could have saved them, given them immortality, possibly even cured my mother. It was my fault now, my fault that they were dead.

"My fault."

"No," the woman whispered. I hadn't realized she heard me. "It is the fault of nobody but Castlebar."

They were all I had, the only things in life I had truly loved. I was alone now —alone and even more lost. I came back from the thoughts of pain and back to the thoughts of the beautiful woman in my house. How could I be so sure she was telling the truth? How could I be sure she wasn't the one who had murdered my family? After all—she *was* in my house and knew my name.

16

"Who are you?" I demanded.

"Please," she started. "I followed Castlebar here. I came here for him. He killed my father as well. I am no murderer, Clem."

"How can I know that?"

"I guess you can't," she answered, almost with a smile in her voice. "You can either trust me or not, but either way, you cannot kill me, and if you decide it, I may have a way to help you escape your pain."

I was confused for a moment, processing everything she had said. "Take away my pain?"

She nodded.

"How?"

She put her hand up. "I can't explain now. I will tell you all you need to know in time."

"Will you?"

"Come with me. We can do no more here. Everything will be sorted out. You are up for inheritance, Clem."

"How do you know that?"

She tapped her finger against her temple. "I know how to make things happen."

I shook my head slightly. This was too strange and all happening so fast. I didn't know what to make of it.

"My name is Luna," she said.

"Last name?"

"Is not important," she answered. "I am Luna. That's all you need to know. Come with me."

"Where?"

"To my home."

"What about *my* home?"

"It will be yours once the law has taken care of it."

I pressed my fingers to my temples, trying to get my head to stop throbbing from the grief that was quickly turning into anger.

She led me outside to a silver Honda parked crooked at the bottom of the long, curvy driveway.

"Nice parking job," I muttered.

"I was in a rush."

"Uh huh."

"Just get in."

The drive was silent. It wasn't a very long drive but long enough to make me irritable and uncomfortable. She drove to a house that almost looked like it was in the middle of the forest. She opened the door, and the house was beautiful.

The front room was spacious with old-fashioned, upholstered furniture—a couch, loveseat, and chair—which all appeared to be from the mid-1800s, with redwood and floral patterns. The light was dim, casting soft shadows on the walls. There was a china cabinet to the left of the redwood door, filled with elegant artwork. *I would love to be a painter*, I thought. The carpet was beige and completely spotless.

"It's—"

"I know." She laughed. "A nice home is an important thing to have."

A smile forced its way across my face when I looked at her. "Beautiful."

She laughed. "Are you all right?"

I pulled my eyebrows together.

"I'm sorry," she said. "Of course you're not. I'll make us some tea. It will make you feel better. I promise."

"I doubt *tea* is going to do much," I said, sitting on the redwood-framed couch.

"Sure it will." She disappeared into the other room.

I sighed and looked around again. There was a coffee table in front of the couch, packed with books. There was no television on the desk against the wall. Not that I minded that; I had grown up without it. I was lost in my thoughts and had almost forgotten where I was until Luna came into the front room with two steaming mugs.

"It's a special herbal tea," she said. "It will make you feel calm and may help you sleep."

I took a sip. "It's sweet."

"Rosemary and lavender. I picked up the recipe recently from a friend of mine, a witch down in Coos Bay."

"Interesting."

"It has a bit of spice in it too," she continued. "Small sips."

It did help me to feel calm, perhaps mind over matter, but the numbness I was feeling had become comfortable. My grief had exhausted me, and the tea had relaxed me.

"You need rest," she told me. "You've been through quite a lot."

"You have no idea," I mumbled under my breath.

She led me into the bedroom down the hall. It wasn't big, but it was spacious. It had a queen-sized bed with a floral mattress and a wrought iron frame. The walls were a sky blue color that matched the blue in the bedspread. There was a vanity in front of the bed, against the wall with a large, round mirror. Perfume bottles and pictures were crowded together, yet it still looked elegant.

"I will make sure to retrieve your things from your home. Leave that to me," she said.

I was too tired to argue over her being in my room around my treasures. For some reason, I trusted her. It was like she was all I had now. I fell asleep within minutes, still in my clothes.

Luna woke me late in the morning the next day. I gasped, sitting up instantly, my hands up defensively.

"It's okay," she soothed. "Just me. I didn't mean to startle you."

I sighed. "Sorry."

"I got some of your things for you, clothes, mostly, and this."

She handed me a brown teddy bear with a red ribbon around its neck. It took everything in me not to cry. My mother had given me that for my birthday one year, before she had gone too insane to drive. It meant a lot to me. I snatched it from her hands. I didn't want her touching it.

She smiled. "So...I did okay?"

"I'm sorry, Luna. Thank you."

"Are you hungry?"

"I don't know."

"I'll make you some breakfast. I put your clothes in the dresser. The bathroom is just down the hall. I think you can take it from there."

"You don't need to take care of me."

"Well, right now, Clem—somebody does." I heard her quietly laugh as she left the room.

She was probably right; I needed *somebody* if only for a while. Luna was sweet, but she wasn't beautifully innocent like Vivian. She seemed like there was a dark, ghastly secret she was hiding from me. Sometimes I got a grim feeling when she looked at me. I tried to ignore, but there was something interesting I was waiting to learn about her. I was hoping it was something good, something that could help me.

The bathroom was huge. There was a white marble tub bigger than any tub I had ever seen. I wasn't comfortable enough to relax here yet, so I settled for a quick shower. I daydreamed about resting in that tub with Vivian; my mind even brought Luna into the picture but pushed those images away. I would never see Vivian again. I would never be able to look at her that way again. I could feel myself becoming numb to those emotions I had felt. I knew it was wrong before it had happened, and now for some reason, that mattered. I never wanted to let myself hurt again. I would guard my heart as best I could. I would never fall in love. Didn't I promise her I would come back? Didn't I promise her that I loved her? Maybe I would have to break that promise—to protect myself. Maybe that was the right thing to do. If protecting myself meant protecting her too, then I had to. I would only hurt her in the end.

I wrapped myself in a towel and headed back to my room. Luna came in without knocking.

"Good God, Luna. Don't you knock?"

She laughed. "Sorry. Thought you were still in the bathroom. I was just going to put some more of your clothes away for you."

"Um...thanks."

She chuckled again. "Nice towel."

I was frozen still for a moment. She closed the door, but the look she had given me had paralyzed me for a moment. She had given me a crooked stare, keeping me wondering what she was thinking. Nobody had ever looked at me so solidly before, so...unyielding to anything I could have said. It made me uneasy. I cringed and got dressed quickly.

I walked into the kitchen, and she was just setting the plates on the table.

"Hope you like this," she said, not turning to look at me.

"I'm sure I will."

She turned then, smiling, wiping her hands on her little white apron. She pulled it over her head. "Getting chilly out today." She pulled the pin from her hair, and I watched the blood-red locks fall perfectly in place over her shoulders. I didn't respond. I was mesmerized for a moment. She seemed not to notice my reaction and sat down. There were only three chairs at a round, wooden table. The cabinets and drawers were white with red trim, making it look very bright and lively. She was a wonderful cook too. She made fried potatoes and bacon to go with the perfectly made omelets.

"It's delicious," I told her.

"I'm glad you like it, but if you don't, no reason to be too nice. I can always make you something else."

"Don't be ridiculous. If I have a problem with it, I can take care of it myself."

"I suppose you could. Sorry if I baby you. You seem very fragile right now."

"I guess I am."

"So, tell me about yourself, Clem. I know almost nothing about you."

"That's true. You don't."

"Would you prefer it that way?"

I smiled and shook my head. "You've done a lot for me. I guess I at least owe you as much as to tell you who I am."

She raised her eyebrows, waiting.

"I'm seventeen years old. I know—younger than I look. My father was a banker—this you know. It was also clear to me that you knew my mother was sick."

She nodded.

"I don't want to talk about them," I said. "Not yet anyway. I want to tell you about Walter Redline, the professor who has become my friend and mentor. I need to get back to him as soon as I can to tell him of my mistakes."

"What kind of mistakes?"

"The kind that destroyed my dreams."

I spoke to her about Walter and my fear of death. I told her about Vivian and the temporary madness I had suffered. I told her everything I could think of. I opened up to her with almost no fear of what she would think. I didn't shed a tear, but when I was finished with my story, she embraced me and stroked my hair.

"You'll be all right," she told me. "I promise."

It was like she could read my mind and knew I was more hurt than I seemed. It felt wonderful to be held and to be comforted. I never had a mother to take care of me; I always took care of my mother.

Chapter Three

AFTER THE DEATH of my parents, I was beginning to think nothing could ever hurt me again. There was a strange comfort in that thought. To never feel pain sounded wonderful, but at the same time, I feared going numb. My thoughts were jumbled, and I wasn't sure what I believed anymore or what I wanted from life, from science, from Walter—from Luna. I didn't know anything. I was lost. I stayed with Luna for what seemed like longer than it was. I was there for at least two weeks and decided enough was enough.

"Luna, I want you to sell the house."

"What?"

"You heard me. Sell my house."

"Clem...why—"

"Just do it, Luna. Please?"

She nodded. "Are you all right?"

"I'm pretty far from all right. I don't want to look at that house again. I can't. It can no longer be my home."

"This can be your home," she said. "This can be where you stay."

I shook my head. "I don't know."

She stepped close to me—too close. "Stay with me," she whispered. "Please."

"Why are you asking me to stay?"

"Don't you know?" She sounded hurt, almost angry. "I've wanted you since the moment I met you."

Suddenly, I felt repulsed. Yes, she was beautiful, but there was something about her that made me feel sick. Something that meant I could never look at her like that.

"Luna...I'm seventeen years old."

"I don't care."

"I have that effect on people it seems."

"Clem..."

She moved closer, and I walked away. I concealed myself in my room. She didn't follow right away, but about ten minutes later, she knocked on the door. I sighed, trying to ignore.

"You know, your door doesn't lock," she said.

I grumbled, hiding my face in a pillow.

She opened the door. "Hey."

I looked up at her. She looked normal, like she always did.

She sat on the edge of the bed. "I'm sorry. I didn't mean to make you uncomfortable."

I just nodded.

"You're just...very charming." She brushed my hair back from my face, and I pulled away from her again even when I had enjoyed it. I always enjoyed being touched just not by her. She took my hand. "I can't help it. If I can have you—just once—I would be forever in your debt."

I smiled, almost laughing. "It can't happen that way. You need to leave."

"Clem—"

"Luna, just go!"

She almost stormed out. I flopped down with my face in the pillow again, trying to think of something I could say to her, something to make her feel less offended. There wasn't a real reason I had denied her after all, only that the thought of her skin against my own repulsed me for some completely unknown reason. Maybe I could ignore that fact; maybe I could think of something other than her. I owed her something after all, didn't I? For rescuing me and taking me in? I should give her *something*. I brushed off those thoughts, sickened again, and I shuddered.

"Can't happen," I whispered to myself.

I let my mind wander away from the discomfort and fell asleep.

It was late in the night or early in the morning when I awoke to her brushing her fingers across my face.

"What are you doing?" I groaned, still not fully awake.

"I don't give up that easily."

"Oh, for the love of God, Luna—"

She cut me off by pressing her lips against mine harshly. Something heightened in me. I was unsure what. The air turned warmer, the atmosphere thicker. I parted my lips, accepting her kiss. It was long, passionate, and as her tongue slid into my mouth, my breathing quickened, and my muscles tightened.

Can't happen. Can't happen. CAN'T happen!

Oh, but I wanted it to…so badly. My entire body burned for her the way I never thought it could.

She ended the kiss but wasn't finished. She crawled into the bed beside me and started kissing my neck. I instantly began to feel sick again. She wasn't clean or beautiful to me. She was dirty and sordid. I loved Luna—I did, but not the way I loved Vivian. I couldn't let her touch me this way.

"That's enough," I whispered to her. "Enough, Luna."

She stopped but only for a moment. I tore her away from me and heard her quietly laugh.

"All right, Clem," she whispered. "I'll leave. You have wonderful self-control, love. Did you know that?"

"Goodnight, Luna."

She chuckled again. "Goodnight, Clem."

I rolled over and couldn't even fall back asleep. All I wanted was a hot shower to help me feel clean.

The morning came faster than I expected, and Luna didn't bother me once. I took care of myself until she knocked on the bathroom door, announcing break-fast as if the night before hadn't even happened. The entire meal was silent. She put the plates in the sink and finally said something.

"Tell me," she started. "When did it stop being important to you to talk to Walter?"

I had actually forgotten about Walter. "When I realized I couldn't bear to tell him of my mistakes."

"Don't you think he would understand?"

"I don't want to talk about it," I said. "Please."

"I know what you need."

"What I need?"

"Yes," she answered, turning to face me. "Your life has no meaning."

"Like you would know what meaning is," I snapped, standing up from the table.

"I meant no offense," she said calmly. "I'm just trying to tell you that I know of a place you can go…we can go—a place where life has meaning, a place where you are taught the true ways in which the world works. I have lost a lot in my life as well, Clem. Neither of us have anything more to lose. I can't see why not."

"What...place?"

She smiled. "A man leads this group—a group of people like us...who need guidance and purpose."

To have purpose was all I ever wanted. My dreams of science were destroyed. What else did I have? I was able to say only one thing.

"When can I meet him?"

Her face lit up, and she stepped toward me, brushing her fingers through my hair again. "How does tomorrow sound?" she whispered. She kissed my cheek.

"Tomorrow sounds fine," I said and stormed past her. I wasn't getting used to her touching me; I still hated it.

Anxiety was creeping in, and I awoke the next morning eager to meet this man Luna had talked about. My eagerness quickly turned to apprehension when she mentioned he didn't know her.

"I was told about him by a friend of mine," she said. "I wasn't sure about his teachings or his beliefs, but my friend had assured me that since meeting him, her life turned to pure bliss. Everything made sense and became so simple."

"What are his teachings?" I asked. "And his beliefs?"

"Well...I don't know."

"How can you be unsure of something you don't know?"

"Clem...just trust me, okay? I did meet him once. I get a good feeling about him."

There was clearly something she wasn't telling me. What if it was something ghastly—evil? What then? I shook off the negative thoughts and tried to let myself feel excited for something to finally help me. I knew Luna was lying about something, but it stopped mattering almost instantly. It was as if nothing could frighten me anymore. I had nothing left to lose.

Chapter Four

SHE WAS DRESSED in a silken gown, almost see-through and bordering inde-cency. I tried to ignore.

"Choose something nice," she had said. "You want him to notice you."

I nodded and took her advice. I dressed myself in a nice pair of slacks and a button-up shirt, not wanting to dress *too* nicely. Luna led me out to her car.

"Now listen, Clem," she started. "This man is very important. He under-stands things that you and I don't. So please do your best to listen. He is smarter than anyone we are sure to ever meet."

I kept my thoughts inside. More vile ideas came to mind. I was doubting her again. What if this man was going to kill me? What if that was Luna's plan all along? To get my parents killed and then end with me? Again I shook off the thoughts. *If I am going to die, that's all right,* I thought. I had nothing here anyway.

When we arrived, it wasn't at a house or even a flat. It was a small woodland area about an hour away. There were about twelve men standing in a circle with their heads down as if they were praying. There was a large stone on the ground, surrounded by a circle of other smaller stones. Leaves fell from the trees, gently resting on the rocks.

"Wait," Luna whispered. "He knows we are here. Wait for him to speak. Do not speak unless spoken to."

A man immediately turned around. He had dark hair down to his shoulders and was cleanly shaven and dressed as I was dressed.

"Ah," he said, "Luna."

He walked toward her and took her hand. She smiled and bowed her head.

He looked to me. "And you are?"

I hesitated before responding, not knowing if I should bow. I mimicked Luna.

"Clement Thortan," I said quietly, lowering my head.

"Look at me, boy," he said kindly.

I brought my gaze to his.

"Abraham is my name. And what is it you want from me?"

Luna answered. "We wish to be part of your order. We wish to be members of your remarkable studies and rituals."

Abraham smiled. "Oh, Luna, I knew you would come my way. You look lovely as always."

She smiled again.

"And you, my boy," he started, "you have something about you I have never seen before." He began circling me like a vulture.

"James," he said.

"I'm sorry?" I questioned.

"Luna, I want this one," he said, ignoring me.

"Sir...?" she said with a gasp.

He nodded. "I want this one."

I said nothing, just waited as Luna had instructed.

"Do you want to be part of this order?" Abraham asked me.

"Yes, Sir," I stuttered.

"Do you have the courage to learn the ways of the world that others do not understand?"

"Yes, Sir."

"Do you swear an oath to obey me as your father?"

I hesitated. *Father.*

"Yes. Yes, Sir."

He pulled out a knife and led me to the circle of stones. The men crowded around the boulder and instantly looked up at me. They were all different ages, some younger than me and some much older.

"I have made my choice," Abraham said. "I have found the one I feel is right."

The men all stared at me solidly. It didn't feel natural. Something wasn't quite right.

"Take a seat," he told me, gesturing to the stone in the center.

I pointed to it and looked at him questioningly.

"Yes," he said. "Sit."

I pushed through the crowd and sat on the rock. Abraham came closer and took my hand in his.

"Pain is life," he said and sliced my hand with his knife without warning. I gasped and wrenched my hand away. He grabbed it back and held it over a goblet of wine or some other dark liquid. My blood dripped quickly into the goblet.

"Pain is life," he said again. He gave the goblet to Luna. She took a drink from the cup and passed it along. After all of them had drunk from the goblet, he handed it to me.

"Drink."

I didn't answer, just took a small sip, disgusted by the idea of drinking my own blood. This was too strange for me.

Abraham beamed at me. "Then I take you, Clement Thortan, as my son, and your name from this day on shall be James West."

"James..." I echoed.

Luna bowed her head. "Are you sure about this, Sir?"

"Have I ever given you reason to question my choices?" he hissed.

"No, Sir, you have not."

He nodded and kissed her cheek. "Take James. Start his lessons. He trusts you."

"Come," she said to me. "Let's get you established here."

She led me to another part of the woods. There was nobody around, but it had to have been an important place. The air was still, and it all seemed so quiet. Again came that feeling, that foreboding of evil, the thoughts that she was hiding something from me. Something wasn't right. She refused to make eye-contact.

"Luna?" When I said her name, it frightened me that my voice didn't cut through the stillness like a knife. Everything still seemed so—dead. I wanted to scream, wanted to yell and flail my arms, anything to cure the silence. I begged for something to happen, for the floor of the forest to writhe as if in life, for the trees to fall and threaten to crush me, for lightning to come crashing through the leaves—anything, anything but silence.

"Luna," I said again.

Finally, she turned to look at me.

"I'm not sure about this."

"What?"

"I'm not...sure about this anymore."

She almost laughed. "Uh...Clem—James, it's a little late for that now."

"Why are you whispering?" I asked her.

"Because..." She sounded furious and moved until she was only inches away from my face. "Because you have *no* idea what Abraham will do if he finds out you aren't sure. You swore an oath, James. There is no way out of this now."

"No way out?"

She shook her head. "Look," she started. "It's fine, okay? You have nothing left to lose, right?"

I sighed and nodded. There was nothing I could say to argue that.

"Must you call me James?"

She smiled. "Yes," she said immediately. "Get used to it. Now let's get started, okay?"

"All right."

It was strange the way she acted. She refused to make eye contact and stood there just silent for many moments.

"Luna?"

She finally looked at me.

"What are you hiding from me?"

"Don't be ridiculous," she hissed.

"Don't play games!" I yelled. "Tell me what this place is, who these people are."

"I told you." Her voice was a whisper again. "The ones who understand the ways of the world."

"What must I do?"

"You must understand." She placed her hands on my shoulders. "You must understand their ways. Abraham knows how things work, the one thing that gives us strength in our days of weakness."

Her words intrigued me. I loved the sound of that. *Strength in our days of weakness.*

"Tell me. What is that one thing?"

"The thing that has sustained you since before you were born. The thing that kept you alive while still in the womb."

I narrowed my eyes. "What?"

"Blood."

"Blood?"

"Yes, James. Blood."

She smiled at me and hesitated before speaking. "Abraham has instructed me to ask you a series of questions."

"What kind of questions?"

"The personal kind."

I sighed and tried to keep from cringing.

"James, you won't have any kind of privacy here—you'll need to get used to that. It's okay though. I won't judge you."

"That's not what I'm worried about." I didn't care what she thought.

"Listen," she started. "I'll spare you under one condition."

I raised my eyebrows.

"You have to answer *one* question—truthfully." Her dark blue eyes were big, and she looked extremely serious, making me wonder what was really going on in her head. She pulled her red locks of hair over her shoulder and stared at me solidly, waiting for me to respond.

I nodded hesitantly. I felt a sudden reluctance to tell her anything.

"What is the *one* thing that would hurt you the most?" she asked. A smile spread across her face, and I had to avert my gaze. Her smile could have meant so many things. She had just asked me about pain, and now...she looked happy.

"Nothing could hurt me anymore."

"Think about it!" she demanded. "Then answer me again."

I stared at her, shaking my head. I lost my family, Walter would never care for me again, and I left the only woman I ever loved. What more did I have?

"Really, Luna. Nothing."

"Very well."

She led me back to Abraham. "He's ready, Sir."

Abraham grinned; it was a smile I had never seen anybody express before. It seemed like the true meaning behind it was hidden from me and was meant to be hidden. His followers were all cloaked in black and were surrounding the stone in the center. Their backs to me, they were perfectly still, like statues, humming some nonsense.

"It's time," Abraham ordered. His words weren't spoken loudly, but his people seemed to understand and moved aside to reveal what was there for me.

I couldn't breathe at first. I couldn't move. I choked on the last bit of air left in me. She was there...for real this time. I didn't have to close my eyes to see her. How could I have told Luna that nothing could hurt me? How could I have been such a fool? The very sight pained me more than I thought anything ever could again.

I heard her gasp. "Clem!" Tears were pouring from her eyes.

"Oh my God!" I tried several times to say her name, and when it finally came out, I was already crying.

"Vivian!" I rushed to her side.

"Clem," she said again, sobbing.

"Oh God!" I cried. I looked up at Abraham. "What is this?" My voice swelled into my throat and exploded. I heard myself screaming now. "What the hell are you doing!"

I felt like I was going mad again. The pain, fear, and anger could easily have driven me right back to where I was when Vivian had first rescued me. I owed it to her to rescue her now. But how could I? How could I stand against Abraham and all of his followers? I tried to speak, but all I could do was cry. I stroked Vivian's hair.

"It's all right," I said. "It's going to be all right."

"Who are you, Clem?" she whispered.

"This isn't what you think, love," I answered. "I swear to you. I would never do anything to hurt you."

She didn't answer, just stared at me. She looked so helpless. It made me sick to see her that way. Her beautiful dark eyes were red and swollen with her tears. Her shadow-colored hair was sticking to the moisture on her cheeks. Yet even as she looked this way, I couldn't take my eyes off of her. Her face was flushed, yet her lips were pale and colorless.

"What have they done to you?"

"Nothing," I heard Luna say. "They haven't done anything to her, James— not yet."

"Not yet?" I growled. "How could you? I trusted you!"

"Please..."

I stood to my feet. "I trusted you, Luna! I knew you were hiding something from me, but this? Her? How could you?"

"I had nothing to do with this!" she yelled back.

I backed away. "What?"

She sighed. "This...it wasn't me. This was not my plan."

Abraham chimed in. "She is a follower. She did only as I instructed, and so will you."

I shook my head. "No."

I heard the crowd of followers break out into a verbal yet quiet disbelief, and all of them turned to look at me. Had nobody ever said no to him before? I looked to Luna. Her hands were over her mouth, and she looked terrified, like she was about to cry.

"No?" Abraham echoed.

I shook my head, too afraid to repeat the word.

He struck me hard across my face, so hard that I toppled over and fell right beside Vivian. I sat up, coughing.

"Would you like to tell me 'no' again, boy?"

"Please," I pleaded. "Let her go. I beg of you. Anyone but her."

He smiled. "Anyone?"

I nodded, sobbing. "Anyone." I tried to keep my voice even, but it cracked through my tears.

I heard Luna whisper something to him. I looked up to see he was nodding. He looked to a young boy who I saw walking toward me.

"Go ahead," Abraham said to him.

The boy leaned down beside me and pulled out a knife at least four inches in length. I saw Vivian close her eyes. It took everything in me not to scream. I pushed him back with all the strength I had. I felt Luna grab me by the shoulders.

"Let me go!" I cried out. "No, don't. Please!"

The boy just looked at me almost sadly—disgusted.

I watched as he inched the knife closer toward the woman I loved. I screamed and shut my eyes.

There was a moment of silence—a moment I wasn't sure I wanted to be alive.

"Clem?"

I heard her voice and opened my eyes. How was it possible she was alive? I saw the stranger still staring at me sadly with her bounds in his hands. She sat up, rubbing her wrists.

"Run," he murmured.

I tried to yell, but my voice was caught in my throat and came out in a throttled plea. "Vivian—run!"

She stood up and inched toward me. "Who are you?" she whispered.

"You wouldn't understand," I said. "Please, my love, just leave this place. I'll come back to you someday like I swore I would."

She shook her head. "Clem—James, whoever you are, do not find me."

"Viv—"

"Please." She started backing away from me. "Leave me alone."

"Run," the boy repeated.

She turned and ran, almost stumbling over her feet. I watched as she disappeared into the trees. I had this maddening urge to chase after her, to lose myself in the forest, with her in my arms. The thought left the very instant I heard Abraham's voice.

"Yes, Luna," he said. "Fair enough."

"Come," Luna murmured.

"Where?"

She gestured me with her hand, a look of sheer disappointment on her face. I couldn't pay attention to her. My thoughts were fixed on Vivian. How did they find her? How could they have known? The answer came to me before I finished asking myself. Luna. She told Abraham everything—before this day. Of course she had lied to me. I knew she was lying. Why didn't I run? Why was I following her now? Wasn't Vivian some kind of test I failed? Wasn't she going to kill me now?

"James?"

"Yes?"

"We are alone now. Abraham has left me with specific instructions."

"Luna, if you are going to kill me, just do it quickly."

She laughed. "Kill you?"

"Aren't you supposed to kill me?"

Her laughter hadn't ceased. "Of course not. Vivian was an attack on your heart. Abraham does that to us all. He wanted you, remember? He chose you."

I couldn't respond to her. I just kept thinking about Vivian.

"Look," she began, sighing. "You need to start slowly. How do you feel this very instant?"

"Distressed. Devastated. Lost."

"Good."

"Good?"

"Yes. That means we can begin now. Do you remember what I had said about blood?"

I nodded.

"It gives us strength and helps protect us when we are emotionally broken."

I narrowed my eyes.

I watched as she leapt into the air. I gasped and stumbled backward. She twisted her slender body as she floated to the ground, her gown disguising the movement of her legs. It was almost…inhuman the way she had moved.

Before I could speak, she was there in front of me like she hadn't even moved at all. She brushed her red hair from her face and looked into my eyes.

"What…?" I wasn't sure what I was planning to ask her.

"Look."

She opened her hand to reveal a bundle of feathers. There was blood running down her wrist, contrasting wonderfully with the snow whiteness of her flesh. That's when I realized it was more than a tuft of feathers; it was a bird—an actual bird torn right out of the air. It took a moment for me to process what I had seen.

"How—?"

She put her hand up to silence me. "Practice".

"Practice?" I almost bellowed the word. "You *practice* snatching birds right out of the air?"

She smiled. "Yes. Are you surprised?"

I didn't know how to answer that, so I didn't. She reached into the inside pocket of her jacket and turned her back to me. When she faced me, she was holding a tiny, silver goblet. It looked Greek perhaps and very old. It was designed with winged horses and clouds. It was beautiful. She handed me the cup. There were bloody fingerprints where she had been holding it, but I tried to ignore the disgust it brought from me. I peered inside.

"Luna, is this…?"

She grinned at me, almost mischievously.

"I… No. Luna, no. I'm not drinking this. I'm not drinking…blood."

"Yes, you are. You are, James."

I shook my head and held the goblet out toward her. She sighed heavily.

"Listen to me carefully," she said. "This will help you."

"How?"

"This is more powerful than you know. You may not understand yet, but I promise you—this will help. It may take time for you to notice the effects, but it *will* make you better."

"I don't understand."

"Neither did I. But I do now, and I know now that *this*"—she pointed to the goblet in my hand—"is power."

Chapter Five

HIS NAME WAS ALEX, and he looked quite young with light-colored hair and a very round face. I recognized him instantly as the boy who cut the bounds off Vivian's wrists. He greeted me warmly.

"Hello," he sang, lending me a childlike hand.

I nodded my head once and shook his hand.

"Clem," I said. "Err—James."

"Which is it?" He chuckled.

"James. My name is James."

"So you're my brother now. That's what Father said."

"Yes—I suppose we are family."

Alex smiled widely. "I've always wanted a brother."

"Yeah...uh...me too."

I dropped my hand, and Alex was still smiling. My mind was still focused on Vivian, and slowly, the pain of losing her was diminishing. Shouldn't I be weeping for hours? Shouldn't I be chasing after her, begging her to listen to me? I couldn't understand why I was suddenly so numb to the grief that was trying to swallow me alive. Even the death of my parents was a memory that seemed so far away that I rarely even cared anymore. Something wasn't right. But this was what I had wanted, wasn't it? This was what I had asked Luna for. I wanted someone to help me deal with my pain and my grief, and now, that's what I found in Abraham and his followers. I couldn't turn my back on them now. I couldn't betray them. There was a reason for all of it. If I left, my grief would consume me. I felt I had no other choice but to stay. Days, weeks, even months passed quickly, and the blood Luna gave me every day began to taste sweeter and sweeter until it came to the point that I craved it like a child craves chocolate. It was like I couldn't be without it when my heart began to ache.

Abraham taught me to fight, taught me that I didn't feel pain, that I did not know the meaning of fear. He explained that guns were not our way. He said guns were barbaric and impersonal. Blades were the way we killed. He assured me that he loved me, that I was his son and nothing could change that, but he struck me almost every day—every time he ordered something of me that I denied or refused. Alex just stood by, almost afraid of his father. The day with Vivian was the first time I remembered Abraham had hit me. If I did as he said, maybe he would love me, maybe he would love me as I loved him. Maybe he would need me as I needed him.

Chapter Six

ABRAHAM TAUGHT us that there were people out there who were made for us. He talked to us about how he would choose them.

There were others who helped instruct me, others who Abraham felt were a better fit than Luna. David was one of them. He was older than me but still very young. I didn't like the way he treated me. He never struck me, Abraham wouldn't allow that, but he *was* harsh with me. Every time I asked a question, he would yell at me to shut up and listen. He told me that any question I had was irrelevant. I hated him. I avoided him when I was able to and spoke to Jason and Arthur. They were calm and supportive. Jason even helped continue my fighting lessons. We quickly became friends, and it felt encouraging to have people to look to for answers and guidance.

Abraham called together a meeting. Jason and Arthur stood beside me as he spoke.

"If they are beautiful and if you want them, take them," he said. "It is our right."

He explained that the beautiful and the innocent were the ones the world had made for us.

"You must kill him, James," Abraham said to me the first time, handing me a knife. "He is pure."

"Pure?"

"Do you hear his pleas?"

I listened to the boy's pathetic whimpers of innocence and nodded. "I do."

"He is pure. Do you not wish to take that beauty into you?"

"Oh, I do," I answered.

It all sounded gripping to me as it always had. To take in beauty and innocence, to steal purity and, at the same time, make Abraham love me and become like him—strong and powerful. Oh, it was heroic. The boy strapped to that stone, slowly began to take form into a monster, into a foe. He transformed in my mind as someone I needed to kill. He made me almost…thirsty for his blood as if I were some nocturnal, undead predator risen from my grave to feed off the blood of the innocent. And that was what I was going to do, wasn't it? Feed off the blood of the innocent.

I looked to my father, and he nodded his head. The boy looked into my eyes, and suddenly, I felt myself returning to the day my parents were murdered. I saw in his eyes love and fear. I was violently ripped from the visions of the fiend I was going to destroy, and all I saw…was a boy. What was I doing? How could I destroy a child? How could I inflict the same pain that almost destroyed me? What was happening to me?

I did not feel pain, and I did not know the meaning of fear. That is what Father had told me, so why now was I feeling so weak and powerless?

"We don't have all day, James," Abraham hissed.

"I…I don't think—"

"That's right, James," he growled. "You *don't* think. You obey!"

"Father, I mean…I do not think I should kill him."

"What?" my father spat back. "There is never a time it is okay for you to question me, James. Never!"

"Then *you* do it!" I snapped.

I instantly covered my mouth and braced myself to get hit. I felt his hand harshly crash against my face. I cried out, and he tore the knife from my hands.

"You don't want me to do it, James," he said. "I promise you."

I didn't respond, just glared at him. His eyes appeared darker than usual, and I could see something vile behind them. He smoothed back his long hair and sighed as if he were trying to calm his irritation.

"Listen to him," I heard Luna whisper. "Spare the boy, James. Please."

"What are you talking about?"

"He'll suffer if Abraham does it. Spare him his wrath."

So now my killing of him was suddenly turned into an act of mercy? Abraham had always been brutal as I had noticed from the beginning. I knew Luna was right. I knew this boy wouldn't die well if he became Abraham's.

I grabbed the knife from my father. He looked to me, and his expression changed from confused and incensed to pleased. He smiled at me.

"Good," he said. "Good."

"What must I do?"

"Into the heart, son. That's our way."

It wasn't over after him. It was like it would never be over, and I didn't have a choice. I obeyed my father as if it were just the way things were, as if I had never lived any other way. There were others I killed. Others whom I regretfully could not remember—save for one.

Luna woke me very early one morning.

"Get up," she demanded.

"What?" I groaned. "Luna, go away. It's still dark outside."

"Come on, love," she sang. "It's morning, and we have things to do. Get up."

"What kind of things?"

She laughed. "You don't want to be late for your own party, James, do you? Come on."

I got up slowly, irritated as usual by Luna's constant mothering of me. I walked into the kitchen where I was sure she would be.

"Hmm…no breakfast today?" I teased.

She turned around, smiling. "Don't worry about that yet. You'll feel fine once we get there."

"So what kind of event is this?"

"It's sort of your right of passage. Like an initiation."

"Initiation? I was welcomed into Abraham's group ages ago."

"Yes, but if you ever want to be chosen for a mission, you need to prove yourself."

"What are you talking about?" I yelled. "Nobody ever said anything about missions."

"That's what it's all about. To help spread the beauty of the peace The Sevren brings. Come now."

"I am to do things for Abraham?"

"If you wish."

"Of course I do," I said. "I never thought I could free myself from grief as easily as I have. Abraham's words make me realize things I never knew."

"That is what I promised you, James."

"And these missions, is this a way to make him love me?"

"James, he loves you already."

"He struck me," I said sadly. "The day with Vivian was only the first time."

She put her hand on my shoulder. "I know, love, but it's all right. He's your father, remember? He just needs time to realize that you are loyal to him, that you will repay him for all he has given you. That is what today is for."

I was willing to do anything for Abraham. After what he had done for me, I felt I owed him something. I didn't know what it was I had to do, but it didn't seem like it would be something I couldn't handle. After all, he had taught me to be strong. I did not feel pain, and I did not know the meaning of fear.

"Today is for you," he began slowly. His expression remained blank. "Today is the day you swear to do my bidding."

I nodded in obedience.

"Come," Luna whispered.

Abraham led the way to the clearing with the circle of stones. Luna held tightly to my hand the entire way.

Abraham halted and turned to me. "This," he said, "is for you."

He moved aside to reveal something almost as horrific as Vivian strapped to that stone. This time, it was somebody I did not know.

Abraham smiled at me. "He is connected to the enemy, James, a group of people who seek to destroy everything we have created and died to protect. Do you want to let that happen?"

"Of course not!" I retorted. "Of course I want to protect us."

The boy began muttering something; all I was able to make out was his denial.

"I don't know anything about you," he said. "I don't know anything about what you have said."

Alex leaned toward the boy. "Do not speak. You will make it worse."

He wasn't whimpering or crying. All he said was he was innocent. I could see he truly was. He had dark, shaggy hair and lovely blue eyes. He was young —younger than me. I didn't know what I was doing anymore. He was so young and so small. I was torn back into the memories of my parents. Once again, I was feeling weak and powerless against this guilt gnawing away at me.

"Daniel Callahan," Abraham announced. "This is his last day."

"Spare him his wrath," Luna whispered.

I looked to her, trying to hide the pain it was causing me, trying to disguise the way Daniel's eyes were burning through my skin.

"What's the matter with you?" she hissed, still trying to keep quiet. "Do it."

Without memory of what happened, I stood stone-cold paralyzed with a bloody knife in my hand, staring down at the innocent boy I had killed. Abraham praised me, and that's when I realized—I couldn't remember killing anyone before him. I couldn't remember a single other victim. They were *all* Daniel.

Strangely enough, his blood was sweet—thick and powerful, the way Abraham said it would be. I didn't know why I did it, why I agreed to drink from the goblet my father gave me. Fear, I believe—fear of not believing in him, fear of him not loving me, fear of being…wrong.

"I love you, son," he said as I took the cup. "You know that, don't you?"

"I do," I answered, "and I love you as well."

He smiled and kissed the top of my head. It was all I wanted from him—his love. It was all I had asked myself for. *Just make him love you, James.* And now he did. I sat beside Luna in a circle around the stones.

"Alex," my father called. "Alex, I want you to do something for me now."

He nodded obediently.

"I want you to take the boy back to California."

"Sir?"

"Do it, Alex."

I looked to Luna, almost baffled.

"Abraham believes they belong where they came from," she said. "It's his…*way.*"

"Luna," Abraham jeered, "do you feel a need to speak?"

"I was informing James, Sir," she said. "As you instructed."

He didn't respond.

This wasn't right. Something was very wrong. I never believed in *killing* people, did I? But I did. I killed before, didn't I? I killed others before Daniel. Birds were one thing, but people? A young boy? That couldn't be right. I couldn't tell this to Abraham, of course. I couldn't even tell Luna. I knew without a doubt that something was wrong.

"Daniel Callahan," Abraham announced, "was only one of the family members. The rest as well need to be stopped."

I didn't respond.

Stopped? He was going to kill the entire family? The pain was real, the guilt and the grief, but it didn't matter anymore—it couldn't. I killed for him; I did it every time he asked me to. Every single person he forced me to hurt was Daniel. It was maddening. He told me it was my job now to find the rest of his family and bring them.

"Bring them here?" I stuttered in response.

"They reside in California."

"The boy wasn't enough?"

"Of course not!" he spat. I winced, thinking he was going to hit me again, but he placed his hand on my shoulder instead.

"You're still learning," he told me. "He was the enemy, James. That is why he had to die. The rest of his family are just as much the enemy as he. Jane, Ethan, and Carol Callahan all must be put to an end.

I hated myself for what I must do. What was I turning into?

For the following months, Luna was like a spirit guide. Every time the pain felt like it was going to destroy me, she was there to once again explain that this was the way things were meant to happen. We serve fate, a higher authority than the law. These people were meant for us. I knew she was right; that's what Father had taught us.

Alex was the one I sometimes felt didn't understand. He was good at obeying Abraham—most of the time. Alex was never struck, not like I was. Father once hit me so hard my eye was swollen shut for days. I didn't let that happen anymore. I took care of Alex a lot, saved him from Father's wrath. There was one time I found him in the clearing, examining and studying something.

"Alex?"

He spun around, startled, and stared at me, unmoving. I took a step toward him, pointing to the pistol in his hand.

"Where the hell did you get a gun?"

"Does it matter?"

"Yes!" I shouted back. "It does, Alex."

"I just—"

"Stole it."

"No!" he retorted. "Okay…okay, yes, but I was going to return it."

"Give it to me."

"No." He turned around like a child, clutching it to his chest.

"Alex, give me the gun. You *know* it isn't our way."

He sighed, dropping it in my outstretched hand. "Maybe it should be," he grumbled as he walked away.

I thought seriously about turning him over to Father. I was sure he would talk to Alex—reason with him. I was also sure he would hit him. I didn't want that for Alex. I gave the gun to Luna when I returned home.

"How was your walk?" she asked as I stepped inside.

"Fine. I'm guessing this is yours," I said, handing her the pistol.

She sighed. "Who?"

"Alex. Of course."

"Did you tell Abraham?"

I shook my head.

"You can't keep covering for him, James."

"I know."

"I'll tell him."

"No!" I yelled. I almost grabbed hold of her as she headed toward the door.

"James, relax. It's Father we're talking about. It's okay."

"Luna, please don't. This one time, let it go."

"If Father finds out, we will both be in trouble—in a lot more trouble than Alex."

"I'll take full blame, Luna. I swear! He will be furious if he finds out you have a gun for *any* reason."

She sighed. "This is a bad idea. But fine. This once."

"Thank you."

She gave me a flaccid smile.

"What?" I questioned. "What are you thinking?"

She turned away from me. "It hurts you," she murmured.

I took a step closer to her. "Luna, look at me," I pleaded softly.

She turned back around, and I could see she was crying. Her face was so innocent when she was sad. It hurt to look at her.

"It hurts you—when you kill."

I couldn't respond. It was like the air was stolen from my lungs.

Her voice fell to a whisper. "It hurts me too."

Chapter Seven

"I AM GOING to tell you something you may find confusing," she started. "The Sevren is threatened by a very strong enemy. It's an organization of people who are against our beliefs. They have been around since the 20s, and we have been fighting them for our rights to do what we do."

"Who are they?"

"They call themselves The Silver Wing."

"The Silver Wing," I echoed quietly. "Led by whom?"

"That's the thing I was truly terrified of telling you."

"Luna, what are you talking about?"

"James, we have to get out."

"What?"

"We have to leave." Her voice had fallen to a whisper.

"We can't..." I broke off. "Luna, we can't...leave."

"Yes," she spat. "Yes—we can, James, and we must. We just can't let Abraham know."

"How can we keep something like that a secret?"

"You know it's wrong," she said. "I can see it in your face, James. I can see the way it haunts you."

"I'm being sent away to find Daniel's family."

"I know. I'll help you, but we need to find the leader of The Silver Wing, and hopefully, he can help us."

"Who is he?"

"You have met him before, James."

"Have I?" My voice swelled with sarcasm.

"You have. Be ready to talk to him, James. Prepare to tell him of your mistakes."

"My mi… What?"

"Your mistakes," she repeated.

My head spun, and everything started piecing itself together.

I was forced to leave him to protect him.

"Luna…"

She wouldn't say anything more.

"My God," I whispered. "Walter!"

"I know about The Sevren," I said to him.

"How?"

"It's a long story. Tell me why they are here, why you haven't stopped them."

"Oh, we tried," he grumbled, turning away from me and staring at a painting on the wall of a horse running through grass.

"What do you mean?"

"We established a treaty. It was a long time ago. Apparently, it meant nothing to them."

"Did you actually expect them to agree to a treaty, Walter?"

"Oh, well, they did"—he chuckled—"for a while anyway."

"Well, there certainly isn't any kind of loyalty to that now."

He let out a sputtered chuckle again. "Looks like it may be something for you to be worried about after all, eh, Clem?"

I tried to smile, but I couldn't. "We need your help."

He narrowed his eyes. "What are you saying?"

I stuttered and choked on my words. "I…I'm his son."

"Whose son?"

I swallowed and looked away.

"Tell him, James," Luna whispered.

"James?" Walter retorted. "You didn't!"

I turned back to face him and slowly nodded.

"Oh my God!"

I tried to look at him. I tried to say something—anything. I opened my mouth to speak, but nothing came out. I instantly started crying, and he pulled me into his chest.

"I don't know what to do," I said through sobs. "I belong in Hell!"

"Don't say that, Clem," he coaxed.

"I've killed," I told him. "Walter, I've murdered innocent people, more people than I can count."

He pushed me away, but his face remained tranquil and sad. "Clem, you're a good person. I know that, and you know that."

"That's not all," I said. "I fear now you will never again love me."

"What are you talking about?" he bellowed. "There is nothing you can do to make me not love you."

"I messed up."

"Talk to me about it, Clem."

I shook my head. I tried to tell him, but it was like I had forgotten what I was going to say. I had rehearsed it in my head for hours, and once it came time to say it, my fear had paralyzed me. Walter was the only person I had now. He was the only one who could help us. I knew I had to tell him.

Do it for Daniel.

I mustered all my courage and tried again. Still nothing came out of my mouth when I tried to speak. It seemed like days that I stood there, completely paralyzed and dumbfounded until I heard Luna speak.

"It's okay," she said. "Tell him."

I brought my eyes to his and forced the words from my mouth. "I destroyed our dreams." My voice was stifled by sudden tears. "Oh God, Walter. I'm so sorry. Our dreams of science, they are dead!"

"Ah, my boy," he started, smiling, "dreams don't die." He spoke calmly with a kind expression on his aged, furrowed face. He made me smile when he looked at me that way.

"Here"—he gestured to the couch—"have a seat, and tell me what happened."

I started from the beginning with my sickness and the death of my parents, leading all the way to the over three years I had spent with The Sevren.

When I was finished explaining my mistakes, I knew I had to tell him about Abraham's plans for me.

"I've been chosen for a mission," I said.

"What kind of mission?" His eyes narrowed.

"You need to help us get out," Luna interrupted.

He nodded. "I understand. I know somebody who can help. But tell me what *kind* of mission?"

I sighed and lowered my head. "I have been sent to kill this family."

"What family?"

I struggled to remember the last name and turned to Luna.

"Callahan," she said.

49

I nodded. "The sister, mother, and father."

Walter nodded. "I know that family."

"You do?"

"Of course," he answered. "Abraham wants them dead because they are connected to The Silver Wing. My father was the one who established The Silver Wing, and after his death, I took it over, so of course I know the people involved."

"How well?"

He bowed his head.

"Walter?"

"I had this old chest," he started, "filled with pictures and letters. A friend of mine, who joined the Silver Wing around the same time as I did, took it from me. He said it was for my own good. He couldn't stand watching me shuffle through the contents. I was making myself miserable with the memories of the ones I left behind, so he took it. He is dead now, tragically. It will not end with him. They will set out to kill everyone connected to him. As far as I know, the chest was given to his son. It's locked so nobody can find the secrets hidden inside, but that doesn't mean his family is safe."

"There was a boy," Luna said.

Walter looked to her and pulled his eyebrows together. "Young?"

"Yes."

"His grandson," he whispered. "He's dead?"

My throat constricted, and I felt physically sick.

Luna nodded. "The Sevren is now after the rest of the family. The job was offered to James to kill them."

"I understand," he answered.

"What do we do?" I asked.

"Get away. You need to get away. Stay here for a while. It's far enough away from them for now."

I nodded, still unsure of how this was going to end.

Chapter Eight

THE DAYS PASSED EASILY ENOUGH. For two weeks we stayed with Walter, but nothing yet had been planned on how we were to get away from him unseen. It was almost as if we were all too frightened to even speak of it. It was always so quiet; we all went about our days in silence, speaking when only essential. It got to the point where I couldn't stand it any longer. I had to get out.

"Luna, I'm heading out," I told her.

"Are you out of your mind?" she questioned, almost sarcastically, crossing her arms and cocking her head.

She made me laugh. "No, really," I said. "It's all right. I'll steer clear of Abraham."

"How are you planning on getting there?"

"What do you mean?"

"You don't have a driver's license, James."

I laughed loudly. It was completely unnecessary. "Do you not know Father at all?"

"What?" Her voice swelled with tension.

"I have a driver's license, Luna—three to be exact."

"You have...what?"

"Don't worry. I've taken care of it. I'm borrowing Walter's car. I'll just be out for a cup of coffee. I'll be back in less than an hour."

"James..."

"Luna, don't say anything," I demanded, almost harshly. I was sick to death of her tending to me like I was too incompetent to take care of myself.

I looked over one of the IDs and decided Aidan Summers fit me well enough for the time being in case anyone asked. I left quickly, driving to Books by the Bay for a cup of coffee and perhaps a quick read. I walked in, and the place was practically empty. I strolled around to the fiction section, hoping to find something interesting to keep my mind off Abraham and the betrayal that was eating away at me.

That's when I saw her—a quiet girl flipping through random books and tossing them back on the shelves. She was plowing through them as if she knew exactly what she was looking for. Her movement slowed, and I watched her eyes move to the top shelf. She reached for a thick book with a green binding and broad gold letters reading, *Selected Works of Charles Dickens*.

Nice choice. She tugged at the book hastily while grumbling to herself. I almost laughed at her reactions. She was very interesting to observe. Suddenly, I noticed the shelf slowly leaning toward her. I rushed over and gently pushed the shelf back upright and rearranged the books, handing her the one she had been tugging at.

"Are you all right?" I asked, still amused by her.

"Fine," she answered reluctantly. "Thanks."

"I couldn't let the shelf topple over on you like that, now could I?" I smiled at her, trying to ignore her chestnut eyes that were almost burning into my own. I couldn't help but to stare. I saw her quickly avert her gaze. I felt I was making her uncomfortable, but something about her just roused a strange curiosity in me.

"Sorry for being so impatient. I'm feeling a little anxious today," she said, possibly hoping to leave without seeming rude. She didn't seem like she wanted to speak to me at all.

I put my hand up and tried to sound pleased and carefree. "No worries."

She didn't respond right away, and I realized I was staring at her again.

"Well...um...thanks again," she said and turned away.

I knew I should have left it at that, but for some reason, I ended up introducing myself. "The name's Aidan!" I called before she disappeared around the corner.

She turned back around meeting my eyes but said nothing.

"This is the part where you tell me yours," I teased.

"Maybe later," she said, smiling.

I smiled back, unsure if she was trying to be charming and funny or if she was really uncomfortable. I decided it didn't matter and bowed my head. I headed out the door, realizing I couldn't stay there without bothering her. She was beautiful, though not in the way women in magazines were beautiful, but she had this elegance even with her amusing and inept movements. I couldn't stand not at least knowing her name.

I halted in front of the bookstore, going over things in my head. It was finally sinking in how wrong Abraham was. She was one he would have asked me…*ordered* me…to kill—a lovely young girl seemingly completely innocent. There was something sad about her, something that made her turn away from me without so much as her name. It was gnawing at my nerves. I wasn't used to people ignoring me; in fact, I had never been turned down that way in any situation. Who was she? What was she about? I couldn't even understand my own thoughts, couldn't decide why I cared.

I tried to calm my nerves before driving. I concentrated on my surroundings for a moment to straighten out my thoughts. The air was misty, but I enjoyed the small beams of sunlight piercing through the clouds.

My thoughts scattered back to burning curiosity and confusion when I saw the girl walking out of the bookstore, toward the parking lot. Her pace quickened when she heard be behind her, but I caught up.

"Hey," I breathed, trying not to startle her.

"Can I help you?" she asked, clearly irritated.

I was silent for a moment, suddenly not sure what I could say to calm her annoyance. "I…uh…I just wanted to know if I could get your name?" I stuttered, feeling like a fool.

"Actually, I'd much rather not tell you," she answered, still with irritation rocking through her.

"Why not?"

She averted her gaze and pursed her lips before responding. "I don't like *humans*." She turned away before I could think of a response.

Definitely clever. Surely a good way to end a conversation. I sighed, still looking in her direction, trying to see if I could possibly find a glimpse of what she was thinking. Her expression was unreadable just as it had been in the bookstore. *Strange.* I was usually good at reading expression and emotion, but the only thing I got from her was the fact that she was clearly uninterested in engaging in conversation. I tried to brush it off, not wanting it to turn into some ridiculous obsession.

As soon as I got home, Luna rushed to the door. Her breath exploded when she saw me.

"Fine," I told her, suppressing laughter. "I'm fine."

"Why is everything so amusing to you?" she snapped. She tore the keys from my hand and tossed them in the wicker basket on the table by the door.

"You really need to relax. I know how to avoid Abraham, at least for now. Walter will figure things out in the meantime."

She sighed. "You're probably right, but it still makes me nervous when you leave like that. At *least* come up with a clever lie you would tell if Abraham *were* to actually find you."

Of course, I thought. It was very unlike me for that to not have crossed my mind.

"Understood," I said. "Now settle down?"

She huffed and walked away, shoving past Walter in the hallway.

"What's with her?" He laughed huskily.

"She's…tense," I told him. "A little nervous to see me leave."

"Ah, you can't stay cooped up in here all the time. You'll go mad."

I smiled as I always did when Walter spoke to me. "She'll get over it. I tend to ignore her until she gives up fighting with me." I broke into laughter.

Dinner was silent that night, and Luna hardly acknowledged me at all. I guessed she was still angry. I just kept to myself, trying to keep my mind off of the odd, intriguing girl from the bookstore. I slept well that night, and when I awoke, my mind instantly launched back into the day before. How insane was I to *still* be thinking about her?

I sighed and got myself ready for the day, prepared to talk to Walter about The Sevren. For some reason, I couldn't bring myself to say anything to him. I knew things were brewing in his head and he would fill me in once he had everything figured out. I didn't want to nag at him. I focused on those thoughts so my anxiety wouldn't drive me insane. I understood why Luna had been so frustrated with me, but either way, I couldn't stay locked inside. I spent sixteen years of my life locked away; I was determined to at least try to interact with the world during the day.

The girl started gnawing away at my memory again, and I decided to head down to Books by the Bay on the off chance she might be there.

I wasn't at all surprised when I noticed her across the room, chatting quietly with another girl. Her friend seemed highly interested in whatever was being said. Her friend was clearly pretty but in a different way—a more…conventional way. She was in a black, tight-fitting top and a short skirt while the girl I had seen before was in jeans and a T-shirt. I was very intrigued and found myself staring again. I thought they may have noticed me, so I decided I should try to look away and just look through some books to calm my nerves. I browsed mindlessly, my eyes glazing over the titles, unable to focus. That's when I spotted her, the beautiful girl reading a book on Wicca. I couldn't stop myself from trying to make conversation with her.

"Reading?" I asked.

"No," she answered immediately. She tossed the book back onto the shelf. "The book and I were just having a conversation."

I laughed, thinking for sure she was flirting but still slightly annoyed by me. "All right. I asked for that one."

She picked up another book and opened it to some random page. I tried to let myself just leave her alone, but I hadn't satiated my interest.

"So, what's new with you?" I asked, trying to sound normal and casual.

"Why?" she asked, curtly. "It's not like you're actually interested."

Her response took me off guard. My mood shifted by her sudden rudeness. I felt almost offended.

"Why do you have to be like that? I'm just trying to be nice to you," I demanded.

"I'm not interested in being nice, okay?" she spat. "I just want to be left alone."

"Nobody likes to *always* be alone."

"Then does that make me nobody?"

I prepared myself to respond, but she spoke before I had the chance to come up with anything.

"I'm sorry," she said. "I just—I just want to be left alone."

"Well...can I at least get your name?"

She sighed. "Jane Doe," she said quickly and turned away.

I was expecting to be pleased by simply knowing her name, but instead I felt like a knife had just rushed through my heart. Jane... I was almost paralyzed until I realized by her attitude that she was simply being sarcastic. Ha! Jane Doe —how original. Really funny. Something in me still wouldn't let me leave it alone. They said she was in California, but... Now I *had* to be sure.

"Is that your real name?"

"Aidan—please!"

That name...Aidan. Had I really introduced myself as Aidan? I shuddered.

"Nice meeting you," I grumbled.

I thought I saw her turn back around toward me but ignored. I decided to leave her alone for a while, at least while my burning curiosity was satiated. Even though she was being cynical, at least she cared enough to try so hard. She left shortly after that, so I felt there would be little harm in talking to her friend, just to at least find out her name.

"Hello," I said, approaching her friend.

"Oh, hey," she said sweetly, cocking her head and smiling at me. "Have a seat."

I took the chair across from her.

"Why don't I know you?" she asked, flipping her long, brown hair.

"I'm new here," I said, completely uninterested by her attempted flirting. "The name's Aidan."

"I'm Becky," she squealed overly cheerfully. Her gray eyes brightened. I instantly realized exactly what I had to do to keep her interested—talk about *her*.

"I saw you earlier," I started, making it sound like I was noticing. "Who was that girl you were talking to if you don't mind me asking?"

"Oh, Jane?" She laughed.

"Yeah...I guess."

"What about her?"

"I was...wondering about her name."

"Yeah," she yelped. "Jane."

"Ah, nice," I mumbled. Of course she would have told her exactly what to say to anybody bothering to ask.

I huffed and got up from the table. I walked out suddenly, more irritated than anything else. Jane crowded my thoughts the entire drive home. I was willing to believe her name was Jane, but she couldn't be Jane Doe—could she? What parent with the last name Doe would name their daughter Jane? I asked myself a thousand other questions but came back to one conclusion. I *had* to be sure. Something was drawing me to her, like some energy she had. She was lovely and different. Even through her sneering remarks, I found hidden charm in her witty responses. She always had some interesting answer to my prodding questions. But if she was Jane Callahan, there could be trouble there for not only myself.

I walked inside.

"Walter?" I called, tossing his keys into the basket.

"In here," he yelled back.

I followed his voice into the bedroom, and my feet froze in place, almost pulling me to the floor. His hands were up in front of his chest, and beads of sweat rimmed his brow. The gun pressed into his back was like an assault on my nerves. I instinctively raised my hands.

"You really thought you were that clever?" David hissed.

My God. How did he find us? He pressed the pistol harder into Walter's back, forcing a quiet groan from him.

"What name did you give her?"

"What are—?"

"What name, James?" he yelled out. "I saw you sitting with a girl. What name did you give her?"

I took a deep breath, feeling the truth being torn from my lungs. "I told her —Aidan. Aidan Summers."

Why couldn't I lie? How was it The Sevren still had such power over me? So much power that I felt guilty for my treachery?

"The gun, David," I breathed, my voice blocked and difficult to hear. "Please."

His face was twisted into fury, but he put the gun down.

"Our laws no longer apply to you, James," he said. "I will kill you with a gun if I wish. You are not deserving of a personal kill. I will destroy you with any vile weapon I choose."

I knew he couldn't kill me. David was a lower ranked member than myself. He wasn't sent here for that. Walter, however, he could easily kill with nobody having a second thought.

"Abraham is enrolling you in school."

"What?" I bellowed.

"Shut up!" he spat. "You and Mike are going to North Bend High. The Callahan family is here—in Oregon. No need for you to go gallivanting off to California and disappear. Your mission is here now."

No! It couldn't be. It couldn't be her. Jane Callahan? The sister of Daniel? My head spun. She would surely despise me now no matter what was to happen in the following days. It didn't matter. If only I could have left her alone. If only she didn't bewitch me so effortlessly. Oh God. I was going to kill her.

"Be smart, James. Make her trust you first. The kill will be all the sweeter."

I nodded robotically. He shoved past me and out the door before I was able to say another word.

Chapter Nine

IT WAS the last day of summer break, and all I could think about was how angry Luna would be and how angry Walter was for becoming part of my problems. We were lucky Walter's involvement with The Silver Wing had not been revealed. The resistance against The Sevren was not as strong as Walter wished to believe.

As far as everyone knew, he was my uncle and legal guardian. I had a social security number and was in the system as seventeen-year-old Aidan Summers. How could I pull off a carefree, seventeen-year-old junior in high school? None of that was me. I was twenty-year-old Clement Thortan going by the name of James West, carrying twelve IDs and credit cards all issued to different names and social security numbers. "Genius," my father always said, didn't he? I could figure this out. I *had* to. Jane was in my blood now. I had to protect her. That's what I vowed to do the second David threatened me with that vile gun. The goddamn bastard. A gun of all things? Such a sick, man-made torture device. I shuddered and brushed off the thoughts. This would work itself out. I was sure of it.

School was a haze the first day. I knew I had to stay as far away from Jane as possible. Mike passed me in the hallway a few times, acknowledging me with a nod or a stare. I knew what he was saying—*it starts now.* I pretended like I was doing my job and more than prepared to kill Jane and her parents when the time came. Maybe if I stayed away from her, they wouldn't know who she was. David had seen me with Becky; couldn't they believe *she* was Jane until I figured out a way to get the Callahans out of North Bend? It seemed a perfectly logical idea.

Mike was masquerading as a sophomore, meaning we would have no classes together—all the better to conceal our association. It was all done well, and the only thing left were my orders. I was not James West any longer. I refused to be. I would never harm an innocent again. Every time a kill reflected in my memory, I saw Daniel even when I strained to remember the others—they were *all* him. It was driving me mad. Why him? Why did it have to be him I couldn't forget? Why must I live with the guilt of his death weighing on my shoulders when I was intrigued and infatuated with his sister—the girl I was supposed to murder.

Before I raveled out of my thoughts, the day was already halfway over. I walked by myself to the lunch room, noticing the stares and whispers about the "new guy." I spotted Becky happily snapping pictures of Jane as Jane desperately tried to hide her face.

"Come on," I heard Becky squeal, full of energy just as she was when I first met her. "You look adorable."

It seemed the perfect opportunity to be seen speaking to Becky, my false, make-believe Jane. I was sure Mike was watching from somewhere in the cafeteria.

"Hey," I said, just loud enough to be heard.

"Oh, hi," Becky answered.

I saw Jane slowly move her eyes to mine. I glared at her and averted my gaze. I couldn't let her know what was going on. I had to pretend she meant nothing to me. I didn't know her anyway, and I couldn't let myself. I had to leave her alone, which was what she had asked for from the start. I chose a table by myself as far away from Jane as I could get. I could see she was mumbling something to Becky. Becky let out her usual perky response, rendering her at best intolerable.

I tried to look away, but just as it had always been, it was almost impossible not to stare at her. I couldn't keep myself from noticing the looks she had unintentionally passed my direction. I had no idea what she was thinking, no idea what was going on behind her delicate, elegant face. My God, she was stunning.

My infatuation with her irritated me deeply, and I tried to shake it off. I could feel the actual annoyance creeping into my features, and before I even realized I was uneasy, I found myself glaring at her again.

"What did you do?" I heard Becky grumble. The rest of her words were too difficult to perceive, but surely enough, Jane looked over at me and quickly looked away. I didn't want to hurt her feelings, but it was better than getting her killed.

When I finally got to my last class, I was beginning to think ignoring Jane would be much easier than I originally thought. That thought lasted only until I saw her enter the classroom. She was late, so she rushed to the first seat she could get to before the bell rang. I noticed the sickness on her face when she realized she took the seat next to me. My face burned. She was so close to me now. All I had to do was reach out and touch her.

"Hey," she murmured.

There was no way she would be speaking to me. I turned to look at her, forcing myself to pretend like I was angry, pretend like I wanted nothing to do with her.

"Oh, you're talking to me now?" I snapped.

"Well—"

"Don't bother." I broke eye contact.

I wanted to say something to her so badly. *What are you thinking? How do you like North Bend? What are you about, Jane?* I clenched my hands into fists and gritted my teeth, fighting the urge to speak to her. I kept glancing over at her even as I tried not to. Oh God. This would be harder than I thought. It was like I wanted to kill her, while at the same time, I wanted to protect her—I wanted her. I wanted to take her beauty and her innocence. She was made for me, wasn't she?

NO! Of course not. Abraham was wrong. He has always been wrong. You are not James West!

"I'm sorry," she whispered.

"Yeah," I answered, sarcastically. "I'm sure you care *so* much more than you did a couple days ago."

"Really, Aidan—"

The bell rang, and I grabbed my books and raced out of the classroom as fast as I could.

The next day was the same as before. I could barely keep myself away from her. I ended up staring at her more than I had the day before. Sometimes my thoughts would turn insane and senseless, back to the thoughts of killing her. Of course, there was no way I could. Even when I wanted to, the thought of actually doing it made me sick. The day ended quickly, and Becky approached me in the parking lot. Perfect. Maybe Mike would notice.

"Hey," she said.

"Hi," I stuttered.

"You know, you really should have accepted Jane's apology."

"You don't say."

"Look, she really is sorry for acting that way in the bookstore. She understands you were just being friendly. I've known Jane since first grade. We met during the summer when we were kids. I know she comes across as rude sometimes, but once you get to know her, she's really great."

I was sure of that already. "Okay."

"You know, Aidan, it is okay to be friends with people." She smiled.

I saw Jane striding our direction, so I left, quickly walking to my car.

Friends. That was not a logical idea was it? Every day it was getting harder and harder to ignore her. The next day, I failed altogether.

"Hi," I said a little too cheerfully, smiling at her.

"Hi." The look on her face made me uneasy.

"I didn't realize you knew Becky for so long," I said. "She mentioned you were summer pals since the first grade."

She nodded.

I was hoping she wouldn't think I was crazy. It wasn't a good idea to be speaking to her at all, but I couldn't help it.

"Well...she's nice."

"She is."

We didn't talk much after that. She seemed to be avoiding conversation. It was for the best, and I often found myself glaring at her or clenching my hands into fists to keep from touching her.

When I got home that day, Walter instantly knew something was wrong.

"Okay," he started, sitting down on the couch. "Come here and tell me what's wrong." He smoothed back his white hair and smiled at me.

"I don't know what to do," I said to him. "I can't kill her, Walter."

"The girl? You've found her?"

"I knew who she was before I started school," I confessed.

He sighed. "And now?"

"She isn't at all social. I'm hoping nobody else will know."

"Have you spoken to her?"

"I said 'hi.' That's about it. It's hard not to, Walter. You should see her. She's so...amazing."

"Amazing?" He burst into a sputtered laugh. "That's a little heavy, don't you think?"

I shook my head. "I don't know. There's just something about her. It's almost impossible to stay away."

"Being friends might make things easier for you," he answered.

"Yes, but can I be her friend while still being able to protect her?"

He shrugged his shoulders. "Only you can decide that."

I couldn't sleep that night. I lay in bed, driving myself crazy with thoughts of Jane. I decided to go for a walk to clear my head. I focused on staying as far away from the clearing as possible and just walked along the trail. My mind was more relaxed as I focused only on my breathing and the movement of my steps.

Suddenly, something pierced my senses. I remembered the night I had been mugged in the alleyway on my way to work, the night when I first realized I could sense danger. Now it was almost suffocating me. I could feel clouds of troubled and uncontrolled emotions collapsing around me. Something was wrong.

I continued walking through the trees, following the danger that was, by then, almost bringing me to my knees. I tried to fight off the fear that was pulsing through my veins and find out what was going on. Why was I walking toward danger? I couldn't even think about it. All I knew was I had to. Something was telling me to follow my senses and keep treading through the mud. I was nervous over the rain that had begun to fall rapidly. The very sound of the water hitting the trees was as if I was being taunted by mother-nature herself.

I kept moving until I heard footsteps—panicked footsteps. I followed, picking up my pace. I saw the shadow of a figure about twenty feet away, running aimlessly into the trees. I followed still, chasing the silhouette through the darkness.

I heard a muffled thud and a groan as the stranger fell hard into the mud and leaves. I froze and peered into the eyes and knew at once who it was. I would recognize that face anywhere.

"Jane?"

"Aidan?" Her voice was muffled, and she almost sounded relieved to see me.

"What are you doing in the woods?" I asked.

"What are *you* doing in the woods?"

"Oh my God, Jane!" I whispered, kneeling down and looking at her ankle. It was clearly swollen, and I could tell even in the dark that it was turning colors.

"I'm fine," she said. She was a terrible liar.

"I'll carry you."

"Ha!" she burst out. "You most certainly will *not*. I can walk."

"Jane, your ankle is broken. You *can't* walk."

"Watch me." She gave me a hateful look and stood to her feet, but she couldn't hide her accelerated breathing and the pain in her expression.

"Yeah," I said, laughing. "Don't complain. I'm just trying to help."

I lifted her into my arms, and she felt almost weightless. She was very small and tender. I felt anxious to touch her with my strength. I would never want to hurt her.

"Put me down!" she screamed.

"Don't be a baby."

"Put...me...*down!*"

I followed my senses but still almost forgot North Bend and was thinking I couldn't find her house. I just kept walking, slowing my pace so I could feel her warmth for a little longer. When I spotted the house, I recognized it instantly. I had seen it before on my normal walks. The man who lived there was a doctor. Oh good God—he was Jane's father. I set her on the porch and moved aside, away from the light of her house.

"Oh! Jane, where have you been?" her father demanded as he stepped outside.

"I just went for a walk in the woods," she said, turning to look at him. "I think I broke my ankle."

"All right. I'll be right back." He disappeared inside the house.

I moved back out of the shadows.

"You don't have to hide." She looked like she was trying to smile.

I smiled back.

"Um...thanks," she said.

I quickly moved into the darkness again, not wishing her father to know anything about me. The fewer people who would recognize me, the better.

"I don't think it's broken," I heard him say, "but you twisted it something terrible."

I watched as she withdrew into her house. I stood there, almost wishing I could stare through her windows. I shook my head and laughed at myself. No need to get weird and creepy.

Chapter Ten

I GOT HOME LATE that night and ended up with a few hours of sleep. School was a haze until lunch. I found Becky and Jane, but there was somebody else. I recognized him as one of the students in my history class, the only class I had with Jane. I tried to fight back the unexpected sting of jealousy. I felt as if I had to break her attention away from the other guy, whoever he was. I sat across from her.

"How's your ankle?" I asked.

"Fine."

"What did you do to your ankle?" Becky interrupted.

She didn't look up, just shook her head mechanically.

"Well, you certainly did a number on it," I said, trying not to laugh. Annoying her was what I was trying to avoid.

"Really, it's fine," she said, refusing to look up at me. "It only hurt for an hour or so."

I didn't care if she was lying or not. I just wanted to keep her attention on me.

The boy laughed. "Do things like that happen to you a lot?"

Becky laughed back. "She's been a tomboy her entire life."

"I never had any sisters, except maybe for you, Becky."

"I know," she answered. "Still true."

She continued staring down at her almost empty plastic tray, not making eye contact with anybody.

The lunch bell rang, and I watched hatefully as Jane and the new boy walked together to her next class.

I daydreamed through science. The lessons were nothing I didn't already know. Abraham could have at least put me in advanced classes. It would have kept me a bit more interested.

I was anxious to get to history next, to make sure I kept the new guy away from Jane. I walked in, seeing him ready to take the seat next to her. I nearly shoved him out of the way and took the chair. I almost felt bad when I saw the look on his face.

"You can sit here," Jane said to him, gesturing to the seat at her other side.

He shook his head. "It's all right."

He moved closer to the front of the room. Jane glared at me for a split second before covering her face with her hands.

"Hi," I said. "I hope I didn't upset him."

"Aaron."

Aaron. At least now I knew his name.

"Yes," I answered. "Nobody has been very friendly to me, save for maybe Becky."

She chuckled.

"What?"

"It's nothing," she answered but was still laughing.

I didn't blame her for laughing. Becky was a plucky, promiscuous teenager who truthfully drove me crazy more often than not. Of course she was friendly to me.

"Becky is friendly to anybody of the male species," she said.

I smiled. "I thought you'd say something like that."

"Did you?"

I changed the subject. "How's your ankle?"

"I already told you—it's fine."

"Are you sure?"

She just nodded.

"You can tell me if it's bothering you."

"Aidan, please!"

I immediately regretted trying to get an answer from her. I didn't have to speak to her to keep Aaron away. She looked tense and anxious. I couldn't help but to ask her one thing.

"Are you all right?"

She locked her amber eyes into my own, and her pale cheeks blushed lightly.

"If I were to tell you yes, I am guessing you're going to ask me if I'm sure."

"I'll take that as a yes."

66

She was out the door right as the bell rang. I walked slowly, watching her in front of me. I saw Aaron catch up to her in the parking lot. I couldn't hear what they were saying, and it drove me near mad. Her brave little suitor was making me almost furious. It was becoming an unhealthy obsession. She was beautiful and different, and I could tell now just as I could the moment I met her...she was also worth it. I wasn't sure how, but I knew she was. I wanted her. I wanted Aaron gone. I halted my thoughts when my mind flashed with pictures of me with a knife and Aaron strapped to that stone. I shook my head to erase the visions. I couldn't kill Aaron. Not for her. I wasn't James West, right? I didn't want to be—and she couldn't make me!

I stayed in bed the next day. I couldn't be near Jane again. I had no idea what I might have done if I got too close. Luna made dinner that evening for me and Walter.

"No school today?" Walter asked me, sitting at the table.

I shook my head.

Luna stared at me, giving me an accusing look. I sighed heavily and got up from the table.

"James," she called. "James, you have to eat something."

"No, I don't, Luna," I called from the other room, "and my name is Clem!"

I would even settle for Aidan, but James—just the very sound of it made me sick.

"I'm going for a walk."

"Wait!" Walter pleaded, grasping my arm as I reached for the door.

"What?"

"I wanted to know," he started, "if you...well, my...grandson."

My heart sank. "Oh...Walter, I haven't seen him yet."

"If you do...?"

I nodded. "Of course I will watch out for him."

"Thanks, Clem. Um...enjoy your walk."

I put my hand on his shoulder and gave him a formal nod. Again I stayed away from the clearing, not sure if Abraham had called together another meeting. He didn't seem foolish enough to call a meeting in the woods, not now that the Callahan girl was here in North Bend, but I couldn't be sure. Abraham worked in odd ways. I was enjoying the quiet and the serenity, but the sound of that odious name pulled me out of it. I turned around.

"James!" Mike was running toward me. "James..." He put his hands on his knees to catch his breath.

"What is it?"

He stood upright and smoothed back his tousled blond hair. "There's something going on tomorrow night."

"What do you mean?"

"There's a party," he said. "I'm sure the Callahan girl will be there. She seems overly social."

I nodded. So he *did* think she was Becky. Perfect.

"So you're coming, right?"

"Where is it?"

"About three blocks away," he said, pointing behind him. "Andrew Gallagher's." He handed me a slip of paper. "That's the exact address in case you can't find it."

"Sure, Mike. Thanks."

I sighed as he sauntered away. Great. Now I would have to suffer through a party. Anything to keep Jane out of trouble. I was thinking about heading to the bookstore for an innocent cup of coffee, this time wishing Jane wouldn't be there. I decided against it when I realized it was Friday and school was out. That's probably exactly where she was. It was like her refuge, her safe haven. I had to stay away—at least until Monday.

Chapter Eleven

BY THE TIME Saturday night approached, I was already completely prepared to try and stay unnoticed at the party. People seemed to notice something about me was different. Not that I minded much. It was better that way. It was strange but better that quite a few people actually seemed afraid of me. Oh, if they only knew. I ran down to Pony Village Mall to rent a costume before the party. Dracula. Simple enough and traditional. Nobody would think twice.

I threw the costume on and didn't worry about my hair or any kind of accessory necessary for Dracula. I left slightly early, and when I got there, the house was already flooded with people. I could hardly identify anyone through the flashing black lights.

"Hey."

I looked up. "What's up, Andrew?" I yelled over the pounding music, doing my best to sound casual—and seventeen. He gave me some lame high five and offered me something.

"What's this?" I asked.

"E," he said.

"What?"

"Um...E...ecstasy?"

"Oh!" I laughed and put my hand up. "No, thanks, man." I wasn't here to take drugs or get drunk.

"Whatever," he murmured and walked away from me.

I kept glancing at my watch every ten minutes and eventually began to think Becky wasn't going to show up. She probably had a date with some senior.

Either way, I couldn't stand the atmosphere. I walked outside, feeling as if a boulder had been moved off my chest. It was so congested inside. I stepped down the steps, taking intentional notice of the well-carved jack-o-lanterns set on the steps.

I was almost to the end of the driveway when my senses started screeching inside my head again. Jane? No way! I raced to the house as fast as I could just in time to launch myself forward and grasp her arms as she fell backward off the steps of the porch. High heels do not help uncoordinated people like Jane.

"You're a walking accident," I said, setting her down in the grass.

She thrust her hand to her chest. "Oh, Aidan."

I could tell she was glad to see me. Exactly what I wanted but was still hoping not to receive.

"Quick hands," she breathed.

"Only when there is a need. Are you all right?"

"Fine, thanks to you."

I smiled at her.

"I didn't even know you were behind me," she said.

I couldn't respond. I had no logical reason I could tell her.

I noticed she was staring at me, so I saw no harm in staring back. She was wearing a tight, black corset, which could have easily driven me insane if I were to focus too hard on it. Her legs were covered by a black skirt and fishnet stockings. Her red hooded cape matched the dangerous red heels she was wearing. Her skin was perfect as it had always been, but the pounds of makeup I was sure were courtesy of Becky.

"You look...beautiful," I murmured before I could stop myself.

I saw her cheeks blush. "Loving the Dracula costume. We match."

I chuckled and figured I would come up with something to make her smile. I held back my satin-lined cape, bowing formally.

"Vladimir Dracula," I said, forcing the Romanian accent, which I was sure was a terrible attempt.

She laughed, which was exactly the reaction I was looking for, and responded with a curtsy. "Elizabeth?"

"You know your history."

"Sort of. So what's it like in there? Anything going to jump out at me when I walk in?"

"I don't think so, but"—I glanced at my watch again—"I was just leaving."

"Why?"

The truth was enough to get her to leave as well. "I don't care for the atmosphere. Drugs and alcohol are not really my idea of a good time."

"I'm not sure I want to be here either," she muttered.

"But Becky—"

"I know," she mused. "She tried so hard to get me here."

Not at all what I was going to say. I was going to say it was more Becky's thing and that I was sure she wouldn't mind if Jane left. I left it alone.

"To be honest, I'm surprised to see you here," I said.

"I'm surprised to see *you* here."

I tried not to laugh when I saw her press in tooth caps she flashed as she smiled at me. I didn't want her to stay. In fact, I wanted the opposite. Jane shied away from attention, so I came up with a perfectly believable scenario to get her to just go home.

"You should stay," I said.

"Why?"

"Well, there's a costume contest later, and you look very beautiful. I'm sure it would be a lot of fun."

"Becky would *crush* my hopes," she said, "and nobody else would have much of a chance either."

I laughed. "She looks great, I'll admit, but honestly, Jane, you don't give yourself enough credit."

That much I meant one hundred percent.

"I'll make an appearance," she said, "but I don't plan on staying long."

Perfect.

"Well, can I get you a drink?"

"Sure."

"Be right back."

I picked up a red, plastic cup and filled it with punch, which I was sure was spiked. This party wasn't turning out exactly like I had planned. I saw Mike approach Jane over by the staircase about twenty feet away from me. Oh, no, you don't. I walked back to her quickly and glared at Mike, amused by his Indiana Jones costume. I could tell he was high. So much for Mike following orders. He wasn't here to have fun. I hoped he didn't have a chance to get her name. I doubted very seriously she would have told him, considering how hard it was for *me* to pry it out of her.

I handed her the cup.

"Thanks," she said and downed it in one quick gulp.

I laughed. "Want another?" I asked, offering her my drink.

"Oh, no, thanks. I have to drive, remember? I owe you one for rescuing me again."

"It was nothing."

I followed Jane's gaze and saw Becky across the room, fall hard onto the floor as the guy she was dancing with dropped his entire drink all over her devil costume. She just laughed like Becky usually did. That was one thing I actually found amusing.

I knew that second that Jane had no intention of leaving. She would suffer just to make sure Becky was all right. I could see that kind of love in her. I had to get her away from this party before anyone took too much notice of her, particularly Mike.

"Hey," I started, more nervous than I thought I would be to ask out a girl. "I don't think I could tempt you into a movie, maybe dinner?"

She forced a smile. I could tell it was artificial.

"I don't know, Aidan. It's late."

"You said you owed me," I pleaded, "and we both know you have to come back for Becky."

"Like this?" she said, putting her hands up, displaying her costume.

"Yeah." I laughed falsely. "We won't be the only people dressed up. It *is* Halloween after all. People dress up at work all the time." That part I knew was true. *Come on, Jane. Just say yes.* I smiled at her again, hoping she may find me charming.

My body almost forced me to leap into the air when I saw her nod. "I'd like that, Aidan."

I couldn't hide the huge smile that spread across my face. I shouldn't be so happy to get my target to go out with me.

I stepped outside and draped my vampire cape over her shoulders.

"You must be freezing," I said.

"I'm all right. Thanks."

Very like Jane, always putting on the strong, independent act. I knew it was an act simply because it wasn't difficult to get her to agree to something. She wasn't one who enjoyed confrontation even though she could get sarcastic and cynical.

We walked to her car.

"Don't you drive?" she asked.

"Oh, I live just a couple blocks away. I walked here." That was an easy truth to tell. It felt good not to have to lie to her, at least not yet.

"I see," she answered, clearly uninterested.

"I'm guessing you want to drive?"

"Right."

"Do you know where you're going?"

"I'll know where to go once you tell me."

"Well, I can't argue with that," I said, smiling.

She turned on the light and started taking out her unattractive cat-eyed contacts and plastic fangs. I took off my gloves and sat there, waiting a moment before speaking.

"They're having what they call Flashback Week at the theatre," I started, "showing old horror movies. What did you think of *Halloween*?" I was hoping for a classic movie. One I had already seen in case I couldn't focus on it.

"Loved it," she said.

I nodded. "Sound good?"

"Perfect! You know," she started, changing the subject abruptly, "you're quite good at rescuing me. You're not stalking me, are you?"

I laughed and shook my head. That was the Jane I was waiting to see. "You're different," I said.

"Yeah, as if I haven't heard that before."

"No." I laughed. "That's not how I meant it. I meant different than you were in the bookstore the first time I rescued you. But it's a good thing."

"You're different too," she said, "but also not so different at the same time."

"So why did you come to North Bend?" I asked.

"I lived in California, but my parents divorced, and I couldn't stand living there anymore after my brother died."

My heart plunged into my stomach, and my throat tightened. I had to remain composed. "Your brother died?" It was a struggle to keep my voice steady and torture to make her explain.

"Three years ago."

My chest burned.

"Murdered and dumped in an alleyway."

An alleyway? Oh, Alex, you bastard!

"I'm sorry," I forced out, my voice half caught in my throat. "That's awful. Did they catch the person who did it?"

"'The bastard fled. They *still* haven't found him."

They won't, darling. I wished I could have told her that. I wished in that moment I could have told her everything. I was silent.

"What about you?" she asked. "Why did you come here?"

Time to lie.

"My family wanted to move here—for some God unknown reason."

"You don't like it here?"

"Oh, the place is fine. The school is fine too. It's just the people. They seem to find me…intimidating."

She laughed.

"What?"

"Intimidating doesn't even begin to cover it. You captivate people's attention, Aidan, almost effortlessly."

"Have I ever captivated yours?"

"You have," she answered. "After saving my life a number of times."

I tried to laugh but wasn't at all amused. I was anxious of where all of this was going and what kind of trouble my betrayal was getting me into. "So…what kind of movies do you like?"

"Scary," she said.

"You're different, and this time I do mean it that way." I snickered.

"I know."

Chapter Twelve

IT SEEMED most everybody who worked at the theatre was dressed up. People stared more often than usual. The room was dark and lit by lights on the stairs, and my shoes stuck to the floor. I hated it. I had only been to the movies a few times as a kid; I didn't remember it quite like this. The red seats were hard and not comfortable. I kept my eyes locked on the screen, trying to act interested in the movie when my thoughts were just scrambling around trying to come up with ways I could organize this mess I had gotten us into.

It was a relief when the movie ended, though I could have used more time to think. Jane instantly started with the questions.

"So why did you act that way the first day of class?" she asked as soon as we walked out of the theatre.

"I don't think I know what you mean," I answered, hoping she wouldn't catch on that I was lying. It was obvious I couldn't tell her the truth. *Well, Jane, because if I was nice to you, my former cult of assassins would strap you to a stone and serve your blood in silver goblets. I'm sure you understand.*

"Never mind. It was probably my imagination," she said.

"Do you need to get home?"

"I'm tired, but thanks for getting me away from the party. Should I take you home?"

"Back to Andrew's," I said. "I left my jacket there."

She nodded. "Okay. I need to go back there anyway. I need to make sure Becky can drive."

I laughed. "I can guarantee Jared can't."

She chuckled quietly. I wasn't sure if she was actually amused. "Oh, you saw that?"

"Who didn't see that?"

When we got back to Andrew's, Jared was passed out on the bathroom floor. I had Jane help me carry him to the couch. I watched as she rushed over to Becky, who was what she would call "dancing" with a guy dressed as a Jedi Knight. I was surprised to see she wasn't also passed out on the bathroom floor.

I couldn't hear their conversation, but it wasn't hard for me to see that Becky was clearly not sober, and Jane was making sure her Jedi friend would make sure she got home all right.

Jane didn't even say a word to me before rushing out the door. I slung my vampire cape over my shoulder and started down the street, replaying in my mind how I had actually asked her out. Was I crazy? I had definitely planned on finishing what I started in the theatre, thinking of ways I could fix this, so a walk was the solution I came up with.

Mike found me at home again and told me that I had the wrong girl.

"We were wrong. That girl at the party, the one you gave a drink to, she's the one," he said, drama in his voice.

Damn! I screwed up.

"No," I retorted, "I don't think so, Mike."

"James, I swear to you. I'm sure of it."

"Look, Mike," I started, standing up from the couch, "this is my mission, all right? You're great as my right-hand man, but stay just that. Let me take care of this my way."

"As you wish as long as your way won't get you killed by Abraham."

I shunned him even though I knew he was right.

I avoided the bookstore but *had* to do something. I went for a walk again, this time just down the main streets. It was such a quaint town; I'd have actually adored it if it wasn't for everything constantly being so soggy. The rain didn't bother me, just the glumness of it all. I was minding my own business, and one of Abraham's men recognized me. It was Jason.

"What do you want?" I demanded.

"Come this way," he said. He led me into the woods off the road. "What are you thinking?" he hissed.

"What are you talking about?"

"You're in love with her, James! Aren't you?"

"Of course not, Jason. Not at all. I am simply doing what I was told."

They all knew who she was now. This was not my intention. God, if only I could have stayed away.

"I need you to come with me. You need to talk to Abraham."

"About what?"

"About your betrayal," he jeered.

"Betrayal?"

I felt his hand crush my cheek, and I almost fell to the ground. He hit almost as hard as Abraham.

"Do not hide behind the fact that you are his son. He will kill you if he chooses. Though I do think he would be proud of me if I took care of it myself."

He reached into the inside pocket of his jacket and pulled out his knife. I punched him as hard as I could in the face, and he fell backward. I leapt toward him until he was on the ground and sat on top of him, wrenching the knife from his hand. I plunged it straight into his chest. He let out a weak, soggy groan and fell still. I wasn't sure if he was dead yet, but it didn't matter to me. I dragged the body to the clearing, placing it in front of the alter. There was nobody there, which gave me a chance to deny my involvement. It didn't seem to matter; Abraham would know it was me.

I continued walking, now on my way back home to get some cleaner clothes. My shirt was covered in blood, but I was hoping my jacket could conceal most of it until I could change. My mind was now haunting me with the murder I had just committed. It was justified this time, wasn't it? He was someone I considered a friend up until the very minute my knife punctured his heart, and that was hard to deal with. He was better than David, of course; he never threatened me with a gun. It shouldn't have been Jason.

I continued walking, and as I was strolling past Jane's house, I did everything I could to resist the urge to knock on her door. I kept my eyes locked on it and saw two people slowly opening her front door. I knew Jane lived with her father, and neither one of the guys who entered was him. I tried telling myself it wasn't my concern, but I couldn't let them hurt her, could I? Hopefully they would just take what they wanted and leave. Maybe they wouldn't hurt her at all. I knew that if she ended up hurt, there would be no way I could forgive myself, and because of the way people looked at me, I would be the first suspect. I was supposed to kill her though. Maybe I wouldn't have to. It would be much easier this way if it were to just happen. That thought ate through me like acid. Was Jason right? Was I...in love?

I pushed that thought to the back of my mind and slowly crept up to her front door, gently pushing it open. I was about to call her name when I was attacked. A boy swung a rake at me, slicing my shirt. I backed away, and he came at me again.

"Eric!" another shouted. "I got him!"

He pulled me inside by the neck of my shirt and shoved me against the wall. He seemed not to notice the blood. The smell began to make me sick. It brought me back to the days when I was James West and proud to be. I felt dirty and vile.

"Rudy!" Eric shouted. "Be careful!"

Rudy? Damn it! He was Walter's grandson. I couldn't hurt him. Rumor also had it he was friends with Jane too. Perfect! He hit me a few times in the face, and I didn't even move an inch to fight back. I could have killed the guy in less than five minutes, and maybe I'd just kill Eric for pissing me off with that damn rake he swung at me, but Walter would never forgive me.

"You won't leave here alive," Rudy growled, shoving me against the wall and hitting me again. "I won't let you hurt her."

I felt myself sinking into dizziness—not from his punches but more from the madness of everything that was happening. I needed rest; my thoughts were overwhelming me.

"Rudy?"

He turned around to see Jane in the doorway.

"Oh my God!" she cried. "Rudy, stop! Are you crazy?"

"No, Jane! He's crazy. I saw him sneaking into your house. I was trying to protect you."

He grabbed me again by the neck of my shirt and shoved me even harder against the wall.

"Rudy, what the hell is wrong with you?" she screamed.

"Jane, I tried to tell you before. He isn't human."

"What?"

"He's a hunter. You *have* to keep him away from you."

The words flooded into me, and it made me sick to realize he was right. Walter had told him about The Sevren for a reason. He taught him well.

"Rudy, you're my friend," she said, "and I would *hate* to call the cops on you."

"Jane—"

"Get the hell out of my house, Rudy. NOW!"

"Jane, please!"

"Three numbers, Rudy. That's all it takes."

"Fine," he growled.

He let go of me, harshly pushing me back into the wall.

"But do me one favor," he said. "Keep yourself safe. Avoid him."

He stormed off, completely livid.

She rushed to me, but I put my hand up.

"I'm fine."

"Oh my God, Aidan. What's your definition of fine?"

I managed to smile. I wasn't hurt very badly. Most of the blood wasn't my own.

"Lie down," she said.

"Really, I'm fine."

"Okay, then humor me and lie down."

I went to lie on the couch. I sighed and got up, walking to the kitchen.

"Jane."

"Oh, for the love of God, Aidan. Would you please lie down?" She brushed her lustrous dark hair from her face, and I could see the beautiful shape of her cheekbones. I suddenly found myself captivated by her again.

"Jane—look."

I took one of the towels from her and wiped my face. I took off my jacket and wiped the smeared blood off my arms. The blood came off, and there were no marks just like I knew there wouldn't be.

"I could have torn him apart with my bare hands, but all I could think about was you and how you would never forgive me." I left out Walter for obvious reasons.

She shook her head and stared at me through slanted eyes. She just kept her gaze locked on me without saying a word.

"What?" I asked. "What are you thinking?"

"At this point, I'm trying to figure out what you are."

I didn't know how to respond. I was amused by the possibilities of what she could be thinking. It appeared a lot stranger than it really was. I smiled at her and bowed my head. Her direct gaze was making me nervous. I never knew how to respond to her.

"Oh!" she said with a sigh. "Aidan." She touched the bottom of my shirt, seeing it was sliced into strips.

I held back my laughter. It would only be amusing if she knew the whole story, which I clearly couldn't tell her. She wasn't fooled.

"Aidan, how on Earth do you find this funny?"

"Really, Jane, I'm fine."

"What happened?"

I chuckled. "Uh, business end of a garden rake."

"What?" she bellowed. "What is wrong with him?"

"Actually, that was…Eric," I said, struggling to remember his name. "I'm guessing Rudy's older brother?"

She nodded.

"It's because of Rudy, Eric is alive. One more swing and I would have killed the guy."

She just stared at me again in that same baffled way. It was best I stayed a mystery.

"Thanks," I whispered, "for rescuing me."

"Aidan, why—?"

I put my hand up. "I was trying to protect you."

"From? And...why me? Why were you here? You live by Andrew, don't you?"

"I don't have many friends here, Jane. There isn't much to do, so I walk... sometimes for hours, sometimes even all day."

"So what do you mean protect me?"

"I noticed that your dad had forgotten to lock the door when he left."

"What? No—Ethan would never forget to lock the door."

"Well, he did," I answered. "I thought I saw a burglar entering your house, but when I opened the door, that's when Eric came at me with the rake. Rudy stopped him but pulled me inside and started hitting me—among other things."

She stared at me again, this time with her mouth hanging open in shock.

"Why would Rudy have been in my house?"

"He was yelling at me, telling me I wasn't going to leave here alive," I said. "Saying that I better not hurt you. He thinks we're friends, and when he saw me walking down the street, I guess he thought I was coming to visit you, so when he noticed the door was unlocked, he hid inside until I walked by."

"*Thinks* we're Friends?"

I nodded. I hated the sound of that. *Friends*. It was such a deceiving word. I shouldn't be friends with Jane; I would only end up hurting her in the end.

"Are we not friends?"

"That's one thing Rudy *was* right about. The other is that you should avoid me," I said.

I knew I couldn't do it myself. Maybe if she avoided me, I could more easily stay away.

"Why? You were the one who was so persistent about wanting to know my name. You could have just left me alone like I asked you to the first time we met."

"I know, but I couldn't help myself. I was so intrigued by you. I didn't mean to captivate your interest if I have."

"You interest everyone," she whispered, "even maybe Rudy in some way, though negatively."

"I'd love to be your friend, Jane, but I don't think Aaron Raines would like that too much."

"Why does *that* matter?" she groaned sarcastically, crossing her arms in front of her chest.

"Because you don't want to lose him," I told her. "Friends are hard to come by. Be careful, Jane...who you rescue."

I halted at the doorway and walked back toward the kitchen. If I was to have her avoid me, I figured I should say goodbye, mostly to cure myself of the burning feelings she was inflicting upon me.

"Jane?"

She spun around, gasping and thrusting her hand to her chest. "Oh," she breathed.

I laughed. "I'm sorry."

"You're still here."

"I couldn't leave without thanking you properly."

I pulled her against me and could feel her body quaking. She was more nervous than I was.

"Thank you," I whispered in her ear. I planted a soft, brief kiss on her cheek, which sent electric shocks through my limbs.

"If you were to wish it, Jane...you would never see me again."

"I do not wish that," she whispered.

I bowed slowly and left, wishing more than anything it wasn't Jane who I was sent to kill. Why couldn't it have been some insignificant cookie-cutter Barbie who bored me to tears? I wouldn't wish for Becky, of course, for no other reason than her being Jane's best friend. I still didn't quite understand that bond. I hated thinking about Jane—she made me feel so guilty.

I walked home, reciting in my head the words I would say to Luna about Jason. I repeated it so many times that it began to fall into a rhythmical, meaningless chant. I had to tell Walter about Rudy too, didn't I? Rudy—superstitious, imprudent child. Unfortunately, I disliked him mostly because he was right about me. Well, except for the part about me not being human; that was just plain ridiculous. I couldn't imagine all the crazy stories he was telling Jane. She probably thought I was some mythical monster with inhuman powers. How cliché. It was definitely something Rudy would say. I had heard gossip from random conversations I picked up with my insanely keen hearing. He had half the school thinking he was nuts.

I got home in the evening, and Walter raced to the door. He pulled me into his chest.

"Walter," I said with a laugh, pulling away from him. "What's with you?"

"You've been gone all day. I worried, waiting here all day like an anxious parent."

"I'm fine. Have news for you by the way."

"What sort of news?"

I dropped the keys in the basket and sighed, taking a seat beside him on the blue upholstered loveseat.

"Your grandson decided to try and beat the crap out of me today."

"What?" he bellowed. "Rudy?"

I nodded.

"Why?"

"He thinks I'm a hunter," I said, giving him a weak smile. "I thank *you* for that."

He laughed. "That's Rudy. Looks like he's a good judge of character."

I glared at him.

"I embellished those stories for him. I never knew he believed them."

"He looked up to you. I'm sure he still does."

"I'll bring him back to me when the time is right."

"I know."

"Let's take a look. You don't look too banged up," he said.

"Like I said...*tried* to beat me up."

He frowned. "You didn't hurt him, did you?"

I didn't answer.

"Clem?" He sounded almost frantic.

I shook my head. "I didn't even move to fend him off."

His breath exploded.

"You can thank Eric for my shirt."

Walter smiled flaccidly. "Ah, him too?"

I raised my eyebrows and nodded. "Didn't expect it?"

"Never was very close to Eric," he answered. "It's too bad. He's a good kid."

"You can still change that, Walter."

He shook his head. "Maybe someday."

Chapter Thirteen

"HE'S DEAD?" Luna whispered.

I nodded, and she turned away from me.

"I'm sorry," I murmured.

She spun around, causing her red locks to become tousled over her shoulders. "Good God, James!"

"Luna, I had to."

"Had to? Had to kill Jason? He was our friend."

"Yes, and he was going to turn us over to Abraham."

"Killing him wasn't the only solution."

"Luna, you know it was," I argued. "Since when were you not on my side?"

"Don't be that way," she demanded. "I *am* on your side, but you are not being careful."

I shunned her. She was right, but hearing her lecturing me about it wasn't going to help. I walked away, shutting myself in my room. That's when my thoughts ran wild and locked into order like a jigsaw puzzle, and one thing became clear—the one thing I realized I had known since that first day at the bookstore. I was falling in love with Jane Callahan.

I had to be close to her now; it was like a burning need to have her with me. But at the same time I knew I loved her, it was for that very reason I was also contemplating killing her. It may spare her a lot of pain and possibly even heartache. I was hoping I wouldn't have to do that.

Being close to her was the greatest feeling I had ever known, even stronger than my adoration for Vivian. Ah, poor Vivian. Jane would end up like her, wouldn't she? That was a good enough reason I shouldn't be friends with her. People were already beginning to take notice of how beautiful she was. She wasn't so invisible anymore. Mike was loyal to me and hopefully wouldn't find out what I was up to. Maybe me wanting to protect her was a good enough reason *to* be friends with her. I wasn't sure yet what I was going to do.

At school the next day, I felt unnaturally happy. Just knowing she was near made me smile like some brainless, lovesick teenager. I walked to her class before she left and leaned against the wall, waiting for her. As soon as Becky saw me, she smiled at Jane and skipped away, almost bouncing like her usual, energetic self.

"Hello," I said, cheerfully.

"Hi," Jane stuttered.

"I have decided to do what I want," I said. "I want to be friends even if Aaron and Rudy don't want it. It isn't up to them."

"Good," she sang. "Does this mean you are finally going to tell me how you do those crazy things you do?"

I chuckled. "What do you mean?"

"Like can you fly with that vampire cape you wore?"

I laughed even though I was unsure how serious she was. "Is that what you've been thinking?"

She shook her head. "No. I don't know what to think."

I just smiled at her.

"At the party, were you even standing behind me? When I fell?"

"Of course I was."

"I'm sure I was alone, Aidan. How did you know I was in danger?"

"I didn't," I said, keeping my voice even and emotionless.

"I really want to know how you do those crazy things."

"You need to stop listening to Rudy." I chuckled, raising my eyebrows.

She sighed. "Probably."

After every class, I was there waiting for her. We didn't say much. I couldn't think of anything relevant to say, and she realized it was hopeless to try and get answers from me. People stared, of course, but it stopped mattering to me. I wasn't going to let anyone hurt her—except maybe me if I eventually decided I had no other choice.

I walked with her to the cafeteria and gestured to the seat opposite of me. She sat down and glanced over at Becky and Aaron, who were snickering and stealing looks at the both of us.

Jane looked down at her hands, chipping away blue nail polish on her short fingernails. She finally looked up at me and immediately launched into a question.

"So why—?"

"Hold on." I chuckled, raising my hand. "Don't you think it may be my turn to ask the questions, Jane?"

"If you can think of one."

I hesitated, trying to think of something I didn't already know about her. Maybe being interested in her life outside of school was acceptable, though I didn't want to pry.

"How do you know Rudy?" I asked. That was a logical question.

She laughed. "That's the best you can come up with?"

I smiled and shrugged my shoulders.

"He lives a few houses down," she said. "He was really good friends with my brother when we were kids."

Oh God. I had to ask. I couldn't resist. I had no idea how much I had affected her life; I was sickeningly fascinated by the thought of finding out. "How old was your brother when...when it happened?"

"Fourteen," she answered, looking down at her hands.

He was a child just as I thought.

"You said three years ago," I answered. "Wouldn't that have made *you* fourteen?"

She nodded. "My twin."

I sighed. Even worse and now I could see she was in agony.

"I'm sorry," I said. "You ask the questions."

"I was just going to ask why you acted that way the first day of class. What did I do?"

If she only knew. "It wasn't that you did anything. I was just in one of my moods, and in some ways, I was upset with you for ignoring me, but everything is fine." I smiled at her and noticed the blood rush to her cheeks. I was overwhelmed by the way I was able to make her blush. She had no idea how beautiful she was.

"Also," she continued, "those green eyes of yours—contacts, right?"

I laughed quietly. I had gotten that before. "Now why would you think that?"

"They seem...unnatural."

I leaned forward, begging my mind to stay sane so I wouldn't find myself giving in to the urge to kiss her. I was completely lost in her eyes for a moment, and it seemed as if she were lost in mine. I stayed in position, wanting desperately to close my lips around hers.

I leaned back, staring at my hands. I couldn't look at her. I had very little self-control when she stared at me that way—so solidly with her face completely unreadable.

"Wow," she whispered.

"They often absorb the colors around them. That's why they may sometimes look dark or even violet on occasion as I have been told." At least that was the truth.

She nodded and smiled.

"But your cuts," she said, "when Rudy and Eric attacked you."

I didn't want to answer. She was definitely noticing there was something not right about me. I hated it.

"The rake didn't cut past my shirt. I backed away. And Rudy really isn't very strong. The reason I looked so dizzy and disoriented is because the smell of blood makes me sick."

"Uh huh."

I noticed she was staring down at her chipping nail polish again, and her eyes appeared almost...turbulent. I was burning with curiosity of what was going on inside her head.

"Now what are you thinking?" I asked.

"Why do you always want to know what I'm thinking?"

"Well, what good are thoughts with nobody to share them with?"

She mirrored my smile.

"It's just that you're always so passive," I continued. "It's so hard to read you."

"Can't be that hard."

"Oh, it is. You hide so much." I felt guilty for saying that, considering how much *I* hid.

She looked away from me again.

"Like Becky for example," I said. "She's contemplating coming over here just to see what's going on." I had no idea if that was true, but it seemed like something Becky would be thinking.

"How do you know that?" she said, not turning around to look at Becky. "Maybe she is just daydreaming about something completely out there."

"Well, that's obviously possible, but I don't think so."

"How do you know?"

"She's just one of those people who is easy to read. You have to admit yourself Becky isn't really too hard to figure out." I laughed.

"But I am?"

I nodded.

"Why?"

"I don't know."

"I have a question."

Of course she did. "More questions?"

"Well, just one—maybe two."

"Okay."

"What were you doing in the woods that night?"

"I told you," I said. "I walk. I don't sleep well, so sometimes I just walk all night."

"How did you know how to find me? Um…two questions."

I bowed my head for a moment, unsure how to answer.

"And at the party…and the bookstore."

"That's more than two."

"Aidan…"

It was still strange hearing her call me Aidan. I wanted to tell her the truth. I wanted more than anything to tell her every single thing about me. Since that wasn't possible, I decided I could tell her about my bizarre gift. The worst that could happen was she would think I was insane.

"All right. You want the truth?" I started.

"Of course."

"I have this thing…where I can feel when danger is close. When there is a strong possibility that someone may be hurt. I don't know how it happened. It was just…one day I woke up with this odd new feeling. And to think of you being hurt…" I broke off, shaking my head and lowering it again.

"How does it work?" she asked after a brief moment of silence.

She *did* believe me. I shook my head. "I don't know. I usually can't feel it unless it involves you."

"Me?"

"Yes."

"Why?"

"You obviously are, as I have said before, a walking accident," I said, laughing.

She didn't seem amused. "Just a little clumsy."

"That's an understatement."

She just glared at me. It wasn't threatening at all. She was too pretty to look mean.

I was torn back into my worries. I knew this was wrong. This whole conversation was wrong. Even looking at her was stupid.

"You know, Jane…my knight in shining armor act shouldn't have made you want to talk to me."

"It didn't. *You* talked to *me* remember?"

"I'm just saying that Rudy was right—well, about one thing. You really should avoid me."

"Why?"

"I'm not a very good friend." That seemed like the most logical reason I could give her without being forced to lie.

"Aidan"—she paused—"you're strange."

I smiled, finding her charming as usual. "I know. But you should, and *that,* to answer one of your first questions, is exactly why I acted that way in class."

"Maybe I will then!" she retorted curtly.

I ignored her angry tone and nodded. "It's probably better for you."

"Okay, so now it's suddenly better for you to *not* talk to me?"

"I'm sorry."

"Don't worry about it. At least you warned me this time, so don't be mad when I don't talk to you," she snapped.

"It's not that I *want* you to avoid me—"

"Make up your mind, Aidan."

"It's just that it would be best," I continued, still ignoring her anger and staying composed. "It's just that...well, as a person, I like you...enough to be good friends, but I would let you down. It's in my nature. So logically, you *should* avoid that. I don't want to hurt you." This sounded true enough. Of course, she wasn't aware that I saw her as much more than a friend. Of course, she didn't know that I was foolish and hopeless for her.

"Maybe this time, I'll do what I should," she spat.

"Be careful who you choose to rescue, Jane."

She glowered at me, but I bolted out of the room as soon as the lunch bell rang.

I wasn't expecting her to speak to me, but when she didn't, it drove me near mad. I found myself missing her. I still stared at her obsessively and tried to make eye contact. She avoided it. The tension between Jane and me seemed to please Aaron more than I was keen on, and he usually took the seat at her other side. They talked quietly on occasion, usually about the English assignments from their other class. I wasn't interested. I had told her to avoid me, hadn't I? I didn't realize how easy it was going to be for her to ignore me when I looked at her. She was so close that I could have reached out to touch her, and it took everything in me not to try.

Days passed, and slowly my thoughts of Jane became more and more irrational. I still had this sick desperation to kill her at the same time I wanted to protect her. I was terrified of what I would do to her if she were to trust me. It was much better this way.

"I don't know what you're up to," Mike started, "but if we lose track of the Callahans again, it will be your head."

I sighed. "Did you know Alex left Daniel in an alleyway?"

Mike nodded. "Yes…and?"

"And? And…that's sick!" I yelled.

"James, since when have you started caring?"

I grumbled. "I would appreciate it if for just once you wouldn't call me James."

He laughed. "Oh, and would *Aidan* suit you better?"

"Better than James," I murmured.

His face fell. "Oh, James…are you…?"

"Am I what?"

"Oh my God. Father is going to kill you."

"Mike, please," I pleaded. "Please don't tell him."

"I'm not going to betray you. You know that, James, but if you don't finish the job…I will *have* to tell him."

"I know. You are more loyal than I am."

He huffed. "James, you cannot disappear."

"I haven't."

"Abraham doesn't know where you are," he retorted. "He didn't find you at Luna's. He thinks you are doing something creative with the Callahan girl."

I was, though nothing that had to do with loyalty to Abraham or his followers.

"Finish the job!" he shouted and stormed out.

Jane made me feel mortal again, made me feel that human feeling of what it was like to feel as though you would die without that person by your side. Because of her, I was finally alive again. I couldn't betray her now. She had given me back my humanity, that thing that Abraham had stolen. Finishing the job was not an option.

I missed the sound of her voice over the weeks she had been avoiding me, so I walked to her house one night. I contemplated throwing pebbles at her window, but I noticed Becky's truck in the driveway. I sighed to myself, suddenly wondering what I was doing there in the first place. It almost hurt me to let her out of my sight for more than a few hours at a time. I worried constantly over the thoughts that The Sevren would find her and hurt her.

I heard Becky at lunch the following days jabbering about a trip to California with Jane during winter break. She seemed thrilled about it. Again came the nagging urge to try and keep Jane within my sight. I guessed there was only one way to do that. When winter break came, I packed a small suitcase with a couple of shirts and a jacket, grabbed my money, and prepared myself for a very long drive to Southern California.

Chapter Fourteen

I FOLLOWED CLOSELY BEHIND, trying to ignore the rain and concentrate on not losing sight of Jane's car for more than a few minutes at a time. I watched the road behind me, making sure I wasn't being tracked by Abraham's men. I was doing this simply to protect her. The drive was agonizing. I would occasionally move to the back roads when I thought she may have noticed my car. I'd hop back on the freeway when I was sure I wouldn't be seen. I felt ridiculous for what I was doing. But it was the only way I could be sure she wasn't being tailed by one of The Sevren's assassins.

When they arrived, I wasn't sure what I was supposed to do. I hadn't planned that far ahead. I decided to head down to a cheap motel until she was leaving. I rented the room under the name Josh Alexander, and my ID said I was twenty-five, which was good enough. Missing Christmas didn't matter to me, though Walter seemed a bit more disappointed than I expected, and Luna was furious with me for what I was doing.

"You are being reckless," she had said.

True enough but it didn't matter to me. I spent the days making sure Jane's car stayed in the driveway of her mother's. I checked every other hour since the day after Christmas to make sure I wouldn't miss her leave. It was a maddening routine.

It was three days after Christmas when I noticed her car wasn't in the driveway any longer. I rushed down the road, driving much faster than the law allowed, and eventually found her car about twenty miles away at a gas station.

I sighed in relief and followed a bit behind as she headed down the road. It was warmer outside than I expected. Santa Monica was much warmer than North Bend in the winter. I was enjoying the warmth and the lack of rain; I had been deprived of sunlight for far too long in my life.

My heart started pounding, and waves of panic swept over me when my senses began electrocuting me with terrible feelings again. That's when I saw a truck rushing toward Jane's tiny Aveo, and without a second to think, they collided. The Aveo spun and hit the divider, flipping over on its hood.

My mouth fell open, and for a moment, I was paralyzed with fear. I had to do something to help her. My head spun, and thoughts raced through my mind on what I could possibly do. The Aveo was a crumpled heap of metal, and I wasn't even sure if Jane was alive. I couldn't let myself believe otherwise.

I pulled over to the side of the road. Just as my hand reached to open my door, I saw Jane dragging herself out of the thrashed car through the broken window. She pulled her tiny body over the sharp, uneven shards of glass. Again my body froze. The sound of a siren pulled me into a state of hope, and I watched from about thirty feet away as they hauled Jane and Becky into the ambulance.

I followed to the hospital, still unsure if she was alive. I waited outside for about twenty minutes before walking in.

"Callahan," I said to the woman at the counter. She had brown hair and big brown eyes. She looked sour and unhappy.

"Excuse me?" she said.

"There were two girls brought in about twenty minutes ago," I started. "They were in a car accident, and I was wondering their condition."

She picked up the phone and paged the nurse. A young man in blue scrubs came immediately up to the counter.

"Can I help you?"

"I was wondering about the condition of the girls in the car crash."

"Are you family?" he asked suspiciously.

I had to lie, of course. I couldn't find out a thing otherwise. "Yes. Jane is my sister."

"Miss Callahan has suffered a minor head injury but should be all right. Miss Marshall has some minor cuts and bruises but nothing to be too worried about. I will let you know when your sister is awake. You may have to wait to take her home though. She will probably have to stay overnight just to make sure she has no internal damage."

Awake? She must have lost consciousness after escaping the wreck of her car. The nurse walked away, and I left the hospital. I couldn't take Jane home; I couldn't be any more involved than I was already. I was sure Becky would call someone for help.

I stopped by a small flower shop on the way home and ordered five dozen red roses, thinking I had to outdo Rudy and Aaron. I wrote a brief note and had the roses sent to the hospital, charging it to a false credit card.

I drove home the rest of the way, sure that Jane hadn't been tracked. She would be safe the rest of her way. Well...at least safe from The Sevren.

The entire next week at school, she still never said a word to me. Never even a "Thanks for the roses, Aidan." I found out Rudy had gone to rescue them, and Jane was now driving a dingy-looking '95 Camry. In history class, I would still catch myself trying to make eye contact, but she would ignore it the best she could. Sometimes she would even wring her hands together. I didn't know what she was thinking and why she had actually listened to me when I told her to avoid me.

The next day, I stayed home again, trying to think of some way I could make things right. Luna and Walter both left me alone, probably assuming I was sick. I spent most of the day trying to sleep but kept being jolted awake from an assault of gruesome nightmares. I was continuously seeing messes of blood and bones every time I dozed off. If I couldn't even rest, how on earth was I going to be able to think clearly? I had to tell Jane—I knew that. I just didn't know how or when, but I knew she had to find out. It would be easier to protect her if she knew. That way, she wouldn't question me if I were to ask certain things of her.

When I pulled into the parking lot, Jane's eyes met mine, and she looked away, rushing across to the other side. I just suffered through my boring classes, waiting for history when I could speak to Jane. I had to somehow tell her *something*. Before I was able to even steal a glance at her, Mr. Cornally called on me for a question I couldn't have cared less about.

"Mr. Summers, who led the Reign of Terror?"

"Maximilian Robespierre," I answered.

Mr. Cornally nodded and made some reply, but I wasn't listening. I looked over and whispered her name.

"Jane?"

She turned halfway but stopped before making eye contact.

"What are you thinking?" I whispered.

She sighed heavily. "So you ignore me for weeks on end, and now you suddenly ask me what I'm thinking?"

"I wasn't ignoring you."

"What?"

"In case you haven't noticed, you've been the one avoiding me. Avoiding eye contact—conversation."

"Aidan, don't talk to me," she grumbled.

I laughed.

"I'm sorry," she said sarcastically. "Was I making a joke?"

I was amused again by her attempt at being mean. "Oh, come on, Jane. You're the one who was mad when I said we shouldn't talk, that it was better that you avoid me."

"No, Aidan. I am irritated by your inconsistency. If you want me to ignore you, then let me!"

"I don't want that. I just think it would be best for you. I'm not a very good friend and would hate to let you down."

"You're stranger than me, Aidan," she mumbled.

"Maybe." I laughed happily yet quietly, keeping an eye on Mr. Cornally's back as he wrote on the board. "I wanted to know if you would like to go somewhere with me after school today. There's something I want to show you."

She hesitated before responding and looked away from me, hiding her glorious face behind her dark hair.

"Okay," she said soberly.

"Okay," I repeated. I couldn't hide my smile. "If you're worried about being let down, I'm warning you now."

"I expect it from everybody."

I caught up to her in the parking lot after school.

"Hey."

She turned around. "Oh…hi."

"You didn't wait for me outside your class. Did you forget?"

"No. Just wanted to get out of the rain," she answered.

I nodded, not sure if she was being entirely honest but also not caring.

"Where did you even come from?" she asked with that familiar baffled expression on her face.

"What?" I laughed.

"I mean…you just appeared out of thin air again."

I shook my head, suppressing laughter. Rudy—I was sure of it. "Really, Jane? Rudy is definitely seeding some crazy ideas in your head. I walked, okay? Same as you."

"Mm hmm."

"So are you going to make me give you directions again?"

She shook her head. "I can let you drive, but what about your car?"

"I'll come back for it," I answered, smiling. "You seem highly distracted, Jane. Is everything—"

"Fine," she retorted, interrupting my sentence, which told me that she didn't want to talk about it. She got out and walked around to the passenger's side door, and I turned to smile at her, trying to make her feel a little bit more comfortable. I wasn't sure what her expressions meant, but she seemed nervous and anxious over something.

"Aidan?" she started.

I turned to look at her.

"The roses…"

I chuckled. "Yes, I'm sorry. I couldn't resist."

"Yeah, so I read."

"Well, did you like them?"

"I did," she answered reluctantly. "But…how did you know about the crash?"

"Rudy, of course."

"Rudy said he didn't tell anyone," she answered suspiciously.

"Okay," I confessed, unable to come up with an elaborate lie quickly enough. "You caught me."

"Aidan…you didn't."

I couldn't respond.

"Did you…follow me?" I could feel the anger in her voice.

"I'm sorry," I said almost defensively, trying to calm her resentment. "I have this incredibly annoying urge to protect you. I *only* followed you to make sure you were all right. Unfortunately, I wasn't able to save you from the crash."

She stared at me almost loathsomely through narrowed eyes.

"I really am sorry," I continued. "Nothing creepy, Jane. It isn't like I stared through your windows or watched you sleep."

She sighed, and her face fell soft for a moment. "Really?"

"Yes. Really. I promise."

"I don't know why it's so impossible to stay mad at you?"

I smiled, unable to hide it. "One of my gifts," I teased.

We were silent for a few minutes, both of us waiting for the other to speak.

"Heading to the other side of the woods," I said. "I want to show you where I was walking. There's something I want you to see."

I pulled over to the side of the road and walked around to her side of the car and opened her door. I lifted my open hand, insisting she take it. She lightly gripped my fingers, and her skin felt so warm and soft. It felt amazing to touch her. I stood there, just staring at her again, admiring the light that had turned her eyes to an amazing shade of amber. I felt the need to speak, to tell her how beautiful she was, but I couldn't risk how she would respond. I wanted to hear her voice. My body was burning to hold her close to me, but I couldn't risk that either.

"Come," I whispered.

I was trembling the entire time and led her slowly into the woods. This was not a good idea, but I had to do something to make her understand. I pulled back some branches and moved a little farther into the deeper parts of the woods. I concentrated on the fact that the girl I was sent to kill was being led to the very place where it was supposed to happen. My mind couldn't think of anything else. I couldn't let them hurt her; I couldn't let them find her wandering around in the woods. I was hoping the clearing would frighten her enough to stay away.

I looked straight ahead, ignoring the beauty of the trees. Again I pulled back a few branches, revealing that vile clearing.

"Most people don't just walk into the middle of the woods," I started softly, trying to keep my voice even and keep from trembling. "The trail leads around this. *Most* people follow it, Jane." I smiled lightly and raised my eyebrows at her.

She was still silent and stared at me for a long time before she finally spoke.

"What is this?" she asked, locking her gaze on the blood-stained boulder in the middle.

"It's an old place of sacrifice," I said honestly.

"What?" she whispered. "Sacrifice?"

I nodded. She *was* frightened. Perfect.

I wanted to tell her the story while still keeping myself out of it. "There are stories of a tribe, some say a coven or cult, who would bring certain people here and open their throats and drink their blood."

"Why?"

"I don't know why, but they hunt people."

My God. She was going to think I was completely mad, wasn't she? She was going to laugh at me and walk away. But she didn't. She just started shaking like she was freezing cold.

"Jane? Are you okay?" I asked. "Do you want my jacket?"

"No, Aidan. No, I'm okay."

I nodded and prepared myself to ask her if she was sure since she hadn't stopped shivering, but I stopped myself when I remembered how much she hated that.

"Thanks," she said.

"For?"

"Not asking me if I was sure."

I guess she hadn't realized how badly I wanted to.

"Why did you take me here?" she asked.

I hadn't planned on an answer to that question, so I gave her the best one I could come up with. "I guess to show you where Rudy gets his superstitions. Some things about his stories may hold truth, and I am simply warning you to stay out of the woods—especially at night."

"You said they drink people's blood."

"Yes."

"And Rudy mentioned acute night vision and strange abilities."

Oh, no. I knew where she was going with this.

"Yes," I answered hesitantly.

"You people are talking about vampires!" she almost yelled, suppressing laughter.

I chuckled, almost amused by her assumption. "I'm sure some people might call them that, but since vampires are mythical creatures, we stick to 'hunters.'"

I knew Rudy must have told her the story, so it wasn't anything new. Him telling her may have been a good thing.

"You believe in them?"

"Like I told you," I answered, "to an extent. This wouldn't be here for no reason. It's just an interesting thing to see and hopefully a good reason to stay out of the woods."

"If you knew, Aidan, if you knew that the woods were so dangerous especially at night, why were you there that night? When you rescued me?"

Because since I am one of them, they wouldn't hurt me. I clearly had to lie again. I smiled falsely. "Most people follow the trail. First of all...I'm not like most people, and second, I told you about my ability to sense danger."

"I wasn't sure I believed you," she whispered under her breath, bowing her head.

"Do you now?"

She nodded.

"Anything else?"

She glared at me and cocked her head. "Actually, yes. There are wolves in the woods, right?"

"Yes."

"Why didn't I see them that night? Why didn't they bother us?"

"Wolves usually become active deep into the morning," I said. "It was just after sunset when I found you." I had no idea where she was going with that question.

She looked at me solidly again as if trying to read through my lies.

I changed the uncomfortable subject. "So have you yelled at Rudy yet? I was pretty sure you were going to."

She grimaced. "I'm not on speaking terms with Rudy right now, but when I am, I will definitely yell at him!"

I chuckled, not sure if I was actually amused. "He was only trying to help. You really shouldn't be too hard on him. I came in thinking he was a burglar, and that's when he attacked me." Why in hell was I protecting Rudy?

"You're not angry?" she asked, looking confused as she often did by my inconsistencies.

"Not really. He's a decent guy. He cares about you. That's all."

"Yup, stranger than me," she muttered.

I smiled again. She was so charming.

"Well, thanks for showing me this," she said. "I will stay out of the woods."

"Good." I hoped she meant it.

She stood there just looking into my eyes, and my body wanted her close again. I reached for her hand and ran my fingers over her perfect skin.

"You have very beautiful hands," I whispered. My mood had suddenly shifted, and I felt timid and nervous.

I could feel her uncertainty as she moved her fingers with my own. My heart was pounding the entire time. I interlocked our fingers, and she didn't move, not to help me nor to stop me. I stared at her lifeless smile. She was silent still, so I felt the need to say something.

"Thank you for letting me take you here." I paused. "For trusting me." I had a strange feeling she *didn't* trust me, but with her, I couldn't be sure.

She finally looked at me. I noticed something behind her eyes. I couldn't decide what it was, but it almost looked like fear. She tore me out of my speculations.

"Should I drive you to school?" she asked. "To get your car?"

I smiled and shook my head. "I'll walk."

"To the school?"

"Yes. Then I'll drive home and…probably walk some more."

"Aidan…"

That name again.

"Will you just let me drive you? Please?"

"You don't need to do that," I answered, almost trying to get away from her. I was terrified of what questions she may ask me.

"No, really. It would make me feel much better if you just let me drive you."

I couldn't tell her no when she looked at me with that beseeching look in her beautiful eyes.

I shook my head. "Fine, but only because you agreed to come here with me."

The drive to the school was mostly silent, which was a relief.

"Thanks, Jane." I felt that maybe she wouldn't stop me if I were to touch her again. I leaned over and kissed her cheek. When I felt her acceptance, I lingered for a moment and kissed her a second time, still wishing as always for more.

"Good night, Aidan."

I slung my school bag over my shoulder and shut the door. I drove home, left my school bag in the car, and just walked.

Chapter Fifteen

I WALKED AIMLESSLY and ended up at Books by the Bay—of course. I ended up thankful to be there when I saw Jane yanking her arm away from Mike's grasp.

"Really, Mike," I heard her say. "I have to go."

I recognized the expression on his face all too well; his fury had its own unique look. His cheeks were flushed, and his face was twisted into a mask of what almost appeared to be pain, his eyebrows pulling together.

"All I wanted was one dance," he growled. "Now, I'm offering you dinner and you walk out on me."

"I'm sorry. I just can't tonight," she said with obvious distress etched on her face.

"But you can!"

He was yelling now, and I was wanting more than anything to stop him, but I couldn't give him the chance to think I was there simply to save her. There was no way of denying who she was now.

Jane opened the car door, and it slammed closed as Mike shoved her into it.

"Do not dismiss me again," he snarled.

"Mike, please," she begged. "Can't we do this some other time?"

"Tonight is better."

I saw that fury creeping further into his features, and I couldn't let him hurt her.

"Jane?" I questioned.

"Aidan!" she called.

Mike took another step back.

I nodded my head and glowered at him. He stole another glance at Jane and walked past me. I punched his arm softly, making sure Jane didn't see. He knew I was saying to meet me at home.

She let out a sigh. "Thanks."

"Are you okay?"

She nodded. "My ribs are a bit sore, but I'm fine."

"I should kill him," I growled deep in my throat.

"Nah, I don't think he's all that dangerous."

Shock crept into my face, and I realized I wasn't able to let Jane know anything about us and our alliance, so I tried to hide the expression.

"Found me again," she said, scattering my thoughts.

"Well, maybe you're right," I said, keeping my secrets again. "He probably wasn't planning on hurting you. I was just walking aimlessly and ended up here. I didn't sense danger the way I sometimes do. You're just born for trouble." That was at least the truth.

"You got here fast."

"Did I?"

"Where are you headed?"

I opened my mouth to speak, unsure of what I was going to say, but I was interrupted by her high-pitched gasp. She pressed her back into the car.

"Aidan," she hissed quietly.

I followed her eyes and found myself staring at a little gray wolf.

"Oh, it's all right," I said quietly. "Simply stay calm."

I took a step toward it, sure of the fact that it wasn't going to hurt me. Again I thanked my studies with Walter for being able to pick up emotion. The animal was frightened.

"What are you doing? Are you crazy?"

"It's fine, Jane."

I reached toward it.

"Aidan, you idiot, it's going to bite your damn fingers off."

"Jane, *please*!" I spat, still trying to whisper. "Be quiet!"

I touched its fur, and it became very still, and the growling moved into its throat. I began softly stroking its head.

"Go on," I whispered, waving my hand.

The wolf turned and trotted away, back into the woods near the bookstore.

"My God. How did you do that?"

"Animals can sense fear," I explained. "As long as you don't show them you're afraid, they won't bother you." I wasn't sure if that was true, but it seemed to convince her.

"Can I give you a ride home?" she asked, changing the subject abruptly, which led me to believe she wasn't convinced after all.

I nodded. "I think I've walked enough tonight."

I got in the passenger's seat and slouched down, sighing to myself over Mike's constant annoyance of me.

"Thanks for rescuing me...again," she said, tucking her hair behind her ear.

I smiled. "Always."

"So now I guess we're even."

"How so?"

"I saved you from Rudy, and you saved me from Mike...and the wolf...and maybe a few other times. So see—even." A smile crept along her face, and she seemed to suppress a laugh.

I chuckled, nodding. "Ah, yes. We'll call it even."

"I still don't think I understand why you're not angry at Rudy," she said, reaching for the parking brake.

I smiled and tried not to laugh. "Actually, I found the whole trying to kill me thing quite entertaining."

"Why?"

I was unable to contain my laughter then. "Well, because if Rudy knows so much about the hunters and he believed me to be one, then he should have known that he wouldn't have been able to kill me."

Her mood shifted. I could feel it in my very bones.

"Are you saying you're a hunter?" she asked, her voice quaking.

I didn't want to lie to her, so I couldn't deny it, yet I knew I couldn't confirm it. I didn't know how to respond. "I didn't say that, Jane." The only thing that made sense.

"But you are."

She stopped at the driveway of my house.

"Why don't you just tell me what you are?" she asked.

"Just stay out of the woods, Janie." I wanted to touch her again, so I grasped a lock of her hair and twisted it between my fingers. I resisted the urge to kiss her and bowed formally. "Stop listening to Rudy."

As soon as I opened the door, I called to Mike. "I told you to let me do things my way."

I turned and waved at her, trying to tell her to leave in case Mike tried something stupid again. He approached me at the door.

"Are you crazy?" he spat.

"Mike, please. You promised you wouldn't betray me."

"And I won't," he answered, "but you are making a huge mistake. How much longer do you think I can lie to Abraham?"

"As long as you need to!" I yelled.

"What do you plan to do, James?" I saw his anger almost showing in his features again. "Do you plan to just…run away?"

Run away… Why didn't I think of that? Of course. Take Jane and run away…when the time was right.

"Perhaps I will."

He sighed and turned away from me. "You are such an idiot!"

"No, Mike. I just know what's right."

"Nobody knows what's right when their mind is clouded by love."

"Love is the only thing that has ever made things clear!"

"So it's true?" His voice fell. "You love her."

Damn. "Mike, just let me do things my way—please."

He stormed off but yelled as he walked toward his car. "You are making a huge mistake!"

I didn't even remember school that Friday. I just found myself walking down the street by Jane's house again. I glanced at her door, making sure it was closed this time. I continued walking and heard her voice from an open window a few houses down.

"A coven of people," I heard, "who hunt other people—my guess is that they are insane, thinking they are vampires or…something."

There was another voice I knew, and I strained to listen. "They're sane," he answered, "just not entirely human." His voice was serious, and a tinge of fear trailed through his words. Rudy.

"That isn't possible," Jane said.

"Do you think people just make up stories off the top of their heads? Everything comes from somewhere."

"Most of the books I read are pretty out there," she answered.

"I tried to warn you before, and you wouldn't listen. Do you want to listen this time?"

He paused.

"The legend of the hunters is old and not one you will find at a local bookstore. About forty years ago, my grandfather was in his twenties and traveling the world, studying cultures and their religions. He was an anthropologist of cultures but obsessed with theology. Religion was his true passion. There were several cultures he found intriguing, such as the African tribes in the forests and the Arabs in their clothing styles, but the strangest things he saw happened here in Oregon. People went missing, and my grandfather was determined to find out why. The police and even the FBI were stumped. Sometimes bodies would turn up in alleyways or dumpsters."

I had this fantasy in my head of tearing through the door and beating Rudy senseless for trying to turn Jane against me like that.

"There were even a few cases where the bodies went missing after being sent to the morgue. Those cases ended up cold. The bodies were never found. Eventually, my grandfather did find out what was going on, and when I was young, he used to tell me the story. For some reason, it never frightened me. It was like a bedtime story. My papa was a hero in my eyes, and I would ask him to tell me the story so often that I eventually knew it word for word. There were a lot of details he left out, but I do know that he talked about how he sought out the mysterious people in the woods who called themselves "The Sevren." He explained to me how they hunted people—only certain people, pure people, the most loved and happy. They would sacrifice them with bone knives or axes and spill their blood on the alter in the clearing you have seen. The members would drink the blood of the victims, taking in their beauty and the essence of their lives. It is an incomparable pleasure to them, even the children."

I stopped listening to him. I couldn't stand what he was telling her. It made me want to hurt him—to kill him. I picked up Jane's voice when I heard the name of the cult again.

"So, The Sevren is back?"

"I believe so, yes."

I stopped listening again but picked up my name moments later.

"If the Summers kid is one of The Sevren, he's broken the pact, and there will be hell to pay. Be careful, Jane. They are stronger than us."

"Vampires," Jane whispered.

"They aren't vampires."

"Sounds that way to me."

"They may have some of the same abilities, but vampires don't exist," he demanded.

"Exactly. Thanks, Rudy, but I don't think that listening to your stories is the best idea."

"The night you hurt your ankle," I heard him call. "The night you got hurt and Aidan rescued you."

"How do you know about that?"

"Why do you think the wolves didn't bother you that night?"

"What?" Her voice was acidic.

His voice dropped. "Why do you think nothing worse happened?"

"Rudy, Aidan isn't a vampire, okay? Or *hunter*."

"You *have* to listen to me."

"No, Rudy, I really don't," she said. "Aidan can't...control the wolves."

"I saw what he is, Jane," he yelled, "what he was doing, and it was terrible. Please just keep yourself safe!"

He was clearly lying. Rudy knew nothing about me. Again came the urge to beat him to a pulp. After all, he tried to beat me first. Maybe Jane would understand. I shook off the thought—it wasn't logical. I would end up killing him.

I wanted her to know everything, but I wanted to tell her myself, to let her know to her face that I would never hurt her! I knew what she was thinking. Damn Rudy. I was going to lose her now no matter what. That feeling that grief would swallow me alive flooded back to me, and I knew I shouldn't—especially now, especially when I was sure Jane was going into the woods, listening to Rudy like I didn't want her to do. Perhaps it would help Jane to see it. I wasn't entirely sure she was going to walk into the woods, desperately wanting her to. I also prayed she wouldn't see me this way. I knew I had to tell her somehow. This would be the easiest way. Wouldn't she turn her back on me like Vivian? Wouldn't she turn away in fear and disgust? What was I to do then?

I raced around the back of Rudy's house and past the edge of the woods, making my way back to where Jane would be. The rest is dark. All I remembered was hearing a gasp and pulling my teeth out of the bird and locking my gaze onto hers. She took a couple of steps back with a look of sheer terror on her face. Her eyes were not the beautiful amber color I loved but a dark, deep shade that made me terrified of what she was thinking. I stood up, dropping the bird on the ground. Before I even took a step toward her, she was running.

I chased after her, but she raced into her house and locked the door.

I knocked lightly. "Jane?"

"Go away!" I could hear the terror creeping into her voice, and I felt almost as if it would destroy me.

"Jane, please," I begged. "You have to listen to me."

"Rudy was right about you!" she shouted.

"Jane, I'm sorry," I pleaded. "I had to."

"Just go away!"

"Open the door. Please!"

"No!"

"I'm sorry. I was so hungry!" That was true in a way.

"Then cook a damn cup of noodles, Aidan! Go away!"

"You don't understand!"

"I don't want to."

"Would you just let me in?"

"Why the hell would I let you in?"

"Trust me, please."

"I could never trust you," she answered. "You told me yourself you're not a very good friend."

"Yes, I said that," I confessed, "but when have I ever given you reason to be afraid of me? Listen to me." My voice fell. "I need you," I whispered, leaning my head against her front door. I was unaware I was going to say that until I did. "I know it sounds crazy, but I need you to listen to me—please."

I heard her door unlock, and she opened up, staring at me. She stepped aside and nodded but wouldn't look at me again.

"Thank you," I breathed.

"Are you going to tell me what you are now?" she whispered hesitantly.

"Do I need to?"

She jerked her head toward me but quickly recoiled and settled down on the cushions of her couch in the front room.

"Maybe not," she whispered.

I sat down next to her. I softly touched her hand with my fingertips. She yanked her hand away almost harshly.

"I'm sorry," I whispered.

"You just surprised me," she said but kept her hands in her lap.

"Don't be afraid. I swear to you I'm not going to hurt you."

"What does that mean? Does that mean you will kill me so fast I won't feel the pain?"

My heart sank, and I almost felt sick. What was I supposed to say to that? I was supposed to kill her after all, and in a small way, I desperately wanted to. I pulled my eyebrows together and looked directly into her eyes.

"Jane—"

"I'm sorry," she started. "Just please, Aidan. If you're one of them, tell me."

"One of who?"

"You know who."

I chuckled and shook my head. "Rudy," I mumbled. "Ah Rudy." I had to lie to her still.

"What?"

"My personal opinion is his grandfather was senile," I said. "I don't think The Sevren exist."

"You know the story?"

Oops. "I…heard."

"You were spying?" she yelled.

"Not exactly," I retorted, putting my hand up. "I have good hearing, and yes, I walked by and could hear from the open window. I couldn't help but to listen to what he was telling you."

"What other abilities do your kind have?"

"My kind?"

"Yes. The…well, you know."

"Well, the wolves."

"It's true?" she bellowed. "You can really control the wolves?"

"I wouldn't say I can control them, but they listen to me. They trust me. And my *kind,* as you put it, has nothing to do with that ability. I don't know where that one came from, much like my ability to sense danger. It's just something I have inside me." I wasn't sure if that was true, but it felt right.

"What about the bird?"

"I told you," I said. "I was…hungry."

"You ate the bird? Raw?"

I shook my head.

"Oh my God," she whispered. "You—"

"It's what we do," I said, hoping I was right about her figuring it out for herself.

"Blood?"

I nodded. "I cannot explain everything to you right now, but I promise you I will. I would never hurt you, Jane—or any human."

"Then you aren't a true…*hunter,* right?"

I put my hand up. "Another day."

She just nodded feebly.

"I just had to make you let me in," I said. "I had to tell you to your face that I don't intend to ever hurt you, but I also want you to know that I can."

"That's just it then. That's why you didn't want to be friends."

No. I was protecting her from Abraham and his men, of course. It had very little to do with me.

"Now you understand," I lied.

I stood up and turned away. I felt the pressure of her hand on my shoulder.

"Tomorrow?" she asked.

I turned around and held her face in my hands. I wanted desperately to kiss her. She wasn't resisting my touch, so I very lightly touched her lips, and I felt my body temperature rise. I had to stop before I went too far.

"Soon, Jane," I whispered.

I left then contemplating what everything meant, what could happen now that I told our secrets. I talked to Walter about it, ignoring Luna's snide remarks.

"Clem, what do you plan to do?" he asked.

"I don't know," I said, sighing. "Get the Callahans out of North Bend as soon as I can and…" I broke off, averting my gaze.

"And?"

"And…" I paused and looked back at him. His eyebrows were raised, waiting for my answer. "And…go with Jane."

Luna huffed and shoved herself between Walter and me on the couch. "James, I'm going to say this once." She actually sounded calm. "If you try something like that, Abraham will not only come after her, he will come after you and me and *everyone* you have ever spoken to—including Walter."

I flinched.

"So," she continued, "what are you going to do?"

"I don't know." I shook my head. "I…don't know."

I tried to sleep that night, but my mind kept replaying my day, and I ached to see Jane again. I almost couldn't stand waiting for school the next morning. It was driving me mad. I tried to relax, but after over an hour, it proved impossible.

I got up from the warm blankets of my bed and pulled on a simple pair of blue jeans and a T-shirt, slipped on some simple shoes, and went for a walk. It should have occurred to me before I even began walking that I would end up at *her* house. I *must* have been crazy. If not, there was something severely wrong with me. I had to see her; that much was all I knew.

I climbed the tree that led to her window on the top story and tapped lightly on the glass. I could see even in the darkness of her room that she had hardly even stirred. I knocked a little harder, and light flooded the room as she switched on the lamp on her bedside table.

"Jane!" I whispered just loud enough to be heard.

"Aidan?"

"Open up!"

She sprang up and opened the window.

"Are you crazy?" she hissed.

"I hope so," I said, chuckling.

I crawled from the oak tree into her bedroom.

"Don't wake Ethan," she whispered.

I nodded. "I had to see you," I confessed. "I don't think I'm entirely ready to explain myself, but for some reason…I had to see you."

"You *must* be out of your mind," she said, but I could see she was still smiling.

I *was* out of my mind. After all…what the hell was I doing at her house in the middle of the night? The thought of just leaving without a single word would be better than sitting here with her, not knowing what might happen. I couldn't leave, of course. When I was close to her, all I wanted was to be closer.

I sat down on the edge of her bed, and she came over to sit beside me. I moved closer, and she didn't move away. I felt desperate to touch her again and lightly brushed my fingers across the soft flesh of her neck. I saw her shiver, but she still didn't move away.

"Stay," she whispered, her voice sounding throttled.

"I'm not going anywhere." That was the honest truth.

It was puzzling to suddenly have this desperation for her, so much deeper and intense than it had ever been before. I felt as if the very touch of her skin turned me into something more than human, something more than myself. She was beautiful and strong. I felt addicted to her mentality and her body as if I were meant to study every part of her in every way I could. Her spirit was intertwined with my own, and I felt that she was part of me. *Is this what it feels like to be in love?*

"You're beautiful," I whispered. I touched her cheek and moved my fingertips across her lips and heard her gasp.

"Are you okay?"

She didn't answer but moved closer until I could feel the heat of her skin so close to me I wanted to take her for myself.

I groaned deep in my throat and whispered seriously. "You're tempting me, Jane."

I moved away.

"Stay," she whispered again. "Please."

"You need your sleep."

"I'm not sleepy," she insisted.

"Will you sleep if I lie beside you?"

She nodded, and my heart rate sped up.

I curled up close to her, and my heart was pounding the whole time. I tried to veil my nervousness. I put my arm around her waist, feeling that familiar, helpless need to touch her. I heard her quietly gasp.

"I'm sorry," I muttered, feeling my heart sink into my stomach, and I moved away.

"No, it's okay," she said, sounding almost frantic. "I don't mind."

I smiled to myself and put my arm back around her, pulling her into my chest. I knew what I was doing was going to cause immense problems. I decided I didn't want her out of my sight for any amount of time. I slept for a very short while and awoke when it was still dark outside. I walked home to get my car and was back in Jane's room before she woke. I watched her sleep, trying to imagine what she may have been dreaming about. She stirred lightly and whispered my name.

"Aidan?"

"I'm here."

She sat up quickly and turned in my direction, startled.

I laughed. "I'm sorry. I got my car. I'm driving you to school."

"I wasn't planning on going to school."

I smiled. "Go to school, Jane."

"Just need a shower," she answered.

I tried to shake off the images but still ended up smiling. "I'll wait."

I kept my mind away from the fact that Jane was thirty feet away from me in the shower and focused my attention on what I might tell Mike the next time we would speak, as well as Luna and Walter.

She was dressed and back in her room before I had much time to think. I smiled when I saw her. She was dressed in tight-fitting dark wash jeans and a red top that exposed a very small amount of cleavage. It hit me then that she shouldn't be anything more than afraid of me, all things considered, but she seemed to be swooning more than anything else. It was a wonderful and confusing truth.

Chapter Sixteen

SCHOOL WAS DIFFERENT THAT DAY. *I* was different. After every class, I was there, waiting for Jane. Things felt wonderful when we were at school. I was a normal boy with a normal girlfriend (if that's what she was) and a normal disinterest in my studies.

Aaron ignored me at lunch, which I was used to, and again chose a seat as far away from me in history as possible. I didn't speak much, but I did do my usual glancing or smiling at Jane when she looked my direction.

"What are you thinking?" she asked.

I glanced quickly at her and smiled, amused by her question. "Trying to figure out what you're thinking," I replied, honestly.

She just looked away for a moment.

"Are you afraid of me?" I asked, realizing that during class probably wasn't the best time to ask.

She didn't even hesitate before responding. "No."

"You should be."

"Why?" she snapped. "You promised you'd never hurt me."

"I did. It's just that the logical, safe thing to do would be to fear me."

"I'm not afraid of you."

"I know," I answered. "I'm just saying you *should* be. I know by now... that's never changed your mind about anything."

I smiled at her, and after class, she walked with me to the parking lot and instantly continued the conversation.

"Why would you *want* me to be afraid of you?" she started. "You said before that…you needed me…to believe you, remember?"

"More than having you believe me, more than having you close to me, Jane, I want you to be safe." This was the most honest thing I could have possibly said to her.

"You've saved my life more than once already."

I nodded. "Let's hope I am never the cause for anybody else needing to play your knight in shining armor."

I heard her sigh, but she said nothing. We got in my car and drove in silence for a few minutes before she started with more innerving questions.

"You've never killed anybody before, have you?"

I didn't want to lie to her. "You know I have, Jane. I basically told you I have."

"But…the bird."

"I simply promised that I would never hurt another human again."

"Am I safe with you?"

I pursed my lips. "For now…yes."

She glanced in the side view mirror and peered over her shoulder.

"What is it?" I asked, trying to push aside the tension that was swelling in my voice a moment before.

"That car," she answered, pointing over her shoulder. "It's been behind us since we left the school."

I glanced quickly over my shoulder at the black Mustang, trying to tell myself it was nothing. "Strange. You don't recognize it?"

"No. Should I?"

"No. I'm just expecting Rudy to do something stupid again."

"You wouldn't hurt him, would you?"

"I let him beat the crap out of me, Jane, without moving to fight back. What do you think?" I chuckled.

"Right."

She looked behind us again. The car was still following even after we had turned.

"Where are you going?" she asked.

I was suddenly full of nervous worry. It *was* after all a black Mustang—the same car Abraham had.

"Testing this guy," I answered, no longer worrying about hiding the tension.

"Can you actually see him?" she asked, glancing over her shoulder again.

"Stop turning around!" I snapped. "He'll figure out what I'm up to."

"Can you see him?" she repeated.

I nodded. "Barely."

"Well—"

"Please," I retorted before she could ask anything of me. "Don't ask any questions. I promise everything will be all right."

I was certain at that point it was Abraham. I was definitely in trouble. He must have been getting impatient. I kept driving, waiting for an indication to confirm my thoughts.

"Aidan?" she whispered.

"Shh. Really, Jane. I'm trying to concentrate."

After about fifteen minutes, he stopped following, and I saw his figure in the car turn and stare at me as he drove by. I caught the familiar license plate that confirmed it was Abraham. I had to tell her now. There was really no way around it.

I sighed heavily and pulled over on the side of the road and put the car in park. "I did the only thing I had tried to avoid," I grumbled.

She was silent.

"All I wanted to do was keep you safe, and now I have endangered you."

"What?" Her voice was instantly thick with anxiety.

"I didn't want us to be friends because I wanted you to be safe, but if I leave you now, you will *never* be safe."

"Aidan, what's going on?"

"The license plate of that car…" I started.

"Yeah?"

"Did you see it?"

"I saw there was a seven and I think a…B?"

I nodded. "Yeah, tacked to the end of the letters S-E-V-R-N."

I saw the fear paralyze her for a moment even when she tried to hide it. "It could be a coincidence."

I shook my head.

"I thought you didn't believe in them."

"Yes, I said that," I answered, my voice dropping at the thought of my dishonesty. "I lied."

"You lied?"

"Yes, Jane, I lied. Let's not make a big deal about it, all right? I know the Sevren exist. I know for a fact."

"Because you're one of them!"

"No," I yelled back. "No! Never!"

"Then why are they a problem?"

"Because they are being led by a man who is more powerful than me, stronger than me, and I have history with him."

I sat there, waiting for her to ask me who, anxiously awaiting the answer I wished I didn't have to give her.

"Who?" she finally asked in a strangled voice.

I sighed and squeezed the bridge of my nose, trying to stop the pounding in my head. My voice choked up, and I answered, "My father."

It was silent for a long time. I couldn't figure out what I was supposed to say to her. I ran through several possibilities in my head, but none of them would come out right. I thought about telling her I was in trouble because of my betrayal. I contemplated making her swear to secrecy so I could tell her about Walter. I wanted to tell her everything—but I couldn't.

"I'm taking you home," I finally said. It was the only thing I was able to say. I started the car again. "But I want to stay with you tonight just to make sure you're safe."

She nodded, still with a mystified look on her face.

"If you do not ask me to talk about it tonight, I will tell you tomorrow. Just please not tonight."

Jane walked to the front door of her house, and I came through the window like I had the night before. I was in Jane's bedroom in minutes and heard her telling her father Becky had driven her to school.

I smiled as soon as she walked in. She sat beside me and sighed.

"I shouldn't leave my car in your driveway," I said. "That wouldn't look good."

"Yeah, I don't want to give my dad any reasons not to trust me."

"I'll go park down the street," I said, pointing toward the window. "I'll come right back."

I got in and sped off out of her driveway. I realized it was probably not the best idea to drive when I was angry. I parked against the curb about a block away and walked quickly back to her house. I climbed the oak tree and hopped into her room.

"Aidan!" she yelped, startled again.

I laughed. "I'm sorry."

"No, you're not."

"You're right," I said, laughing. "I couldn't resist."

"How did you do that?"

"Do what? You obviously weren't paying very close attention, and your window is open."

"Uh huh."

"You give me too much credit." I shrugged my shoulders and sat back down. "So...promise me you'll sleep tonight, Jane."

"I'm promising nothing." She broke eye contact, staring out her window.

"Yeah...should have guessed as much from you," I mumbled under my breath.

"What's *that* supposed to mean?" she snapped.

"Exactly what I said," I answered, smiling. "I wasn't insulting you."

"Mm hmm."

I smiled and put my arm around her, pulling her into my chest. It was one of those things that felt normal. It didn't even occur to me until *after* it had happened that it may not have been normal at all.

"If you don't mind, I would like to know some things about you." It was driving me crazy that I was in love with a girl I knew so little about.

"Such as?"

"Such as...your mother."

"Okay," she answered. "My mother, Carol. She's very attached to me. She's the type of person my dad fell in love with when they were young. The problem was Ethan grew up—my mother didn't."

"Kid at heart?"

"You could put it that way," she answered. "She's crazy in my opinion. She *relieves* stress with extreme things like sky diving and parasailing."

I could tell by the tone in her voice that Jane was not the type to indulge in risky things. Me on the other hand—I wasn't frightened of much anymore.

"Not your thing?" I asked.

She chuckled. "Definitely not."

"And your dad? Why did he come here?" This, I actually wanted to know.

"He actually grew up here."

She explained that she met Becky and Rudy when she was out visiting her grandparents, and after they died and her parents divorced, her father, Ethan, moved back.

"Everyone I have ever loved besides my mother lives here."

"Well, then it worked out for the better."

She smiled. "Yeah...I guess it did. People still stare at me like I'm an alien, but I'm getting used to it."

"You notice that?" I asked.

"Of course I notice it. I'm the new girl at North Bend High—the reclusive girl that nobody can get any type of answers from. You're the only one I've told things to, except maybe Becky and Rudy."

I knew that wasn't at all why people stared. She really had no idea how beautiful she was. I let it go.

"Well, then I should return the favor, right?"

"Sure. I'd love to know about the mysterious Aidan Summers. You're famous at school, you know. People make up stories about you."

"More like infamous I'm sure."

"So, what about *your* mother?" she asked.

"My mother was…crazy," I said. "Not crazy in the good way like your mother. She was a little off her nut if you know what I mean. Both of my parents are dead."

"Oh my gosh, Aidan. I'm sorry."

"No, it's really all right. I live with my uncle Walter, who is a professor and a genius."

"How did your parents die?"

"They were murdered," I answered truthfully for the first time, easily able to push the pain from my voice.

"My father's business partner was a thief and destroyed my father's wealth before he killed him…and my mother. I came home to find them dead."

She stared at me for a moment.

"Not really a good time for sob stories," I said. "You'll hear all about it later. I promise."

She pressed her lips together and narrowed her eyes.

"I promise," I said, laughing. "Take your moments. I'll wait."

"I'll be right back."

"Take your time."

I waited for her, clearing my head for only fleeting moments before my brain forced images of Jane into my head. I tried not to think about her naked and in the shower. It was wrong to be lusting over my target. It was wrong to be thinking about it at all, but I couldn't help it. She was what I wanted and all I really thought about. I was also haunted with the fear that she may know I had lied to her about other things, like the fact that I was one of The Sevren at least at one point. It was obvious that she didn't put it together that I had something to do with the death of her brother—but I knew she would also find out about it eventually. I shivered at that thought.

When Jane walked in, my thoughts were completely stripped away. She was in a white silken nightdress where I could actually see every part of her body, though not enough to take away the lovely mystery I was so intrigued by. I could feel the blood rushing to my face.

She sat beside me on her bed.

"Are you going to sleep tonight?" I asked.

"Mm hmm."

I smiled. "Good."

"I have one condition."

"Of course you do."

"You have to lie with me," she said.

I nodded, smiling. I, of course, would not have it any other way. Even more than being close to her, I wanted to make sure I was here to keep her safe. It was too late to stay away now, too late to con Mike into believing Becky was the one. It was my fault, of course, but I blamed her...for being so tempting.

Those feelings and thoughts came rushing back to me when I touched her shoulder. I stopped when she locked her gaze onto mine.

"You're beautiful," I whispered.

I could feel her hands quaking and saw her cheeks flush terribly.

"Are you afraid?" I asked.

"I don't know."

Was that the truth? She had every reason to be frightened of me. She had every reason to be terrified, but even knowing what she knew, she didn't resist my touch. I touched my lips to her cheek, and she turned her head, meeting my lips with hers. She gently pulled away, but I couldn't stop yet. I softly placed my hand on the back of her head and pulled her close. The kiss was deep and passionate just as I dreamed it would be. I felt her pull away and wrap her arms around me. I returned her embrace and felt her softly kiss my neck.

"Are you okay?" she whispered.

I nodded. "Lie with me."

"I want you to kiss me again."

I leaned forward and kissed her briefly, not wanting to let myself get too involved yet. I wanted more than I was ready to take from her.

"I'm sorry," I said, "but you're testing my self-control."

"Then let it go," she murmured.

I chuckled quietly. "Not tonight." I kissed her cheek. "Lie with me."

I felt her nestle close and press her face into my chest as I ran my fingers through her soft hair. I knew she was falling in love with me, and I wasn't sure at the time if it was a good thing or a terrible thing. What would it mean if Abraham or one of the others found out that not only did I love her but she loved me in return? Things were not going to end well. That I was already sure of.

I slept soundly and awoke to Jane running her fingers through my hair.

"Morning," I whispered. I twisted a lock of her hair around my fingers, admiring its softness. "I didn't know you had curly hair."

"I don't. You mistake my tangles for curls."

I smiled and bowed my head.

"What?"

"Nothing," I said. "You act so modest sometimes."

"Do I?"

I raised my eyebrows at her.

She mirrored my smile and turned away.

"It's tomorrow," I said, "and I promised to explain."

She nodded and locked her eyes intensely on me.

"I need you to believe me," I said. "I need you in general—that simple."

"You need me?"

I nodded. "Yes. And I would rather you not go to school today, simply because it would make me feel better for you to stay within my sight at least for a day. I tell you I need you, and if I ever want you to need me in return you deserve to know the truth."

"You lied to me?"

"Yes, Jane, and I'm sorry. I understand that it's going to be hard to believe anything I say now, but that's what I need you to do—believe me."

"Okay."

Even by telling her the truth, I didn't want her being able to find information on my family, so there were a few things I changed, such as my father's occupation.

"It seems like a very long time ago, yet I still remember it as clearly as possible. I was young and still lived with my mother and father. My father was a very skilled surgeon and was very wealthy. His fortune, however, was beginning to diminish thanks to his partner, Matthias Castlebar. Castlebar was a thief, but at the time, my family trusted and respected him."

She moved closer to me and began listening intently. I told her everything, leaving out that Walter was Rudy's grandfather, my love for Vivian Black, the fact that I killed her brother, and the fact that I was meant to kill her. Everything else I was honest about. I explained that Abraham was the one I now called "father" and how my betrayal was not going to help matters in any way for me.

"Abraham is evil. I understand that now," I said. "He enjoys the killing and the feasting. He's not sane."

I squeezed the bridge of my nose and sighed.

"Are you okay?" she asked.

I looked up at her, again being reminded how lovely she was. "Yes. It is just painful sometimes." What she didn't know was I was not haunted by the death of my parents but of the evil of Abraham and even more than that because I was the cause of her misery and pain. *I* was the very reason she was here—ironic.

"I do share your pain," I said. "My mother and father... I know how it feels to lose someone you love."

"I'm so sorry, Aidan," she whispered. "For everything that happened to you."

"You must never tell anybody, Jane," I said almost frantically. "You must never say a word about who or what I really am."

"What about Rudy?" she questioned.

"NO!" I cried. "Especially not Rudy!"

"No...I mean...Rudy already knows."

I laughed, and it was genuine. "Rudy thinks I'm a...hunter."

"He told me where to find you that day."

I nodded. "And I knew that, remember? I wanted you to see," I admitted almost without shame. "I wanted something that would force me to reveal myself to you. I couldn't find the courage on my own." That was the truth.

"You wanted me to see?"

I nodded. "Otherwise, I wouldn't have been there. Don't get me wrong. I didn't mean to frighten you, but you don't seem like somebody who gets frightened easily. I didn't realize how terrifying I must have looked."

"You looked beautiful," I heard her mumble, almost like she was speaking to herself.

"And pathetic, crouched down like an animal."

"But you looked strong," she said. "I liked that. Even if it did frighten me."

"Were you afraid I was going to hurt you?"

"I don't know what I was afraid of," she answered, "but I don't think I was afraid of you hurting me. Otherwise, I wouldn't have let you in."

I was overjoyed to hear that, but what came out was not the happiness but the anxiety I also had in my thoughts. "In a way, Jane, I wish you hadn't," I said softly. "As much as I needed you and as much as I wanted to assure you I wouldn't hurt you, it is because of me that you are in danger."

She didn't say anything. I waited for her to break the uncomfortable silence developing between us.

"Aidan?"

I smiled at the sound of that name and kissed her forehead. "Everything will be fine. I promise." I wasn't sure if that was true, but I knew I wanted it to be.

"Aidan?" she said again.

I looked at her, waiting.

"There is one more thing that you haven't explained."

I sighed, knowing instantly that it was the question I was dreading. "Rudy?" I muttered. "Is this about the day with Rudy?"

"You don't have to tell me," she said, "if it's painful."

I tried to smile, but it didn't last, the discomfort and suffering showing in my features. "I am only afraid of truly terrifying you."

She pulled her eyebrows together. "I really think it's better now if you tell me."

I turned for a moment, staring out her window at the thick layer of clouds, admiring their graceful movement.

"Why were you covered in blood but not cut?"

I locked my eyes on her, being torn almost violently out of the calm state the sight of the gray sky was pulling me into. "As you know, I came in simply because I wanted to protect you. The crazy thing is, Rudy and Eric both thought that the blood was from the garden rake. They came at me instantly as soon as they saw me. The blood wasn't mine, Jane."

I saw her choke up. "What?"

"One of them found me," I continued, "one of The Sevren, a lower ranked member than myself. He was going to turn me over to one of the leaders...and he was going to kill you. I had to protect you!"

"So..."

I hesitated briefly. "I killed him, yes," I said, wishing it wasn't the truth, "with his own knife. I placed the body in front of the alter when I returned to the clearing."

"Which is why you were covered in blood?"

"Exactly. If they find out I killed him, which they probably already know, then they are looking for me."

I noticed she was trembling, so I gently started running my fingers through her hair. "Are you all right?"

"I'm fine," she said. "Worried."

"I know. But nothing is going to happen to you."

I grasped a lock of her hair and smiled, trying to lighten the mood by saying something. "Your hair has gold in it."

"Does it?"

"Jane, why don't you ever say what is in your head?"

"I do."

"I don't believe that."

"I'm...honest. Most of the time."

"Is that really what you were just thinking?"

She sighed. "No."

"Didn't think so," I mumbled. I may not be able to read minds, but I usually can tell when somebody is hiding something.

"I thought you couldn't read me."

I laughed. "I can't. But I *can* tell when you are saying something you are not thinking."

"I sometimes don't even know what I'm thinking or what I'm supposed to be thinking."

"Now *that* was the truth."

"How about another truth?"

I nodded.

"I'm scared."

"Of me?"

She shook her head mechanically. "I was telling the truth when I said I wasn't afraid of you."

"Do you trust me?"

"I don't know."

"If you had to choose to trust me or not, would you?"

"If I had a choice, Aidan, probably not."

"That's probably best."

She paused for a long moment, and I could tell she wanted to say something. I looked away from her—I meant to. I didn't want my gaze to force words from her if she wished not to say them.

"But..." she choked out.

I waited anxiously, bringing my eyes back to hers.

"But...I love you."

My heart skipped a beat, and my insides felt like they were shaking. I realized when she said it that I already knew. It shouldn't have surprised me the way that it did. I felt blessed in that moment. I felt that I could never deserve her love, and I owed it to her now more than ever to protect her.

"I know," I answered, trying not to show my surprise. I wanted to keep things calm. "I've known that."

I could see her face fall in a look of relief. "Still," she started. "It feels good to say it."

"Feels good to hear it," I answered. "I told you that I need you, Jane. That in itself should have told you that I love you."

"You love me?"

"Of course. I thought you knew. That is why I always wanted to be close to you since the first day I met you."

She tried to smile, but she was a terrible liar. "This complicates things."

"Actually, it may make things easier."

"How?"

"Love is strong," I said. "It gives speed." I wasn't sure if I believed it, but it felt good to pretend.

Her face was a collage of hidden thoughts and unfamiliar expressions. I had no idea what was going through her mind. She exhaled slowly.

"What's wrong?" I asked.

"It's nothing."

"What are you thinking?"

"Why do you always ask me that?"

"Because you're one of the few who baffle me when you're in thought," I said, smiling.

She shrugged her shoulders. "I'm not thinking about anything."

"Huh." I smiled at her sweetly and shook my head.

She moved closer and leaned in to kiss me, but before our lips met, we were interrupted by a knock on the door.

"Should I?"

I could almost feel the panic in her voice.

I nodded. "It's all right. It's safe."

She walked out of the room slowly as if she was expecting someone or something to be waiting for her around the corner. It made me sick to know that her fears weren't without warrant.

I heard the door open, and Becky's chipper voice fill my ears.

"Hey!"

I couldn't hear Jane's quiet response.

"You okay?"

Another pause.

"What are you doing?"

I was straining to listen, and I walked toward the door of her bedroom to get a little bit closer.

"I'm a little busy," Jane said.

Becky giggled quietly. "Is Aidan here?"

"Uh…yeah."

She didn't seem interested.

"You won't believe who I've spent the past three nights with. Aaron. You know, he's actually kind of cool."

"Yeah."

"Oh…right…*busy*."

"Shut up," she laughed. "It isn't like that."

"Telling me it isn't like that when I didn't say it was 'like' anything means it's *totally* like that." Becky chuckled back.

"Right."

"Okay, well, I'll leave you to it, but you are coming to opening night, yes?"

"Opening night?"

I didn't bother listening to the rest of Becky's blabber about her play. I wasn't interested. I also felt ridiculous for ever seeing Aaron Raines as a threat.

I parted the curtains and stole a glance out to the yard below, spotting Becky's truck parked haphazardly in the driveway. Within moments, she was scurrying along the walkway toward the driver's side.

I turned to see Jane in the doorway. "Becky?"

She nodded. "Yeah. She reminded me about her play coming up. I'd...love for you to come."

I smiled while inwardly cringing at the thought of having to sit through it. "Sure. So what does she think about...us?"

"I told her it isn't like that, but she doesn't believe me."

I frowned. "Well...isn't it sort of...err...like that?"

She shrugged. "I'm not sure. I guess so."

I chuckled lightly and turned away, noticing a picture on Jane's dresser. The face caught my eye, but I couldn't figure out why. I knew him—that I was sure of. My smile fell. It didn't take long for me to realize he was the face of all of my victims. He was Daniel Callahan. It all became so real in that moment, so painfully real.

"Aidan?" I heard Jane question.

I wanted to be sure—I wanted to hear it from her. "Wh—who...?" I cleared my throat, trying to stay composed. "Who is this?" my voice forced out.

"Who do you think?" She walked up beside me, staring at me and pointing at the picture. "It's Danny."

"Short for Daniel, right?"

She nodded, looking puzzled again.

I cleared my throat again. "Oh, of course."

"What is it?" she asked. "What's wrong?"

"It's nothing," I said, finally able to keep my voice even. I smiled at her. "He just reminds me of someone. Never mind."

She knew I was hiding something from her, of course, but she let it go. I wanted to shatter the picture frame and tear the image to shreds as if it would make the memories disappear. I continuously glanced at the picture even late that night in the dark. It was making me insane. I felt Jane stir and move closer into my chest.

"Did I wake you?" I whispered.

I felt her shake her head against me.

I softly kissed the top of her head. "Have happy dreams, love."

Chapter Seventeen

"ARE YOU GOING TO SCHOOL?" she asked.

I shook my head. "No. But...I think you should."

"I'm not going without you."

"It's safe. You should go," I said, which was true.

She shook her head.

"Will you go if I come with you?"

She nodded softly.

"All right. Let me get home really fast. I'll be back before you're ready."

"I bet." She laughed. "You have a way of appearing out of nowhere."

I smiled, entertained as always by her active imagination. I drove home as quickly as I could, ignoring Luna's questions about where I had been. I threw on some clean clothes and didn't even bother with a shower. When I got back, she was still in the bathroom. I focused again on Daniel's picture until I heard her behind me.

"He was happy," I said.

"Yes."

I tried to smile before turning to look at her. "Ready?"

She smiled back. "Sure."

After a boring, surreal day of uptight teachers and seemingly pointless assignments, I dropped Jane off at home.

"I'll be back," I said, "but I need to check something out first."

She nodded, but her eyes looked far away. I didn't feel comfortable leaving her alone, but I couldn't stay with her every second. I turned away.

"Don't do anything stupid, Jane."

I drove home and called for Luna. She raced to the door instantly.

"What's wrong?" she asked frantically. Walter came in to see what was going on.

I suppressed laughter. "Nothing's wrong. Well, besides the obvious, so you can calm down. Both of you."

"You're not funny," Luna sneered.

Wasn't trying to be. "I need to ask a favor of you."

She narrowed her eyes. "What kind of favor?"

"I know you are angry with me, and to be honest, I don't blame you, but I need your help."

She just stared at me, crossing her arms in front of her chest.

"You are about to be...um...more mad."

"James..." she whined, "what did you tell her?"

"Well, you made that easy," I said, trying to lighten the mood by laughing.

Her face remained hard.

I cleared my throat. "Sorry."

"So?"

"Well...everything," I said. "Only...not everything." I continued before she could respond. "I need to tell her the rest, and I need you to pretend like you don't know."

"What?"

"I need you to stay at your house for a while. Mike will make sure Abraham still thinks we are missing. I'm going to take Jane there. I need you to pretend when I walk in that it's the first time you have seen me since my betrayal. Jane will be a lot more willing to believe me if she were to simply overhear us talking."

"I have no idea what you are thinking!" she spat.

"Please, Luna. Just do this. For me."

She sighed. "You're lucky I can't refuse you. I am guessing you want me to keep her there as well."

I nodded. "Yes. Please."

She huffed. "Fine."

I had to tell Jane everything and had to keep Luna out of it as much as possible while still letting her help me. Again I knew I didn't have the courage to tell Jane the details myself, so I figured if she were just to witness it, like that day in the woods, it would be easier.

I drove back to her place just as Rudy was leaving. Great. Now what was he telling her? He shoved passed me.

"She never *did* have any taste," he mumbled, glancing at me.

I stepped inside, since he left the door open, laughing at his reaction. I knew exactly what he was there for.

I smiled at Jane playfully.

"Don't start," she said acidly.

"Oh, come on, Jane." I snickered.

"It's *not* funny!"

It was actually a lot funnier than she realized. "Don't you like him at all?"

"Yes," she said automatically. "When he's not being his ridiculous self."

I smiled. "I think he's in love with you," I said, trying to pretend I felt no jealousy or resentment toward him. I didn't want Jane to know she had the power to break my heart.

"Eew!" She smacked my arm softly.

I leaned against the counter on my elbows and raised my eyebrows, trying to be charming while still playfully irritating her.

"Oh, *please, Aidan.*"

She walked quickly to her room, and I followed.

"You know, I'm not mad," I fibbed.

"You probably shouldn't be."

My mind erased Rudy as soon as I sat beside Jane on the end of her bed and she leaned against me. I put my arm around her.

"I don't want you to be afraid," I said, trying to make my voice sound soft.

"How could I not be?"

"If you had any conception at all of how much you mean to me, you would know that I would never let anybody hurt you."

"Don't promise me that, Aidan. You said yourself Abraham is smarter and stronger than you are."

"Yes, that's true. But I have my moments. If I'm doing it for you, it's enough to give me strength." That I *knew* to be true.

"I'm not sure I understand exactly what you mean."

"I simply mean that my loyalty to you will kill me before anything bad happens to you."

"That's supposed to comfort me?" she shrieked.

"Just…don't worry."

"I'll get right on that," she muttered.

"No matter what happens, Jane, I love you."

I hoped she believed that even if she were to believe nothing else. Her face became flushed again.

"I want to tell Becky so badly," she whispered.

"I know."

"I don't mean about what's happening," she continued, "but at least about us."

I tucked her head under my chin. "She already knows."

"Still," she muttered. "I wish I could tell her."

"Jane, do we *really* have to do this?"

"Aidan!" she hissed. "Of course. She's my best friend. You have *no* idea how much this play means to her."

I groaned.

"You know, you don't have to come if you don't want to."

"Of course I do, Jane," I answered. "I hardly feel comfortable leaving you alone at home. I'm not letting you do this by yourself."

"Do you really think something bad is going to happen?" she asked. "At school?"

I shook my head. "Actually, no, but I won't be able to relax until I know you're home safe, so that's why I'm coming with you."

She nodded. "No more complaining, please."

"Okay, okay." I smiled at her, and she returned the gesture.

"I'm guessing you want to drive?"

"You guess right," she answered. "I know my way at least to school."

"Are you okay?" she asked, obviously trying to break the silence.

"I'm fine. Just a little bit anxious. I can't stop being angry with myself for not having enough self-control to leave you alone."

"I trust you. I know you will figure this out."

It was not at all the response I was expecting, but either way, I appreciated her optimism.

We waited in line at the little ticket window, and I paid with some cash I had found in the pocket of an old pair of jeans probably from over three years ago. Jane rushed inside as fast as she could to take the middle seat in the front row. I heard Jane's name, and we both turned to see Aaron.

"I'm glad you're here," Jane said.

"Wouldn't miss it for the world." Aaron chuckled.

He made eye contact with me briefly then turned away and sat next to Jane. I decided to have some fun with him.

"Hello, Aaron."

"Um...hi," Aaron stammered.

The tension was almost unbearable, but I found it more amusing than I should have. Jane looked at me, and I shrugged my shoulders. From the very moment that the lights dimmed to the moment they came back on, I was completely inside my head, contemplating what I had asked Luna for, wishing that I had another option that didn't include locking Jane up.

After the play, the crowd exploded in applause as Becky and her castmates bowed gracefully. After the curtain closed, Becky raced over to Jane. I snapped out of it and back into the school theatre.

"I saw you the second I stepped onto the stage," Becky squealed. "It was so awesome seeing you right in front of me."

Jane laughed. "Becky, you were so great!"

"You did do really great," Aaron added and hugged her without a second's hesitation.

I smiled at her, trying to be nice. Becky really wasn't so bad once I was able to get past the loud, unnecessary way she acted.

"Sorry to say we don't have any flowers for you," I said.

Aaron thrust his hand to his forehead. "You know what? I actually do, and I left them in my car."

Becky smiled. "I'll come with you to get them if you want."

She and Aaron walked to his car, and Jane waved as we headed to hers. I grasped Jane's hand, and I didn't even feel a slight shudder from her. It felt so normal and so right. I didn't want to ruin the perfect feeling, but I had to tell her something.

"I have something I need to do once we get back to your place," I said.

"Okay…"

"It's important, okay?"

She nodded. Jane drove us back to my house, and I got in my car.

"You're coming with me," I said.

"Oh…I didn't realize I needed to."

"You do," I answered. "I got you involved rightly or wrongly."

She froze beside the car with a look on her face I had never seen before.

"Jane, are you okay?"

She didn't answer, just stared at me. I got out of the car and took her hand.

"It's okay," I whispered. "Please trust me. It isn't a big deal. I just need to take care of something. I'm not going to hurt you."

She nodded and got in the car as if all I had to do was assure her once more that I wasn't going to hurt her. It had finally come to the point where that was completely true. I had no desire to kill her, no desire for her blood as I once did. She was mine now, and I wanted her love and her life, but I didn't want to steal it away from her the way Abraham would have told me to. I was Aidan Summers now. James West was dead, and it felt good.

"You cannot turn around!" I snapped. She gripped the door as I sped down the road to Luna's.

"Aidan, what are you doing?" she yelled. "You're driving like a lunatic. You trying to kill me?"

"Contrary, Jane. Be quiet."

"Where are we going?"

"I need to talk to Luna. That's where we're going."

I felt bad lying to her, but I felt it was the only way to keep her safe. Hide her away at Luna's and let her find out why from our mock conversation.

"Why are you so nervous?" I asked her when we reached the porch of Luna's little house.

"What do you mean?"

I touched her wrist, trying to make her stop wringing her hands together.

"Don't worry," I said.

"What if…what if she doesn't like me?"

I chuckled. Was she serious? "You make me laugh, Jane."

I stepped up to the door and took Jane's hand.

When Luna opened, she instantly smiled like she hadn't seen me in months —which is exactly what I asked her to do.

"Come in," she said in the voice she used to use when trying to charm me.

"He's in North Bend," I said, stepping inside.

"How do you know?" Luna asked.

"Many ways. The stone has been used, and I destroyed my clean slate, Luna. Forgive me."

"A bird?"

I nodded. "It was like he was inside of me. Like he had invaded my mind and controlled me."

Suddenly, I realized that this was partly true.

Luna nodded and embraced me, keeping up the act.

"For a long time, you believed in the power of blood," she said. "When you feel lost…lonely—"

I shook my head. "I was frightened. I was a coward. I did it because I was afraid to not believe anymore." That was my confession to Jane.

"Never be afraid to be who you are, James."

James! I hated it!

"I'm sorry, Jane," I whispered, turning toward her, "for making you a part of my problems."

"I'd stand by you no matter what, even if you tried to run from me," she said softly.

I smiled. That was why I loved her. Her loyalty and her love were the most beautiful things I had ever seen in a person.

"You look terrified," Luna said, glancing at Jane.

"I'm all right," she answered.

Luna nodded but didn't look convinced.

I kissed her cheek, hating myself for what I had to do. "Do me a favor, Jane," I whispered, pulling her into a hug, "and don't fight me."

"What?"

"I'm doing this for you."

Luna pulled her arms from around my shoulders. Jane tried to struggle, but I held her tightly in my arms.

"I love you, Jane."

Luna handcuffed her and dragged her away from me.

Jane started scrambling toward me like I was going to disappear if she didn't reach me. I could already see I had made her cry. I felt almost sick at the sight of the tears saturating her face. It was the only way I could explain to her the details of The Sevren without lying and the only way to keep her safe.

"We really aren't the bad guys, Miss," I heard Luna say. "He really does love you. This is just his way of doing what he needs to do. Please don't cry. He is only trying to protect us all."

I embraced Luna when she returned to the living room.

"So the conversation didn't work," she whispered. "She's still confused as to why you are locking her up."

"I can't tell her," I said. "It will only terrify her more than I feel necessary."

"Go home, James. I'll take care of Jane."

I nodded and headed back to Walter's. I explained to him the situation, and he had almost nothing to say.

"Did I do the right thing?" I asked him.

"You did what felt right to you," he said. "If you believe she will be safer being guarded by Luna, then you are probably right."

"Luna can be ruthless," I said, laughing. "When the situation calls for it."

He smiled at me. "I know."

Chapter Eighteen

LUNA CAME CRASHING into the house, screaming my name. I shot up in bed and raced to the living room.

"Calm down," I demanded. "What's happened?"

She started shuffling her hands and stumbling over syllables. My heart started throbbing like it was about to tear through my very chest. I had never seen Luna look so distressed. Again came that intense, wrenching of my senses. I felt strained as if someone had placed their arms on the keys of a piano, and the sharp, sour notes pulled at my nerves. I concentrated on keeping my breath even.

"She's..."

"She's what, Luna?" I yelled acidly.

"It wasn't my fault!" she yelled, throwing her hands up dramatically. "But she's...gone."

"What?" I bellowed. "Gone where?"

She shook her head, her blue eyes wide and glazed. "I don't know, but I found this."

She handed me a slip of paper. The words were written from an old-fashioned typewriter.

James,

We know what you are doing, and Abraham has summoned you to his home. You will finish the job if you want to live.

~Dorian

"Straight to the point," Luna said.

Walter came into the room with a puzzled look on his face. His eyebrows were furrowed, and his drawn, little mouth hung slightly open. "What's all this shoutin' about?" he asked seriously.

"Jane's missing," I said.

His face fell, and he looked as if he were trying to speak but remained silent. I handed him the note.

"Oh God," he mumbled.

"What do we do?"

"I know someone who can help."

"What do you mean?" I asked, still with my senses screeching, warning me of danger.

"I know someone," he started, "who has undercover information about The Sevren."

"Walter, I don't even know this...Dorian," I said.

He nodded. "I know. *I,* however, do."

My mind shut down for a moment, and all of my thoughts flooded out of my psyche and into the tension of the room. I got ahold of myself and shook off the feeling.

"What do you mean...*you do?*"

He sighed, picking up the phone on the wall by the couch. "He used to do work for us," he started. "The Silver Wing."

"What?" I yelled. "That doesn't make sense."

He put the phone back down and took one long stride toward me. "He's vicious, sadistic, and almost inhuman. He came into The Silver Wing as a spy for The Sevren. No one saw it coming. He's a very good actor, Clem, better than any I've seen. He speaks about twelve languages and is built like a rock. He's completely out of his mind."

"If he is one of them, where has he been?"

"He's not part of the cult like you were, Clem. He's more of a worker behind the scenes. There are dozens of them."

"I know. So what do I do?"

"Let me phone my friend and see what we can set up."

My insides were quaking. I knew they wouldn't kill Jane; they wanted me to do it. Yet even as I knew she would stay alive, I still had no idea how badly she would be hurt. If something goes wrong, they may decide to torture her to death anyway.

"What?" I heard Walter yelp.

I strained to listen to the person on the other end but couldn't.

"Where?" he asked. "Yes, but I don't know how we can—" He paused after being interrupted. "Yes. Dorian. How could you not know?" He sighed.

Luna whispered something.

"What?" I turned to look at her and could tell she was trying not to cry.

"I'm so sorry," she muttered.

I embraced her. "It isn't your fault."

I couldn't blame Luna, could I? I had the nagging feeling of wanting to. I did leave Jane in her care after all. But this was The Sevren's doing. I understood better than anyone how clever and cunning they could be.

I tuned in to Walter again.

"Well, we have to do something." He sighed. "Yes, okay, but Alex is one of them. We can't trust him."

Alex—my brother. I had completely forgotten about my own brother. I halted my thoughts, reminding myself he was *not* my brother. But I had loved him as if he were and protected him from Abraham. Maybe he would help me.

"Yes, I know that!" Walter yelled. "But again, just because Alex said so doesn't make it true. Just...do something for her. If you believe he wants to help—"

He was interrupted again. "Tell her...tell her James asked him to."

Asked him to do what?

"Here?" he asked. "Yes, that will be fine."

He hung up the phone.

"What's going on?" I asked. "What does your friend know?"

"My friend is a fool," he growled.

"What happened?"

"He's the one who kidnapped Jane."

"What?" I shouted. "Why?"

"He felt he needed to protect her from you and at the same time get some inside information on The Sevren."

"Then why in hell does Dorian have her?"

He sighed. "He handed her over to Dorian, not knowing he was one of them."

I turned away, covering my face with my hands. "What do we do?"

"Ian is on his way here now," Walter said. "We are going to try to figure something out together."

"What did you tell him I asked for?"

"I told him to tell Alex you asked him to do something for her."

I nodded. "I would have."

"I know."

"I'm not sure where she is," Ian started, "but I have a feeling she isn't hidden well."

"Then you don't know Abraham," I said.

He chuckled. "James...where did Abraham tell you to meet him?"

"At his house..."

He raised his eyebrows at me. "I said not well hidden. I'm very sure she is well *guarded*."

"So how do we get to her," Walter started, "if she is so well guarded?"

I felt Luna grip my shoulder, and I touched her hand.

"It doesn't seem fair that this is up to you," she said. "It's my fault this happened."

"Don't be ridiculous!" Ian hissed. "I'm the idiot who took her."

I literally bit my tongue to refrain from saying something to him that might make things worse. Such as stating that he was an irresponsible, incompetent, idiot who may very well have murdered the woman I loved. I didn't think that would help matters. I sighed heavily at these thoughts, and the tension in the room thickened among the maddening silence.

"Dorian has to leave some time," I said, breaking the stillness that was tugging at me.

Ian nodded. "Wait for his arrogance to get the best of him."

"Yeah!" Walter shouted. "Because we obviously have the time. I'm sure Jane is fine in the comfort and care of The Sevren."

"Oh, stop," Luna stifled. "Just listen to each other rather than snapping at each other."

Walter put his hand up. "Then enlighten us."

Ian nodded, his blue eyes tense and focused. "Once The Sevren are sure you aren't giving in to the will of Abraham, they will become sure that a rescue won't be happening."

"They will kill her by then," I said. "Once they realize they can't make me do it, they will do it themselves."

"Yes, but they will kill you along with her, and in order to do that, they have to find you," he answered.

"So...we rescue her when Dorian and Abraham aren't looking?"

He nodded.

Something about that just seemed a little bit too easy. Perhaps things didn't have to be as difficult as I had convinced myself they would be. After all, it isn't like The Sevren were gifted with super-human abilities no matter how often it seemed they were. I decided to leave things up to Ian and Walter and hope that things would work out.

I decided a walk sounded nice as usual. I stepped outside, instantly feeling the moisture from the approaching rain. I pulled my jacket over my stomach and just enjoyed the setting sun. I headed down the streets again and not through the woods. I glanced at Jane's house as I passed, realizing she wasn't there. It made me almost nauseated. I began feeling that familiar self-loathing from what had happened to her and what could still happen to her. It was all because of me.

I pried my eyes away from her house, almost painfully, and forced my legs to keep moving. Before I had even moved five feet, I was startled by the sound of my name. I turned around and didn't see Mike as I expected. Someone yelled again, and I realized that he was calling me "Aidan." I didn't recognize his voice.

"Aidan," he said again, catching up to me, breathing heavily.

Oh God. Rudy. Perfect.

"Where the hell is Jane?" he demanded.

"What?"

"Don't play games!" he shouted, pointing an angry finger toward my chest and narrowing his eyes in resentment to my denial. "I know you did something to her!"

I sighed and backed away from him. "Something's happened. I know I don't need to explain myself to you, considering you already know about me."

"Damn right!" he interrupted.

"Oh, please, Rudy," I said curtly. "I'm human for God's sake, but something I got into by mistake has put Jane in grave danger, so do me a favor and shut up so I can explain." Why was I telling him anything? For some reason, I felt I had to.

"She's been taken—kidnapped by one of The Sevren's assassins. Probably the most dangerous of them all."

His turquoise eyes widened, and I was unsure what emotion had caused it. His breathing quickened.

"My God, Summers…" His voice was frail.

"We are going to save her," I said. "I swear."

"Who is 'we?'"

"Me," I started, "and my friend Ian." I obviously had to leave Walter out.

"Oh no, you don't!" he demanded. "I'm coming with you."

It took everything in me not to laugh. "No offense, Rudy, but this isn't a fieldtrip."

"Shut up," he spat. "I love her, you fool! I'm not leaving everything up to you. I'm coming with you!"

He put angry pauses between his words, and the look on his face told me he was just about as stubborn as I was. I sighed. Maybe he *could* help. Of course not. He would end up killed, and then I would have to face Walter.

"No! Rudy, it's just too dangerous."

"It doesn't matter what you say," he demanded. "I'm coming with you."

"Rudy—"

"My dad is a cop, you know. Don't make me bring him into this."

Damn. He was better than I thought.

"Fine," I hissed. "But you have to do as I say, all right?"

"Says who?"

"Says me!" I yelled. "You *have* to listen to me if you want to stay alive."

"Does that mean I have to trust you?"

"No. Not entirely, nor do you have to like me, but at least...*try* to do a bit of both."

He nodded reluctantly. "Don't count on it."

I felt a flicker of annoyance cross my face but fought it off. This was a bad idea.

"Where is she?" Rudy asked, his face appearing slightly composed and still, which surprised me by the way he had just been so agitated and angry only seconds ago.

I tried to be honest. I hated being forced to lie. "She's here in North Bend, but I'm not sure exactly where she is being kept. That's what Ian is helping us with."

"Is she okay?"

I shook my head. "I don't know. They won't kill her. That much I am sure of. It's sort of against the rules. They want me to do it."

His face flashed with an unbalanced fury but subsided before he said anything. "Oh, well, I feel much better now." His sarcasm turned to anger. "I knew you were one of them."

I bowed my head. "I'm not, Rudy. I used to be, and that's why I am in so much trouble. The Sevren don't take betrayal well."

"I can imagine." His face shifted, and his eyes locked onto mine. "Wait... Do you know anything about—?"

I raised my hand, shaking my head. "I don't. I don't know anything about your grandfather." Forced to lie anyway.

He bowed his head. "Jane?"

I nodded. "Yes. She told me about his disappearance after she went to talk to you."

"And you don't know anything?"

I shook my head. "No."

"All right," he said. "Let's get started then. Save Jane."

I smiled at the childlike way he loved her. It was almost endearing. I couldn't say no to him now. Even though he was one of the most obnoxious people I had ever had to deal with, he certainly wasn't one of the worst.

Chapter Nineteen

"IT'S IMPOSSIBLE!" I heard him yell.

I instantly threw on some mismatched clothes and raced to the living room.

"What's going on?" I asked, seeing Ian standing at the front door beside Walter, with irritation masking his face.

Walter sighed and looked at me. "Dorian is always watching. We need a way to draw him out. Get him away from Jane just long enough to get her out."

"Out of where?"

Ian stared at me as if he was too afraid to answer me. His face was completely blank, but I saw his features harden as he replied. "He has her locked in a basement."

"Oh my God."

"He's done it before," he continued. "A woman named Sharon Walters was kept down there. As far as I know, she's *still* there."

I saw Walter dart his eyes toward Ian with his mouth hanging open.

"Sorry," Ian whispered.

"So what do we do?" I asked.

"I don't know," Ian said, "*yet*—I don't know *yet*."

"There is one thing." I looked to Walter. "Rudy wants to help."

"What?" Walter bellowed.

Ian chimed in. "You told him?"

I shook my head mechanically. "He already knew. He found me when I was walking and demanded to know where Jane was. I told him I didn't know what he was talking about, but obviously he didn't believe me. His father is a cop. I didn't want him alerting the police or the media. That would cause complete pandemonium."

"Well, it won't be long before Jane's father gets worried and calls the police anyway!" Ian yelled.

I nodded. "Which is why we have to act fast."

"Let Rudy help," Walter said.

"Are you insane?" Ian yelled.

"He's strong," Walter continued. "He can handle himself. He can be there for comfort if nothing else."

"It's true," I answered. "Jane does trust him."

Ian sighed. "Fine, but I'm warning you it's a very bad idea."

"Clem…" Walter muttered.

"I promise," I whispered, "I will protect Rudy as best as I can."

He didn't answer.

"So how do we get Dorian away from Jane?"

Ian looked at me but didn't reply. Walter then moved his gaze to me as well.

"Oh…no!" I yelled, throwing my hands up. "No. I'm not going to be bait. Dorian will *kill* me."

"They already want you," Ian said. "Let me do the acting. You can trust me."

I shook my head. "I don't know."

"Just come with me, and…I guess bring your idiot friend, and I'll go inside and tell Dorian you are at the clearing. By the time he realizes you aren't there, we will have Jane out."

"If Abraham wants to find me badly enough, he can," I said. "He's a Sevren. He can find anyone."

Ian nodded. "That's why Abraham has to be…"

"Has to be…"

"Killed," Walter said. "That simple, Clem."

I shook my head. "That won't stop them."

"I know," Ian said, "but it *will* slow them down."

"You didn't tell anyone, did you?"

He broke eye contact.

"RUDY!"

He sighed. "I told Becky. But how could I not? She's Jane's *best* friend. I convinced her to stay behind."

"That wasn't necessary," I said. "She wouldn't be coming anyway."

"I know."

"Anybody else?"

He shook his head. "Ethan thinks Jane is with Becky. It hasn't occurred to him yet that something has happened."

"Good."

"When do we go in?" he asked, fidgeting in his seat.

I was amused again by his odd love for Jane. "We wait for Ian's signal."

"What is his signal?"

"Rudy, just relax. You shouldn't even be here."

"What's his damn signal?"

I huffed. "When he tells us to go in. Good enough?"

"Fine," he muttered. "Good enough."

I sat silently, staring at the windows as if something terrible would happen if I were to look away even for a brief moment. My insides felt as though they were quaking when I saw the blinds in the window of the top story open. My breath exploded when I saw it was Ian. He signaled us to come in.

"Now?" Rudy asked frantically.

I nodded. "Follow me. There is no need to run. Do you hear me?"

He glared at me but didn't object as he often did. I slinked toward the house as calmly as I could, trying my best to keep my mind off of Jane and what she may be going through. I knew I had to keep all of my emotions at bay until Jane was safe. Rudy was following clumsily behind. I tried to ignore his mumbles and sighs.

"Abraham is still in the house," Ian whispered as soon as we walked inside. The house was dim, and the hallways were completely shadowed. I followed Ian through the corridor and toward the basement door.

"Stay here," Ian demanded. "I'm going down. Do *not* move."

I could hear in his voice that he was reluctant to trust me. He still thought I was the bad guy. I tried to trust Ian as he instructed even through his clear and obvious dislike of me. Rudy followed closely behind.

"Rudy," I snarled, "one more step and I'll knock you out."

"Oh, shut the hell up, Summers. I love her."

"That doesn't make it okay for you to be an idiot. One more step. I promise you I could have torn you apart with my bare hands that day at Jane's. Don't make me prove it to you."

He growled deep in his throat but stopped about ten feet from the stairs. I strained to listen to Ian but could only make out some of it.

"Let's go," I heard him say.

There was an almost maddening pause. Oh God. Jane, please say something.

"Jane?"

I heard the softness of her voice, and it almost brought me to my knees. I didn't realize her voice was so familiar until I heard it.

"Dorian left," Ian said. "I'm sorry. I thought he was on our side, that he was fighting against The Sevren, not one of them. He must have been planted within."

"How can I trust you now?" she asked.

"Because I'm the only one who can get you out of here. Come on. Get up."

"By the way," he started, "your friend...is a severe idiot!"

I tried not to laugh, knowing he was referring to Rudy.

"Aidan?"

I was instantly amused. Did she really think I was an idiot?

"Who?"

"Don't remember his name at the moment," he said. "Light, spiky hair, taller than Aidan." There was another pause before Ian continued. "Wow, let me tell you—those two do *not* get along."

"Rudy!"

"Ah"—he chuckled—"there ya go. Rudy. That's the one."

"What the hell is *he* doing here?"

"Well, from what I gathered, he claims he loves you, so Aidan asked him to help."

Not exactly the way it happened.

"Come on," he said, "before Dorian gets back. We have to get you out."

Rudy instantly called her name. Goddamn. Could he not do what he was told just once?

"My God. Are you okay?" he said.

She just sobbed into his chest.

"I'll take care of you. You'll be fine. We have to move."

"You're crazy," she said, "coming here."

"Not crazy, Jane. I just can't leave everything up to Summers. I don't trust him an ounce."

I glared at him even though he couldn't see.

"Rudy, where's Aidan?" Jane asked. I could hear concern in her words.

"Shh... He's just around the corner. Come on."

She raced down the hallway and leapt into my arms. I could feel she was frail and weak but was still able to constrict her arms around my neck as she always did.

"Can't breathe, Jane." I chuckled.

"We have to go," Rudy said. "We have to keep moving."

I was thankful for the dark, not wanting to see Jane in the state she was in.

"I have my car," I whispered. "It's just outside. We have to get you home."

"I'm going to head out," Ian said. "I'll make sure there's no one outside."

I nodded toward him. "Thanks."

"Is Ethan okay?"

"As far as I know, Ethan is fine," I answered.

We walked down the dark hallway, passing several rooms. Jane stopped abruptly and turned toward a closed door in front of her.

My senses were screeching again, and that familiar tugging on my nerves returned. I could hear distinct sounds of sobbing coming from behind the closed door.

"Rudy, listen," Jane whispered after his annoying warnings I wasn't listening to.

"No," he whispered. He grabbed her hand. "Let's go."

"I can't," she demanded. "I have a very bad feeling, Rudy, like I need to do something."

"You have a bad feeling?" he echoed. "You have a bad feeling because if we don't keep moving, you're going to get yourself killed. Don't do it. Please!"

I could feel the evil that was approaching, and it was driving me near mad. My senses again were telling me to follow the danger. I patted the breast pocket of my jacket, making sure I had my knife on me.

"*She* doesn't have to do anything," I interrupted, "but I think you should let me do the right thing—for once."

"Since when are you the good guy?" he snapped.

"Since you tried to steal my girlfriend," I retorted.

"What? Your—"

"Both of you stop," Jane demanded. "I *know* that voice."

"You're making this into something it isn't," Rudy said.

I knew he was right, but I was doing this because I didn't feel I had a choice.

"Why don't we just get Jane out of here? Be logical—for once."

"Look," I started, curtly, "we have to at least try to get along. You can hate me if you want to—that's fine. But until this is over, please at least *pretend* to tolerate me, and I will show you the same courtesy."

"Fine," he growled, "but I'm not doing it for you."

"I'm not asking you to."

I pulled out my knife and turned toward the door again.

"What the hell are you doing?" Jane hissed.

"Jane—close your eyes."

She pressed herself into Rudy's chest.

"It's all right," I heard him whisper.

I kicked open the door and was instantly sickened by what I saw. There was a girl lying across the bed, with her arms over her face and my evil, monster of a father over her body. She was naked and lengthy, but Abraham appeared to still be fully clothed. Rage began boiling inside me, feeling like it would destroy me if I didn't assuage it someway. I grabbed the back of his shirt, pulling him off the bed. My heart almost stopped entirely when I saw it was Becky. She was shaking furiously and screamed Jane's name with the most miserable fear behind her voice. It only heightened my fury.

I pushed Abraham to the floor and shoved the blade into his back. A drowned gurgle erupted from his mouth, and he choked out my name—the hated name that heightened my anger again, forcing it to explode out of me. I growled and pulled the knife from his back, actually watching the blood streaming from his body and emptying onto the floor. I was so full of hate that the sight did nothing but make me want to hurt him more.

I rolled him over and pulled the blade quickly across his throat. That's when the blood really came out. It flooded out the way I never thought blood could. It pooled out around his body, soaking my shoes.

"I told her to stay behind," I heard Rudy murmur. He covered his face with his hands. "She wouldn't listen."

I turned to Jane. "Why are your eyes open?" I asked, trying to remain calm. I just murdered Abraham—there was no way of getting out of this now. My shirt was soaked in blood, so I pulled it over my head and wiped at the stains on my jeans.

"Aidan," Jane whispered, "get her something—please."

I pulled a clean sheet off the bed, and Jane wrapped it around Becky and tied it off in the front. Rudy lifted her in his arms, and she instantly complained.

"No," she said, sobbing. "No, Jane."

"I'm right here. I'm right behind you," Jane coaxed.

A small whimper escaped, but before she said anything else, she fell unconscious in Rudy's arms.

"I'm sorry," I whispered, "that you had to see that."

"How badly did he hurt her?"

"I'm not sure. He was fully clothed when I walked in. She may be a bit banged up, but I think she's mostly scared."

"Abraham?"

I stared into her eyes, realizing Alex had been telling her things. I nodded and continued down the hall to the car.

I couldn't pay attention to anything. I couldn't even look at Jane. I tried to keep my eyes off of her as much as possible. It made me sick to see her that way. She was a haggard wreck. Her face was colorless, and dark circles ringed her eyes. Her hair was a mess of tangles and knots, and her clothes were dingy with a blood stain on the knee of her jeans. And it was my fault.

Rudy put Becky in the back seat, with her head rested in Jane's lap.

"It's okay," I heard Jane say sweetly. "I'm here, and we're going home."

"Correction," I interrupted. "Hospital."

"No," Becky whispered. "You'll be in too much trouble."

"We don't have to tell them exactly what happened, do we?" Jane asked.

Obviously not. I just murdered my own father.

"Aidan?"

"No, we don't, Jane, but either way, in this situation, I am innocent."

"You killed Abraham."

"Self-defense," I lied.

"Thank you," Becky whispered.

Rudy turned to look at her. "You should have stayed behind. I didn't even know you were in the car."

"Well, of course you didn't," she said. "That was the point."

She was slipping in and out of consciousness.

Rudy sighed. "My God," he yelled. "Jane, have you eaten *anything*?"

"I'm okay. I was fed."

"Not as much as I had hoped," I added. "But Alex gave you food, right?"

"Yes," she answered. "Thank you for that."

"I'm sorry I couldn't get you out sooner," I started, suddenly realizing that a bit of food wasn't close to good enough. "I am so sorry I let this happen to you."

"It isn't your fault."

"I should have never gotten close to you."

"I tried to tell you that," Rudy murmured.

"Not now!" Jane snapped back.

"When?" he mumbled under his breath.

"How about when Jane is coherent and Becky is conscious? Sound good to you?" I yelled.

"Jeez," he snapped back. "A little hostile, are we?"

"For the love of God, man. I just found my father attacking my friend, and the love of my life half starved to death in a dirty basement, so I think it would be nice if you could just shut the hell up before I crash this car into a tree. Yes?"

He didn't answer, just slouched down in his seat.

Before we got far, I could feel the car slowing down. I pressed my foot harder on the gas, but nothing happened. I prepared to pull over. Before I had even gotten far enough over to the side of the road, the car stopped completely.

"Shit," I grumbled.

"What's wrong?" Jane asked.

"Damn car's out of gas," I murmured, speaking more to myself than to her.

"What?" Rudy growled. "It was completely full just before we got here."

"Abraham," I said, sighing under my breath. He knew I was here. Great. "Damn—we really do need a car."

"That's not exactly an option," Rudy chimed in.

"Nonsense."

"Okay, another question then. How do you propose we *get* a car?"

I smiled at him, shaking my head. "It won't be too difficult."

I drummed my fingers on my cheek a few times. "Okay... Rudy, I need to go back inside. Stay in the car and look after the girls. Lock the doors. If Dorian gets back, I'll take care of it." *Though I'm not sure how yet.*

He nodded.

I rushed back inside, knowing Dorian would be back soon. I brought myself back to the room where I had murdered my father, trying my best to push back the guilt. There was nothing to feel guilty about. I reached into his pocket, trying to ignore the blood. I turned away, grimacing as the soggy fabric stuck to my hand. I pulled out his car key and a silver cell phone. I wiped my hand on my jeans and returned to the car as fast as I could. Nobody had even moved an inch.

Rudy unlocked the door.

"Let's go," I said, holding up the key dangling from a silver chain.

Jane followed right behind me, and Rudy, with Becky in his arms, followed a little farther behind. The garage was open. Perfect. I looked to Jane, sure she would instantly recognize the black Mustang that had followed us. It was hard to even glance at her looking as awful as she did, knowing it was my fault.

"Are you okay?" I asked.

She choked back then broke eye contact and nodded.

I started the car as Rudy put Becky in the back seat. She hardly moved at all.

Rudy got in the passenger's seat, and I sped off.

"Slow down," Rudy sputtered.

"I'm sorry," I said. "It's a habit."

"I wouldn't mind getting home faster," Jane said.

"Are you *going* home?" Rudy asked, turning around.

"I guess not, but the sooner Becky gets to a hospital, the sooner we all get home."

He nodded. "She'll be okay. You should get checked on too."

"Wait," she started. "Just take her to my house. Ethan's a doctor, you know."

"That's right," I replied in sudden remembrance. "He *is* a doctor."

"Take her to Ethan then," Rudy said.

"I'm still not sure about it though," Jane said. "We're going to need a pretty good cover story."

"Don't worry about that," I answered.

I wasn't sure exactly what my cover story would be, but I had the entire drive home to come up with something. If Ethan *had* to know about me, I figured it was best to make me look more like the hero than the bad guy. I could simply say that Becky had some bad luck with an older guy, which would have been believable, and Jane went over to make sure she was all right, and the guy came back—out of nowhere. Something like that would do well enough.

I parked the car, and Rudy rushed to the back seat to wake up Jane, who had *finally* fallen asleep.

"You're home, sweetie," he sang.

I pushed him aside. "You all right, love?"

Rudy glowered.

"I told you I'm fine," she said, groggily.

"That never means much coming from you."

"Becky," she whispered. "Becky, honey, wake up."

"Are we at the hospital?"

"We're at Ethan's," Jane told her.

"Good."

"How are you feeling?"

"Not sure," she said. "Tired."

"Anything hurt?"

She shook her head. "Just a little sore."

"Can you walk?"

She nodded and sat up slowly.

"Don't try!" Rudy called.

"Really, Rudy, I'm okay," she insisted.

She stumbled toward the porch. "Is…this a different car?"

I laughed. "Yes. The other one was out of gas."

"How long had I been out?"

"A while."

"Ethan isn't home yet," Jane announced, "which is good. Gives us time to come up with a plausible story."

"Already taken care of," I said, tapping my finger against my temple. "Just let me do the talking." Hopefully Rudy could keep his mouth shut.

Becky went straight to the living room to lie on the couch. "Can you call Aaron?" she asked.

Aaron… And I thought he liked Jane.

Jane picked up the phone and quickly dialed his number.

"No, it's Jane," I heard, unable to hear Aaron on the other end.

"Yeah, she's here. Things are complicated, but we're both okay." She paused. "Of course. That's why I'm calling."

She hung up the phone, saying Aaron was on his way.

Becky perked up the second a knock came at the front door.

"Lie down," Jane ordered, but Becky shoved her out of the way and ran into Aaron's arms in ten seconds.

"Oh my God," Aaron choked out. "Becky, what happened? Are you okay?"

She moved away and avoided eye contact. "I'm okay," she said. "No worries."

The tough-girl act always troubled me, but it lasted only until Aaron stared into her eyes, with his eyebrows pulled together. She pressed her face into his chest, sobbing.

"I'd rather Ethan didn't know exactly what happened," Jane said softly.

He nodded. "Can you get her some clothes?"

"Of course. Come on, Becky," she said. "Upstairs. You need a shower."

"So do you," she said, wiping her eyes.

"I'm a little more worried about you at the moment."

Of course she would be. Jane tended to put herself at the bottom of her priority list.

They disappeared upstairs, and Aaron launched into questioning.

"What the *hell* happened?" he demanded, locking his gold eyes on me.

"It wasn't exactly his fault," Rudy said. "Well, I mean, it was, but—"

"Rudy, shut up," I breathed. "It's sort of a long story."

He raised his eyebrows. "Great. I'm patient."

I sighed. "Accepting blame wouldn't make anything better," I started, "so I will simply tell you in my own words what happened, and you can judge for yourself how you feel about it."

He nodded.

We sat down at the bar, and Rudy stood beside me. "I have history with a band of very bad people—people who want to hurt Jane and her family because her grandfather was a member of a rival group."

"What?" Aaron breathed. His voice was hardly coming out. He jolted his eyes to Rudy. Rudy bowed his head and nodded, breaking eye contact.

"You mean…?" His face was tensed and creased. He looked completely terrified and confused.

I nodded. "A friend of mine told me where to find Jane. Rudy insisted on coming"—my voice swelled with irritation—"and Becky, for some *God* unknown reason, hid on the floor under the back seat. I can't believe I didn't see her."

"You wouldn't," Aaron said. It looked like he was trying to smile. "She knew something was up the second Jane didn't call her."

"I know," I said. "Either way, Rudy should learn to keep his mouth shut."

Rudy shot me a dirty look, but I ignored.

"So, Jane was…kidnapped?" He choked up again.

"You could put it that way. I will get us all out of this mess, though. I swear."

"But you aren't…?"

I shook my head. "Don't even think it, Aaron!" I demanded. "I am not one of them."

He nodded, bringing his gaze to his shoes. "And to think," he muttered, "I thought Becky was losing interest."

I actually smiled at his response, but it faded when I saw both he and Rudy give me blank stares.

It was silent for a long time. Sometimes Aaron would sigh or wring his hands together. Rudy took a seat at the bar beside me and just rested his head in his hands. I had to try to think of something other than Jane in a dark basement where Ian had mentioned a corpse. Charming. I knew Jane well enough to know that a dead body was enough to bring actual hatred into her. I only hoped she knew I had nothing to do with it. I sighed at these thoughts, realizing the time had to eventually come when she found out about her brother if she didn't know already.

My thoughts were shattered when I heard Becky yell Jane's name.

I perked up and went to stand by the bottom of the stairs. Aaron flew past me and into Jane's room.

"What do we do now?" I heard.

"Ask Aidan," I heard Aaron say. "Sorry to intrude, but I think the new kid is the only one who *can* know what to do."

Chapter Twenty

JANE CALLAHAN,

We know who you are, and we know that you are the reason for James West's betrayal of The Sevren. Because of your love for him, your blood is tainted, so it is not yours we want. We have your father. Bring us Rudy Thompson, and your father's life will be spared.

~Dorian

P.S. I think it best that you do not disregard this note.

I sighed, placing the note on the table in the kitchen. I knew it was impossible that Dorian knew where she lived. It was most likely delivered by Mike.

"Before anything else is done, Jane, you need to be taken care of."

"Aidan, I'm fine. We don't exactly have time. They're going to kill Ethan."

"No," I retorted, "they won't."

"And why not? How do you know they haven't already?"

"One," I said, reaching into my pocket, "they wait for Abraham's call." I pulled the stolen cell phone out of my pocket. "Two, he's bait to get to Rudy and to get to me." I left Jane's name out of that list for obvious reasons.

"We have to find Ethan."

"We'll get him back, Jane, and nobody will be hurt in the process—except maybe me."

Rudy opened his mouth to speak, but Jane yelled at him not to say anything. He put his hands up and nodded.

"Now please," I continued. "Aaron brought some food. Eat something."

"Thank you."

Aaron smiled and pulled his arm a little tighter around Becky's waist.

"I doubt she's going anywhere," Jane said, smiling.

"Eh—you never know."

I stood beside my love and ran my fingers through her damp hair. She finally looked a little bit more like herself, at least enough for me to see her beauty.

"Why me?" Rudy asked, bringing my attention to him. "Why me and not somebody else?"

I shook my head. "Because they can't use Jane. Her blood is tainted. To them, you are the next best thing." That was true enough though I wasn't sure yet of the exact reason behind it.

"I don't even like you."

"Yes, but they don't know that." I ignored his rudeness as usual. "They are using you to get to me"—I couldn't hold it back—"and Jane."

"Me?" she yelled.

"Even though they do not want your blood, that does not mean you won't end up like…" I trailed off, cursing myself silently for letting my words slip that way.

"Like what?"

I couldn't say anything. I wasn't even sure she knew about Sharon Walters.

"Aidan?"

I sighed. "Like…one of their victims."

"Oh my God." Her voice was completely throttled. "You know about Sharon."

I bowed my head and sighed. Too late. I nodded softly, not able to bring myself to see the look on her face.

"I promise I won't let anything bad happen to any of you!"

Rudy slouched down on the couch with his arms crossed in front of his stomach. I saw the concern in his face and could hardly stand to look at him. I focused my attention on Jane until I saw her get up to talk to Rudy. I put my head down in my hands, trying to ignore their frightened voices.

I couldn't help but to tune in to their conversation when I heard Rudy say he loved her.

"Everything about you, Jane—your courage, your love…your beauty…everything."

Ah Rudy. Still not giving up.

"Rudy…" I heard her mumble just loud enough for me to perceive.

"I know…" he said, "I know as I knew from the beginning that I can be the one to stand beside you—to protect you. You love me, Jane. I know you do. I don't want to die without feeling you close to me at least one time."

"That isn't fair," she demanded harshly.

"I love you, and so does Aidan. That means there will be a fight, Jane, so here I am—fighting. And I don't fight fair. There's little gain in that."

I was prepared for him to fight but wasn't expecting him to be so deceiving. Telling Jane he was going to die just to get his way was so like Rudy. Whatever it took, he was willing to try.

There was a long moment of silence and then Rudy's soft apology.

Jane raced past me and up the stairs to her bedroom. I knew exactly what had happened. I followed her and knocked lightly on the door.

"Go away!" she called.

"We both know you are going to let me in, so either open up now or argue with me for fifteen minutes."

She opened the door and pressed herself against me. I wrapped her in a hug, realizing a kiss from Rudy shouldn't even have me worried. She led me into her room and shut the door.

"What's wrong?" I asked, trying to get her to tell me herself.

"Nothing," she retorted.

I leaned slightly forward, raising my eyebrows. "Nothing?"

She sighed heavily. "I don't want to talk about it. Just be with me."

She attacked me with a heavy kiss, which I resisted, irritated by her trying to convince herself she loved me.

"Stop it, Aidan," she hissed. "Just kiss me."

She pushed me against the door, and I softly moved her away.

"Jane, what's with you?"

"I love you," she whispered. "That's all."

She was never very good at lying. I tried to oppose her still but was completely outmatched by her passion. I welcomed the kisses and thought only of Jane—the softness of her skin and the fragile feel of her tiny body in my arms. I could feel myself giving in. I felt my actual body soften, helplessly lost for her. Electricity rushed through my limbs, and I felt almost mad with desire. I wanted her closer to me, closer than anyone had ever been before.

"I love you, Jane," I whispered, "but just tell me again that you're okay—besides the obvious issues."

"I'm okay," she whispered.

That was all I needed to hear. Whether it was the truth or not didn't matter then. I reached under her shirt, stroking her back, feeling the warmth of her flesh almost burning through me, and the kisses became deeper and more desperate with each movement. They remained soft, both of us aware that there was no need for haste. I felt her love transform from the softness a moment ago to an almost rough-ness in her touch. She moved only inches away from me, removing her white tank top. It was unfair that she had to be so beautiful. How could I resist her?

I stared, almost bewitched by her perfect belly and her small, delicate breasts only half covered with a lacy bra. I tried to look away, tried not to focus on the perfection of her skin. I moved away with all the force and strength I had left in me.

"What's wrong?" she whispered.

My heart sank, almost regretfully. Ruining a perfect moment wasn't some-thing I was good at.

"If you want to do this…" My voice was far away. "I'm sorry, but if you want to do this, I think we should wait until things settle."

"It may be too late by then," she murmured, touching my cheek softly. "What if you don't come back?"

"I'll come back. I know you love me. I am not worried about that. I am not going to let one kiss from Rudy make me even as much as nervous."

She gasped almost angrily, and I suppressed my laughter.

"Damn, Aidan. How do you do that?"

"You ask me that question a lot."

"Well…it's like you have eyes that come out and follow me wherever I go."

I chuckled, shaking my head. "I wish that sometimes. Neither of you were being very discreet. I'm pretty sure Becky and Aaron knew what he was up to." I tried to hide the tension in my voice. I definitely didn't like Rudy.

Her cheeks turned bright red, and she grumbled, pressing her face into a pillow.

"It's okay." I laughed. "I won't kill him. He loves you. I was prepared for him to fight."

"He doesn't *love* me," she said, lifting her face up and staring at me through narrowed eyes. "He just thinks he does."

"Jane, stop being so modest. He loves you, but you *know* I love you, and I know you love me. You don't need to prove that to me, and you shouldn't have to prove it to yourself—not any other way than being with me."

She nodded, pulling her shirt back on, covering up with that horrific fabric. I despised it.

"But don't think I don't want to," I retorted, trying to engrave the image of her bareness in my memory. "I do—of course. But I would rather it not be because of Rudy or The Sevren or your fear of me not coming back—for no negative reasons but because we care for each other. Is that fair?"

She nodded. "I understand…but don't leave."

I smiled and lay beside her on the bed, taking her hand in mine.

"Rest your mind," I said. "Everything will be fine."

I was tense and unsettled. I rolled onto my side and propped myself up on my elbow, staring into Jane's perfect auburn eyes. I whispered her name, unable to say anything else.

"I know," she said. "We should go back downstairs."

Wasn't at all what I was thinking, but she was right.

"We all need to be there for each other," I said, almost annoyed that I couldn't stay lying beside her. "I wish there was some way I could make you believe me that I won't let any harm come to you—*any* of you."

She sighed, closing her eyes. "I wish that too."

I left, feeling anxious to leave her alone even for one night. Walter knew as soon as I got home that something wasn't right. I told him everything, even about my murdering of Abraham.

"I told you he needed to be killed," he said.

"But it was me who did it. I murdered the man I called Father." I felt myself sinking into a sudden sickness. I felt nauseated and cramped.

He pulled me into a hug. "It's all right," he said. "Everything will settle, and The Sevren *will* be stopped—I swear."

I sighed. I loved Walter's faith and his optimism, but it made me more uneasy to realize he had no idea how strong The Sevren really was. I perked up when I heard a knock on the door and grumbled.

"Great. Mike."

I was not looking forward to explaining myself to him. I opened the door, but it wasn't Mike.

"James?"

I stared at his face, not sure who he was.

"James? Yes?"

I nodded reluctantly and stepped outside on the porch and shut the door.

"Who are you?"

He looked older, mid-twenties. He had dark hair and stubble on his chin. He was lengthy and unattractive.

"My name is Joseph. Mike sent me."

"For what?" I spat.

"The girl."

I instantly felt a need to attack him. "What *about* the girl?"

"Doesn't she know you killed her brother?" he bellowed, lifting his hands overdramatically.

"Leave her out of this!" I growled through clenched teeth, moving so I was only inches from his face.

"Oh, but this is about her, James. It always has been."

I stiffened my legs. My breathing was completely irregular, and my hands were shaking. I wanted to rip him apart. I wanted to tear his throat out and leave him a bloody heap on the porch. I restrained myself, trying to stay calm and composed. It was hardly possible.

"You were supposed to kill her," he spat.

"I *never* agreed to kill her."

"Agreed?" he shouted. "You were *ordered.*"

I shunned him and turned away. He walked a few feet then turned back.

"Dorian wants the boy," he called.

I turned back to face him. "I'll kill him first," I growled.

He laughed. "Oh, will you?"

"I will kill him before he touches *any* of them."

"We'll see about that."

I walked back inside, completely livid. I thought seriously about going back outside and hunting him down. Following through with literally tearing him into pieces. I rushed to my room and started fumbling through my dresser drawers. Luna walked in, as usual without knocking.

"What are you doing?" she snapped.

"None of your concern," I grumbled back.

She huffed. "James, listen to me. I'm sorry for being so overbearing and demanding of you, but...I love you. I don't want to see you hurt."

I looked up at her. Her face was soft, and I could tell she was serious.

"I know," I said. "Thank you, Luna. But I need to do this my way, all right? I need to make sure I am prepared for several different outcomes right now."

"What are you talking about?"

"Please don't say anything to Walter, but if I need to get Jane out of North Bend, then I am going to make sure I have the tools to do so safely and secretly."

"The Sevren are smarter than you know."

"I know more than you give me credit for."

"So you're a genius, James," she started. "That doesn't mean you can do everything."

"I know I can't do everything, Luna. I also realize that I don't need to."

I walked past her with a backpack full of clothes. "Don't follow me."

I took the stolen Mustang to Pony Village Mall, trying to keep a low profile, charging dozens of items to numerous credit cards. Bottles of hair dye, wigs, and clothes. When I got back home, I used Luna's outdated laptop to the best of my ability. For hours I sat there, distorting and editing photographs for false IDs and passports. I printed them out and shoved them in a plastic bag. I filled three small duffel bags with all of the items. I shoved the bags into my closet for the time being.

This might work after all.

The next morning, I put all the duffel bags into the trunk and drove to Jane's house. I climbed into the tree, bringing myself to her window. I saw her toss her scrapbook on the floor and lean back on her pillow.

"Jane, you gotta occupy your mind."

I rarely even startled her anymore.

"I really wish you'd just knock on the door like a normal person."

I chuckled. "Normal? Where's the fun in that?"

She shook her head.

"Are you angry?"

"No." She sighed. "I'm sorry. Just irritable."

"I have some ideas in mind," I said, "just to break the ice."

"What kind of ideas?" she asked, sitting up and turning toward me.

"I'm prepared for several outcomes, but…we are going to need your attic."

"Um…okay. Why?"

"I would rather *not* have Walter asking questions."

"What are you not telling him?"

I waved my hand at her, shunning her question. "I need to keep some stuff in the attic for a while. There isn't anywhere at my place to keep it."

"What stuff?"

"Just some things we may need. Please, Jane. I would rather not tell you yet. Just trust me."

"Okay."

I returned to my car and carried the duffel bags into the house. I handed one to her, and she led me to the hallway. I opened the attic door and unfolded the ladder.

"So really, what's all this stuff for?" she asked again.

"I told you," I answered. "For plan A, plan B, and plan C to get us all out of this mess."

"Why don't you just let me see what it is?"

I sighed, knowing for sure it would frighten and upset her more than I could handle dealing with at the time. "The only reason I'm keeping it here is because you have an attic. Remember, I can't have Walter asking questions."

She nodded. "Wow. My dad is *such* a pack rat."

I laughed lightly and glanced at all the stacks of boxes and books covered in dust.

"I wonder how much of my old stuff is in here."

I spotted an old redwood chest in the corner of the attic, sheathed with dust.

"Whoa," I whispered, crawling to the other side. "What's in *this*?"

"According to my dad, nothing."

"Hmm... I think it needs a key."

"Eh, maybe," she answered. "But it's probably empty. It belonged to my grandfather."

My thoughts spun, and that's when I realized exactly what was in that old chest. It was Walter's. It was the collection of things Jane's grandfather had taken so Walter would stop making himself miserable constantly reliving his nightmares. I brushed it off, pretending I didn't know a thing. Lying to her as usual. I was *so* sick of lying.

I shrugged. "Promise me something?"

"I won't open the bags, Aidan, okay?"

"I'm just trying to keep things from getting any more complicated."

She nodded, trailing her finger along the rim of the old chest. "I miss Ethan," she whispered.

I gently took her by the shoulders and turned her so she was facing me.

"I will get him out of this, love. I swear."

She sighed and rested her head in her hands. I wrapped her in a hug, and she fell against me.

"I wish I could tell you not to worry."

"You can."

"Yes...but what good will it do?"

"I'm not sure," she answered. "I'm not sure it will make me feel any better at all, but it's worth a try."

"Don't worry," I said. "I swear to you that things will end up okay."

"Thanks." She moved away from me so she could stare into my eyes. "So, when are you planning on locking me up at Luna's?"

My mood shifted, and I was suddenly amused. "Nothing gets past you, does it?"

"I know you too well to think for even one second you don't have something planned—or *plotted*."

I smiled. "I just want to keep you as safe as possible. And thank you for not complaining. You tend to not trust me enough."

I instantly regretted saying that. Her honesty made me feel so guilty. "Okay, I understand why," I continued, "but honestly, Jane, you're too clumsy to deny you're in danger when you aren't moving."

Her face curled into irritation.

"I'm sorry. I'm doing a terrible job of trying to cheer you up."

"I feel better just being with you," she said softly. "You don't need to try so hard."

I smiled thinly. "It's my job now to protect you in every way that I can."

"I just can't stop thinking about Danny," she whispered. "They killed him, Aidan. I want them dead—all of them."

I felt myself shudder. "I understand, but this isn't the time for revenge."

"How did I know you'd say that?"

"You know me too well," I answered, smiling falsely. "In all seriousness, I just need to focus on getting Ethan away from The Sevren. You need to stay at Luna's. I don't want you here, especially by yourself. They'll find you, Jane."

"They found me at Luna's too. They can find me again."

I shook my head. "They won't. We weren't careful enough before. She'll keep you safe this time. I promise."

"I love you, Aidan."

Her words stung me. It was like I would never again hear her say it.

"It's okay," I said calmly. "You don't have to tell me that."

"I want to."

"Then next time…don't say it like it's the last time."

I felt her running her fingers through my hair.

"Why Rudy?" she asked.

"I told you—because you love him." I turned to look at her.

"And Ethan?"

I hesitated before responding, trying to think of a lie but settled for the truth. "They took Daniel. You and Ethan were supposed to stay safe, but I got involved. I had no idea he was your brother. If I did—well, I don't know." At least mostly the truth. "This is all about me," I continued, "my betrayal of The Sevren and murder of Abraham. My involvement with you as well, especially because you are related to one of our victims—*their* victims."

Damn.

I saw her shudder.

"I cannot tell you why they chose him either, Jane." It occurred to me that it was necessary to tell her that before she asked me, and I gave her a stuttered response. I couldn't risk her reading my lies.

"Why?"

"Well, because I don't know," I lied. "If I did, I would explain it to you in unmistakable clarity."

"Even then it wouldn't make sense, would it?"

"Probably not. It never makes sense for people to be so evil. Stop driving yourself mad trying to make sense of something that there is no sense to be made of." That much was the truth.

I watched slow tears roll down her face. I kissed her cheeks in an attempt to make her stop crying. I heard quiet knocking coming from downstairs.

"You should get that," I whispered in her ear. I wiped away the rest of the moisture on her cheeks with my fingertips.

We climbed down the ladder, and I closed the attic.

"It's probably Becky," she muttered.

She opened the door. It was Rudy. He peered behind her.

"Good," he breathed, stepping inside. "You're here."

"You're happy to see me?" I laughed.

"Not happy," he corrected, "but relieved."

"What's wrong?" Jane asked.

He shook his head. "I've been feeling anxious. I've been spending too much time worrying about myself, and now I'm beginning to worry that we are waiting too long for Ethan. If you have a plan, I'm ready to hear it."

"I don't exactly have a plan, but I'm prepared for a few different outcomes," I said.

Jane interrupted. "What about plan A, plan B, and plan C?"

"I meant mostly that I am prepared for what might happen."

"Which may be what?" Rudy asked, his voice sounding distant.

"I don't know," I answered. "But blood will be involved, which is why"—I looked to Jane—"you have to stay with Luna."

"They can find me there."

"Nobody will steal you from Luna," I said. "We just need to be more careful."

"How can you be more careful than handcuffing me and locking me up?"

I glared at her, not in the mood to argue. "Be quiet, Jane." It was Ian's fault anyway. It wouldn't happen again.

She sighed and walked to the living room. Rudy and I followed and sat beside her on the couch.

"Let's go then," she announced.

"What?" I questioned.

"Let's go," she repeated. "Take me to Luna's, and go save Ethan."

I smiled, amused by her as I often was. "Are you ready?" I asked Rudy.

"I'm ready for anything," he answered.

"Rudy, meet me here tomorrow morning. Jane, I will take you to Luna's early."

"What about Dorian?" she asked.

"Don't worry about it," I said. "They wait for Abraham's call. Dorian doesn't know of his death just yet. If he did, he would have found me by now."

"And if he finds you?"

"I just can't be here when he does," I said. "I won't let him find *you*."

"So tomorrow?" Rudy asked.

I nodded. "Tomorrow."

Rudy left, and I watched Jane sink into the cushions of the couch.

"You look exhausted," I whispered.

"I haven't been sleeping well," she answered, letting her voice trail off.

"Rest then. If you'd like, I'll stand guard."

She nodded and curled up. I draped a blue blanket over her, pulling it up to her chin and hummed to her, brushing my fingers through her dark hair. I watched her sleep, occasionally peering out the windows to make sure we were still safely hidden. I ignored most of the passing cars I heard, but when I opened the curtains again, I saw I had disturbed Jane.

"Oh, I'm sorry." I let the curtain fall back into place to darken the room again. "I didn't mean to wake you."

"It's okay," she whispered, sitting up and yawning. "I need to be awake."

"Why?"

She shrugged. "I don't know. I guess I just don't really feel safe."

"I know." I walked toward her. "You know I care about you, and you know…"

Screeching in, my nerves hit me hard, and I broke off, whirling around back toward the window. They had found us. Damn! I screwed up again.

"What is it?"

"Shh. Jane, get your shoes on."

"What?"

"Just do it," I snapped. "Comfortable shoes. Running may be involved."

She ran upstairs with me not far behind.

"Shit," I grumbled, watching her fumbling with the laces on her shoes.

"What's wrong?"

"We'll have to sneak out through your window," I said, ignoring her question.

"What's going on?"

"It's okay," I said, not wanting to say his name. "But they found me. I knew they would."

"Who?"

"It's okay," I told her again, "but it's him—it's Dorian."

I saw a shudder shake through her. I tried to ignore how terrified she must have been. I needed to focus only on one thing—how to get away from him.

I opened her bedroom window and stepped onto the roof. I pressed my back against the house. I offered Jane my hand. She gripped my fingers tightly and slowly fell against me. I grasped the tree and swiveled my legs around the trunk and climbed down as quickly as I could. Jane reached clumsily for the tree, her shoes sliding loudly across the shingles. She stumbled forward and grasped the branch. She hung in the tree like a three-legged cat. Oh, for the love of God. I definitely had no time or patience for Jane's usual inept ways of doing things. I signaled her with my hand to hurry it up. She started to make her way down the tree, but her hands slipped, and she fell to the ground.

"Oh," I whispered, "are you okay?"

She sat up and placed her hand on the back of her head. "Yeah," she groaned. "Fine."

I crouched down and led Jane into the neighbor's lawn.

"When I say run, you run. Okay?"

"Okay, but what about your car?"

"I can't get to it without him finding us," I said, shaking my head. "Don't worry about it. Just run when I say."

We stooped down, inching across the lawn. I paid little attention to the houses on the street, not even worried about the neighbors asking questions. I glanced back at Jane's house, unable to see where Dorian was. I looked to Jane, then once more at her house.

"Okay, Jane. Run."

I raced down the street, unsure of my decision to simply run away. It seemed that was all I did. We reached the end of the cul-de-sac, and I looked to Jane, who was already breathing like she had run a mile.

"What do we do?" she asked. "Rudy lives only a few houses down from me."

"Oh my God!" I yelled, pulling Abraham's cell phone out of my pocket. Rudy—of course. "Do you know his number by heart?"

"Yes, of course."

"Call him right now."

"And tell him?"

"Tell him to lock the doors and stay inside until tomorrow. We're changing plans. Tell him to meet us at my place. I can give him directions."

"You mean Luna's."

I shook my head. "I mean Walter's. Dorian doesn't know where that is. We can be safe at Walter's until the morning.

Jane nodded and dialed his number.

"Rudy?"

I could hear Rudy on the other end but couldn't tell what he was saying.

"Yeah, it's me."

Jane's face lit up with panic. "No!" she yelled. "Rudy, lock your doors, and tomorrow, meet us at Aidan's. I'll explain tomorrow. Just please don't leave your house."

After a few more insignificant responses, she handed me the phone.

"Tomorrow morning at around nine, meet us at my place. Get a pen. You'll need directions."

"I know where you live," he said.

"Do you?" I asked.

"By Gallagher's, right? Three houses down? I think it's brown?"

"Yes, Gallagher's," I answered. "It's the other house."

"Tiled roof and vines?"

"Yeah, the beige one."

"I'll be there."

"Okay, see you then."

I closed the phone and put it back in my pocket. I had to keep Jane and me safe at Walter's but clearly couldn't let Rudy inside. I still couldn't tell him about his grandfather. This would be interesting.

"What?" I heard Jane murmur.

I looked to her, unsure if she was reading my face or if I had said something out loud.

"I don't want Rudy involved any more than he has to be," I said, "but he wants to help, and I'm sure I will need it at some point." That wasn't necessarily true, but I had to keep him away from Walter for the time being.

"Why can't I stay with Walter?" she asked. "You said Dorian doesn't know where that is."

"Yes, that's true, but Walter isn't the type to kill—Luna is."

"Kill?"

"Yes."

"I don't understand."

There was no point in lying to her now, was there? I told her things so I wouldn't have to lie.

"If Dorian found you there, which is a possibility, he would kill you the second he saw you. You're the one he wants the most, considering your involvement with me. Walter can't protect you the way Luna can."

"So take Rudy to Luna's with me. You don't have to have him help you, do you?"

I knew exactly what she was thinking. "Yeah, that's funny, Jane."

"What?"

"Rudy has a car, and I'm aware of that. Meaning if I tell him to meet us at Luna's, you will escape." I tapped my finger to my temple.

"What if I promise?"

I shook my head.

"Then when *you* drive me to Luna's, or whoever does, Rudy can come along. That simple."

"I don't know, Jane," I said, narrowing my eyes.

"Please?"

I sighed. "Rudy won't have it. He's persistent about helping me save Ethan, and you have to promise me to just do as I say." That was mostly true, wasn't it?

She nodded. "Fine, but if he wants to stay with me, I would feel much better."

"Okay," I answered, reluctantly.

"I'm sorry for being so difficult." She sighed.

"It isn't your fault at all. I'm so mad at myself," I whispered. "I was mad at myself for getting you involved. Now I have gotten you, Rudy, Becky, Aaron, and Ethan all involved as well. I wish I would have never come to this town."

"Please don't say that," she said sweetly. "Hey, maybe it's about time for something interesting to happen."

I half smiled. I loved the way she tried to lighten things up.

"You aren't frightened easily, are you?"

"I don't know—maybe not."

Saving Jane and her friends was the only way I had left to redeem myself.

"This is my last chance to do something good. I'm going to save you all. I swear to it. You are my last chance, Jane."

Chapter Twenty-One

FOR THE NEXT hour of walking, Jane hadn't said much of anything.

"Aidan, where are we going?" she asked, sighing with impatience.

"We need a car. Unless you want to walk the entire way."

"So...?"

"So...how do you feel about grand theft auto?"

"I'm sorry?"

I laughed, easily being able to tell she was not amused. "Would credit card fraud suit you better?"

She groaned and covered her face with her hands. "Aidan..."

"There's no way we're walking all the way to Walter's," I continued before she could say anything sarcastic. "We need a car."

"Aidan, I'm sore and tired, yes, but that doesn't mean I want to commit a crime."

I instantly felt offended. "Though you don't seem to object when it serves you," I spat.

"Excuse me?"

"Abraham, the Mustang..." I meant to continue but realized that insulting her was not going to get us where we needed to be. "I'm sorry. I don't mean to be such a grouch. Just let me do what I need to do."

Trusting me was the only option she had at that point. I was the only one who could clean up this mess, ironically enough, considering I was the one who made it.

I shuffled through my credit cards and IDs and stumbled across Michael London. I had never used that name before and decided it was acceptable for the time being. I settled for something discreet, something that nobody would take notice of or remember. It was a white, Toyota pickup truck. There were enough of those on the road. Who would take notice of mine?

"What about the stolen Mustang?" Jane questioned accusingly.

I shrugged. "Eh…don't worry about it. I have to go back and cover my tracks after everything is settled anyway." Damn. I had almost gotten used to telling her the truth already that things were starting to slip out.

"Cover your tracks how?"

"I'd rather not tell you," I said, truthfully.

"Why?"

"Just because."

"Because I won't like it?"

I hesitated. "Yes."

"At this point, Aidan, I don't think there is anything I can't handle."

"Aidan Summers can go back to not existing just as easily as Michael London rented this car."

Her eyebrows furrowed.

"I told you you wouldn't like it."

"So, by covering your tracks I'd never see you again?"

I nodded. "Yes."

"You're right. I don't like that at all."

I got in the car and put the key in the ignition. Jane still had that saddened look on her face, so I decided to change the subject.

"So," I started, keeping my tone even and relaxed, "are you hungry?"

"Hungry?" She hesitated for a moment. "I don't know."

"Hmm, well, I know I am, and you have to eat *something*," I answered. "There are coffee shops open twenty-four hours. At least eat some soup or something."

She nodded.

I drove slowly, fighting the urge to speed down the road like I was used to. I made my way to a tiny 50s style café that was dimly lit by lamps hanging from the ceiling. I tried to keep my eyes on Jane and ignore the restaurant. It brought memories of my parents and Walter rushing back to me. It was so much like Richard's old place where I had worked. It seemed like ten years ago I had met Vivian and Luna. My body was almost quivering with discomfort.

It was quiet and empty. We took a seat at the bar, and I avoided eye contact with the waitress who was clearly trying to flirt. I smiled at Jane, reminding her where my attention was.

"Do you realize the effect you have on people?" she whispered.

I chuckled. "Sometimes. The reaction I'm used to people having at seeing me isn't normally as positive."

She smiled. "Well, maybe that means there's no threat."

I tried to contain my laughter. She really had no clue. "Like there would be anyway, Jane."

"Well, she was...nice."

She meant attractive. "Was she?"

"Yes!"

I shrugged my shoulders. I hadn't taken notice.

"Ah, come on, Aidan. You don't have to be that nice."

I smiled at her and shook my head.

She smiled back, but her eyes still looked far away. I couldn't tell what she was actually feeling.

"Are you okay?" I murmured.

"I'm fine. Why?"

"You seem distracted."

She shook her head.

"Come on. What's on your mind?"

She sighed. "How far is Walter's house?"

"It's not far. Don't worry."

I could see she had tried to smile. It was a weak attempt. I hated how reluctant she was to trust me. If she only knew how much I needed her. If she only knew what I was willing to do to keep her safe.

The drive was mostly silent. The coffee hadn't sat well with my stomach. It took less than ten minutes to realize it wasn't the coffee; it was my nerves acting up. My senses were being tugged at again, and tremors grew into my chest.

When we finally arrived, the sun was already peeking through the trees. I let myself in to see Walter sitting at the desk in the front room, writing by the light of a yellow lamp.

"You're late," he sputtered.

"I usually am." I chuckled.

He embraced me then immediately looked to Jane. "You must be Jane."

She nodded and shook his hand.

"A great pleasure to meet you," he started. "Walter Redline, as I'm assuming you know."

"Good to finally meet you, Mr. Redline."

"Ah, this isn't a classroom," he sputtered in laughter again. "Call me Walter."

"Walter."

"Clem, you mind giving me a hand?" he asked, directing his gaze back at me. Did he *have* to call me Clem?

"Sure. What do you need?"

"To rearrange the guest room. It's become my storage unit." He let out that familiar chuckle again.

"Sure."

I gave Jane a wink and followed Walter into the spare bedroom.

"Luna's at her place?" I asked.

"Yeah, she's there," he whispered back. "When are you taking Jane there?"

"Not until morning. Dorian...came to her house."

"What?"

I nodded. "I think he came there for me. I think he's waiting for Jane. He wants *me* to kill her. I don't think he's after her right now."

"He'll kill you both!" he hissed. "Once he realizes he can't make you do it... he'll do it...to you both."

"I know!" I spat through clenched teeth. "Just let me do this my way."

He sighed. "I always do."

I walked back into the living room to see Jane staring at the horse painting beside the door. She looked distant and tired.

"You must be exhausted," I said. "Come on."

I took her hand and led her down the narrow hallway lined with bookshelves to the spare room. There was a queen-sized bed against the wall with an old-fashioned floral comforter, courtesy of Luna.

"I shouldn't sleep," she said.

"It's late."

"What if Dorian finds us?"

"He won't. I'll take care of any problems. I'll stand guard."

She shook her head.

I sighed, annoyed, but had this guilt gnawing at me. "I'll lie beside you."

She nodded and brought herself into my arms. The warmth of her skin against my own could easily have driven me mad. I almost regretted refusing her the day she kissed Rudy. Would I ever get that chance again?

I slept lightly, holding firmly to Jane, feeling the need to keep her secure. I thought I was beginning to slip into a dream when I heard familiar voices in my head. I realized it was my name.

I was torn out of my relaxed state and into alertness. I moved away from Jane slowly, being careful not to disturb her. I tiptoed through the hallway and into the living room. I could hear Walter softly snoring from the other bedroom. I walked outside, feeling the chill from the fog.

I opened the front door, immediately irritated by what I saw. Mike was frantic. "James," he stuttered, "you gotta go."

"What?"

"You gotta go. You have to leave here—now. You have to…"

His voice was trembling, and he kept looking over his shoulder. Beads of sweat broke out on his forehead. His hair was down, loose over his shoulders and messily hanging in his face.

"Do you hear me?" he spat. "Leave!"

"I…I have…"

"What?" he hissed. "James, you idiot. Do you have the girl?"

I nodded.

"Then you'd better pray to God that you also have a plan. Dorian beat me to the point of unconsciousness."

It was then that I noticed the bruise on his cheek, and his left eye was black.

"He threatened my life. I had to, James."

"Mike! What did you tell him?"

"Nothing about the—about her," he said. "I swear. I only confessed that I knew where you were. He will be here before mid-day. You *have* to get out."

I sighed and turned away.

"I'm sorry," he said. "I never meant to betray you. I—"

"No, it's all right. It's all right, Mike. Go. Get out of here before someone sees you."

He nodded and bowed formerly as if thanking me for not being angry and ran off. I turned away when I heard my name again. Great. Another.

"James, what are you doing?"

David. Just perfect. "What I am doing is none of your concern," I spat.

"I can't tell Dorian," he growled. "Do you understand that?"

"Why?"

He threw his arms up and huffed. "Because then he will know I've been keeping things from him, and it will be on *me*. Me, James."

"So…don't tell him."

"Yeah, obviously!" he almost yelled. "But whatever the hell you are doing, you are endangering everything we have fought to protect."

"*You* have fought to protect," I said. "Don't you even dare include me in that!"

He sighed again, and before I had time to react, his fist struck me hard across my face, and I stumbled backward. My pain transformed into fury, and I crushed his cheek with my fist and hit him again in the jaw, feeling warm blood splatter onto my cheek.

"Sorry, David," I said, leaving him unconscious in the grass. Hopefully for him, he would wake up in enough time to get away before Dorian showed up.

Crawling back into bed, I put my arms back around Jane's waist.

"Jane?"

"Hmm?" she murmured, clearly not fully awake.

"Jane," I called, increasing the tension in my voice. "Wake up…now."

She rolled over and groaned before waking up enough to respond. "Aidan, what is it?"

Even groggy, I could hear the fear in her voice.

"We can't stay here," I said bluntly.

"What?" she whispered. "What's going on? You said we'd be safe here until morning."

I nodded. "Yes, but something has come to my attention, something I was a fool to ignore. We should leave for Luna's now and not later."

She sat up and switched on the lamp. She gasped and covered her mouth with her hand, noticing the blood on my face—David's blood.

"Jane, I'm all right. I've been betrayed. We need to leave here."

"Betrayed? By who?"

"To be honest…you've met him before."

"What? Aidan, what happened?"

I looked away from her, dropping my head in my hands. "I heard something, a voice coming from outside. When I recognized it was my name, I went out to see who it was. I found a friend of mine who is a member of The Sevren. He's of lower rank than myself, so he has always listened to me. That's why I believed he would never betray me. He told me Dorian threatened his life, so he confessed that he knew where I lived. He came here to warn me of this."

"Who?"

"Do you remember that night at the bookstore—with the wolf?"

"Yes, of course."

"So you remember Mike."

"Mike?" she yelled. "He's one of them?"

I nodded. "Mike and I were enrolled in school here—sort of like an undercover thing."

"Oh my God," she muttered. "This keeps getting weirder!"

"Come on. I'll make sure Rudy gets to Luna's safely, unless I decide I really need his help."

"I'd rather him stay with me," she said, taking my hand and crawling out of bed.

I nodded. "I would too," I whispered, "but he wants to help, and to be honest, I may need it."

She didn't respond. I could see the fear hidden in her eyes.

"Walter will take you to Luna's, but don't worry. I'll be right behind you with Rudy, okay? I need to get you out of here first."

She hesitated for a moment. "Okay."

I opened the cell phone and dialed Luna's number.

"Jane's on her way there," I said as soon as she picked up.

I heard her sigh. "And where are *you*?"

"I'm with Rudy. On my way to save Ethan."

Rudy mumbled something I couldn't identify at the moment. I glanced at him and noticed he was clearly anxious.

"Be careful," Luna said. "And come back as soon as you can."

I nodded though she couldn't see. "I will."

I hung up the phone. "Are you okay, Rudy?"

He jolted his head toward me and cleared his throat. He nodded. "I think so, but"—he swallowed—"I don't know how to fight."

I chuckled. "That is exactly why I didn't want you involved. But I know you, and I knew you would do the same thing you did the first time I told you not to come." I raised my eyebrows at him.

"I know," he answered, nodding, "but I want to help Jane. If this is all I can do for her, then I have to do it. I know you hate it, Summers, but I love her."

I smiled. "I know."

"So what do I do?"

"Stay in the car," I answered.

"What?" he bellowed. "I am *not* staying in the goddamn car!"

"All right," I retorted, putting my hand up. I definitely expected that reaction. "Just do as I say."

"Unless you say I stay in the car," he argued curtly.

I just laughed. "Fine, but if you are so worried about not knowing how to fight, then if staying in the car is how you are going to stay alive, I hope you will be wise enough to realize it."

"I'm no coward," he mumbled.

"I know. I can clearly see that. There is no shame in hiding, Rudy. I have been hiding for months now. Sometimes it's the best thing you can do."

The drive was tense, considering I wasn't exactly sure where I was going. Should I look for Dorian and Ethan at Abraham's place where Jane was taken, or should I check the clearing first to make sure I wasn't too late? I decided it was better safe than sorry and spun the car around.

"Hey, take it easy," Rudy spat.

"Oh, relax," I mused.

I rushed down the road, being thankful I was in the truck, away from the rain that had ceased and been replaced with a thick sheath of humidity. I knew the weather should have meant something to me. I was always one to take everything into consideration, but my senses weren't yelling at me, and my nerves weren't being yanked at. I couldn't decide why my odd "danger radar" wasn't going off like a broken alarm clock. I stepped harder on the gas pedal from irritation and could feel the frustration creeping into my features, pulling my face into a look of anger.

"Please!" Rudy hissed at me. "Slow down."

"Shut up," I muttered. "We need to get there quickly anyway. You shouldn't even be here, so the last thing you need to be doing is telling me what to do."

"Didn't you say they wait for Abraham's call?"

I nodded. "They know of his death by now. They must. If Ethan is already…" I broke off then took a breath and started over. "If I am unable to save Ethan, I need you to let Jane believe I am dead."

"What?"

"You have to promise me, Rudy," I demanded. "If we are too late, I will never again be able to face her. I will still do what I can to keep her safe, but I will do so at a distance. Can you promise me?"

He nodded. "I…I promise."

"You do know that I was supposed to bring you in exchange for Ethan. You remember that, right?"

He nodded.

"Then why the hell are you trusting me not to turn you over to them?"

"I'm not," he answered. "I just figured that either way…I would be helping Jane."

"You're hopeless," I mumbled.

His love for her was more like a teenage obsession. It had stopped being amusing and soon became irritating. His logic was completely clouded by his "love." I can't say Jane was wrong.

He doesn't love me. He just thinks he does.

That proved true.

"So what's the story with you?" he asked, interrupting my thoughts.

"What?" I chuckled.

"Your story," he questioned, slightly raising his voice. "Who exactly are you?"

"You expect me to unburden myself to *you*?"

He laughed. "I'm helping you. I figure I should know what cause I'm assisting."

I shook my head. "Ah, Rudy," I murmured. "So like you."

"So…you gunna tell me?"

I inhaled slowly. "I grew up with an uptight dad and a crazy mom. They were also stolen from me at a young age."

"You mean—"

"Murdered," I interrupted. "I came to the only person who could help me—Abraham. I came into The Sevren, believing they were the family I needed. I grew close to them simply because I had nobody else. Understand?"

He nodded. "Sort of."

"I grew with them, and I grew with their traditions and beliefs."

"So, you are still one of them?"

"I am not. But it isn't easy to reject something you have believed for so long. These people were all I had, and what they believed is what I was taught. I knew very little of anything else." I could feel Rudy's stare burning into my face.

"I understand," he said. "It's frightening in a way."

"Is it?"

"Because you weren't even aware that what you were doing was wrong."

"Well, I was eventually," I answered. "That's why I ran away."

"I can't hate you for it."

I laughed. "Oh, well, thanks so much, Rudy."

He chuckled. "You know what I mean."

"I do."

"Thanks," he said.

"For what?"

"Telling me. Letting me in a bit."

I nodded. "Sure, Rudy."

It felt good to tell him what I was all about, just to sort of clear the air for us. I didn't return the question though. Not only was I uninterested, but I didn't trust myself not to slip up and say something about Walter. He didn't seem to notice.

The air seemed to clear up more than I expected, and by the time we came to the edge of the woods, the humidity was less distasteful.

"Listen to me," I said to Rudy. "You know about this place. You have to promise me you won't act like it."

He just nodded.

"Follow me, and keep quiet."

I slowly crept through the deeper parts of the woods, not even noticing my surroundings. The moss stuck to my hair, but I took little notice. The clearing was empty—almost. I peered around cautiously, just trying to make sure we were alone. Rudy instantly rushed past me and knelt beside who must have been Ethan strapped to the boulder. His chin was scraped from resting against the stone, and his wrists were bleeding. Rudy removed the blindfold, but Ethan's whimpering didn't stop.

"Mr. Callahan?" he questioned.

Ethan tried to mutter something, but neither of us understood.

"Oh," Rudy said, "you don't have your glasses. It's me, Rudy Thompson from three houses down."

His whimpering became slightly quieter.

"What are...?" His voice trailed off.

"We came to help you," Rudy said, answering his unasked question.

"Where is Jane?"

"Jane is safe," Rudy said. "We rescued her and took her home."

"Rescued her?" he choked. "From who?"

Rudy, you idiot!

"Not important," he said. "She's safe."

I took a few steps toward them and opened my mouth to speak, but a voice interrupted me.

"Ah!" he said, emerging from behind the trees. "What other place would James be besides the one place he shouldn't be?"

"I am *not* in a tolerable mood right now, David."

"Oh, nor am I," he replied, leaning against a tree, crossing his arms in front of his chest. "But I see you brought the boy."

"I brought nobody for you."

"You know, James, killing Abraham was a foolish move on your part."

I didn't answer. I just stood there fuming. I had no idea how to get him away in time to save Ethan before the others showed up.

"Bastard," I seethed between clenched teeth. I was unsure he heard me, but I thought I saw a thin smile spread across his lips, pulling wrinkles into his cheeks.

"You know I can't let you take him," he said, almost with cheer in his voice.

"You also can't stop me," I hissed back.

Rudy was silent. At least he was doing *something* right.

"Really, James," David started, shifting his balance from the tree back to his feet. "I don't want to hurt you."

That was a lie if there ever was one.

"Oh, David, I would just *love* to hurt *you*."

I was Abraham's son. I was taught to fight better than anyone for the very reason he wanted me alive, and yet David still wanted to challenge me after my obvious murder of Abraham and Jason? So be it!

He smiled then, finally showing his crooked teeth, and took a step toward me.

"Get back, Rudy," I murmured.

"But Ethan," he whined.

"We will deal with it in a second, Rudy," I snarled, not taking my eyes off David as he slowly approached me. I waited until he was closer to even draw out my weapon. I knew him; taunting was his favorite thing to do.

Don't let him distract you, I thought.

He knew exactly what to say to make me angry. He had done it before, hoping I would go blind with rage and take un-aimed thrusts at him. I wouldn't let that work on me.

Focus on your knife, James.

"I really *will* enjoy killing you," he said, stepping closer, "the way you killed the Callahan boy."

Beads of sweat rimmed my brow as I fought back the irritation of his words.

"It would be fun, you know," he continued, "to watch you die with you knowing it's because of you that the girl you love will suffer mercilessly." He chuckled in a way that promised his seriousness.

The thoughts of him even looking at Jane made me sick. I knew if he were given the chance to touch her, he would be relentless. My body was quivering with anger, and I was almost consumed by the urge to hurl myself toward him in a fit of rage and slice him into ribbons. I fought almost painfully to remain composed, not giving in to what he wanted.

Don't let him distract you, James. Don't listen to him, James!

He could tell I was seething. He smiled at me and drew his knife, taking another step forward. I took a step back, not in retreat but in an attempt to lead him as far away from Ethan as I could get. He followed willingly farther into the trees, out of the clearing.

"Oh, little James," he mocked. "Always Daddy's favorite. Are you actually giving up already? At *least* entertain me for a few moments." He laughed again, this time more in actual amusement.

I drew out my knife and let him continue to advance.

David pulled out his heavy, long parrying dagger. "Are you going to take all day?" he said with a laugh.

"Think of it as a chance to practice patience," I taunted back.

A flash of reflection danced down the lengths of the blade, casting an uncomfortable light straight into my eyes.

"You really want me to make you squirm, David?"

"We'll see who's squirming soon enough." He fell into his fighting stance, his upper body straight and taut, with one leg positioned behind the other. I moved to my left, even farther away from Ethan. David pivoted rapidly after me.

I'll wait, I thought. *No need for haste. I'll let him wear himself out with all his ramblings.*

I barely caught sight of his fist coming in time to pull back. I growled deep in my throat and lunged toward him. There was an outbreak of quick movements as David dove in toward me. I caught his advance with my blade, spinning to my left, feeling the hard resistance of his body as the knife sliced his rib cage. He howled, but it sounded more from anger than pain.

David lunged again, coming up behind me, driving his blade toward my chest. With a twist of my wrist, I caught his knife with mine. With a loud *clink,* they crashed together as though we were fencing. I moved around him and hit him from behind, driving my knife across the other side of his ribs, then moving a few steps back with my blade held tightly in front of me. He turned around, facing me with sheer fury in his eyes. I couldn't fight the smile my triumph forced into my features, but I had to keep in mind I had not yet won.

His movements became inept and clumsy. Drawing a deep breath that brought obvious looks of pain into his face, he attacked. His moves were quick enough to keep me occupied and focused on keeping him away rather than disabling him anymore.

Leaping back, I hid myself behind a tree in a quick movement I was sure David hadn't noticed, and I came up behind him again, slicing through the shirt on his back, drawing a spray of blood.

David's brown eyes grew wide as I moved back and lunged toward him with a cry. I knocked him to the ground and straddled him, shoving my blade into his chest, not yet even feeling the cuts and shallow stab wounds that were scattered across my skin. My breathing was quick and heavy as I sighed and got off of him, standing to my feet. He was still breathing, but moments later, I heard his shallow breath silence.

I immediately turned toward the clearing and walked back to where Ethan was. Rudy was still beside Ethan, but his eyes were full and terrified, and his mouth was hanging open.

"It's all right," I told him. "David is dead. You can relax."

He nodded, but I could see the discomfort in his eyes. "Let's get Ethan," he said. "Please."

I nodded and handed him my blade. He took the knife and stared at it in disgust.

"Um...sorry," I said, realizing I hadn't taken the time to clean David's blood off.

He wiped the blood on his brown T-shirt and sliced through the ropes around Ethan's wrists and ankles.

"Thank you," Ethan stammered out.

Rudy nodded.

"Let's get you home," I said.

Rudy and I helped him stumble to the car and drove in complete silence until we came to his house.

"I don't know what to say to you," Ethan started as we stepped inside. "I don't know what is going on or why those strange people took me, but...either way, you saved my life." He pressed his fingers to his eyelids.

I smiled. "You're welcome."

"We have to go get Jane," Rudy announced.

"Let me come with you!" Ethan shouted.

I shook my head. "She's fine, Mr. Callahan. I promise. We are just going to get her and bring her home. Please stay here and take care of yourself."

"Are you sure?"

"I'm sure," I said. "She's fine."

"Where is she?"

"She's staying with a friend of mine."

"You didn't happen to find my glasses, did you?"

Rudy chuckled and reached into his pocket. "I did actually." He handed them to Ethan.

"Err...thanks," he answered, noticing the crack across the left lens.

Rudy shrugged. "Better than nothing."

"Take care of yourself, Mr. Callahan," I called, walking toward the door.

"We should get him to a doctor," Rudy whispered as we stepped outside.

I chuckled lightly. "He *is* a doctor."

Chapter Twenty-Two

"WHERE ARE WE GOING?" Rudy spat. "We have to go get Jane."

I shook my head, stepping harder on the gas pedal. "Not yet. We need to get back to the clearing. The others know full well of all the murders I have committed."

"And that would make you return why?"

"Because a friend of mine may take the punishment for it. I need to take care of Dorian."

"You mean kill him?"

I nodded. "Yes."

I stopped the car. "STAY here!"

He put his hand up. "I did my part. Just don't make me drive this damn car home by myself." He smirked.

"Thanks for the concern."

The air was moist and humid as usual. The trees were cluttered with moss and vines. I stepped into the clearing just in time to see Mike pinned against a tree just as I expected. Arthur turned to look at me.

"Ah, James," he said. "Come to join your partner?"

I didn't know how to respond. Arthur was a friend of Mike's and of mine.

"What did he do, Arthur?" I demanded, stepping closer to him. "Let him go."

"I can't let him go!" he snapped. "He lied to me. He lied to us all. About you, James. He lied about *you!*"

"This has nothing to do with him," I spat. "If it is me you want, come take *me!*"

He shook his head mechanically. "Get out of here, James," he choked. I could see then he was crying. "Escape while you can. It's too late for me. Run before Dorian returns."

"Arthur—"

"Just go!" he demanded.

I kept my eyes locked on Mike. He didn't say a word to me, and his face was blank—calm. It was almost like he knew what was going to happen and was all right with it. I knew Arthur was right. It *was* too late for him, but me—I could still start a new life away from The Sevren. What was I doing standing in the clearing when Dorian could show up at any moment? I had to run. That would be logical. It was more difficult than I would have otherwise expected to turn my back on Mike. Arthur was going to kill him, and there was nothing I could do to stop him. It was clearly my fault too. That I knew for sure. I forced Mike to keep my secrets for me, and now *he* was paying the price. It hardly seemed fair. The Sevren were still hurting me even after I was no longer a part of them. I couldn't stay. There was nothing for me here, nothing but peril.

I walked slowly through the trees. My sadness was obvious, and I was hoping Rudy wouldn't say anything. Wishful thinking, of course. I knew him too well to think he was capable of keeping anything to himself.

"What's wrong?" he asked as soon as I opened the door to the car.

I sighed. "It's nothing."

"It's not *nothing*." He chuckled. "You look like a kid who just lost his dog. What happened?"

"Rudy…" I murmured, raising my hands, "I don't want to talk about it, all right?"

"Okay. I get it."

I started the car and slammed my foot on the gas.

"Really?" Rudy shouted.

I smirked and slowed down. "Sorry." I chuckled.

"Uh huh. We're going to get Jane now, right?"

"Yes. Would you relax?"

"Sure, sure."

It was just past dawn when we finally arrived at Luna's. The air was moist, and fog had rolled in.

"Rudy," I started, "I need you to do something for me."

He nodded but narrowed his eyes.

"Get Jane for me."

"What about you?"

I shook my head. "Don't tell her anything. If she asks, just tell her you don't know."

I knew I had to return to the clearing and wait for Dorian. I turned away but was only able to take a few steps before turning back to glance at the doorway of the house. Jane was in Rudy's arms, sobbing uncontrollably. I couldn't stand to see her that way. I promised her I would come back. I told her I would see her again. If I returned to the clearing, there was a good chance I would break that promise. I tried to turn away, but it was like the first day I met her all over again. I couldn't look away from her, couldn't bring myself to not speak to her.

"Jane?"

She instantly pulled away from Rudy and raced through the grass. She looked so beautiful running through the fog, almost like a dream. Her hair whipped behind her, and her body moved so elegantly. Her legs lagged behind her body, but she kept pushing until she was in my arms. I embraced her, feeling the need to hold her so close I could hide her within my arms. I felt her bury her fingers in my thick hair and softly kiss my neck.

"I thought you were dead," she said, sobbing.

"I promised you I'd come back, didn't I?"

She moved away from me, and I forced myself to smile.

Jane gasped and whipped around to look at Rudy.

"The blood isn't his," I said.

"You're both okay?"

I nodded.

"And Ethan?" She peered behind me.

"I convinced him to wait for you at home. He'll be there."

I smiled and wiped the tears from her soft cheeks. "We're all okay—"

A rustling behind me cut my sentence short. My muscles ached, and my senses were blaring in my head. My nerves felt that familiar tug, and I whirled around, peering behind me.

"Aidan?" Jane whispered.

This wasn't quite over after all.

"Oh God," I whispered. My voice swelled and exploded in a scream. "Luna!"

Luna ran into the house, frantic yet competent.

"Hurry!" I called. "Jane! Jane, go to Rudy!"

"What?"

"Go!" I demanded. "Now! Run to him!"

She obeyed and started running back toward the house. I wanted to follow her, but I had something I needed to do now. I felt a hard strike into my back, and before I could move an inch, he held me by my hair. He yanked my head back until I started coughing. Damn sadistic fiend.

It was Dorian. I should have realized he'd follow me. I tried to swallow the cry of sudden fear he forced into me, but Jane must have heard because she froze in her steps and turned to look at me.

"When will you learn to do as you're told?" Dorian spat.

"I will kill you first," I choked out. "I swear."

"Oh, will you now?"

Jane didn't move. God damn it. Why wasn't she listening?

"Run!" I called.

Her expression shifted, and she looked almost furious. "Why don't you just admit it's me you want?" she called.

Jane, what the hell are you thinking? This is not the right time to be brave.

Dorian shoved me away from him. I felt the full force of his strength as I collided into the moist, moss of a tree. The firmness behind the moss crushed my muscles. I felt almost as if the impact of my body had broken the tree to splinters. I rolled over onto my stomach, suddenly unable to move.

"I'd rather make *him* kill you," I heard Dorian taunt.

I could feel myself slipping out of consciousness. I tried to move, but my muscles were weak. I forced myself to stay awake even through the burning in my head. The voices began to fade and sound muffled. I couldn't make out words. I could hear Dorian was taunting her. The thoughts of him touching Jane sent electric shocks of rage through me. My vision was dark, and the voices were becoming even quieter.

A panicked, angry yell brought me slowly back to consciousness, and the throbbing in my head was lessening. That lasted only until the sound of gunfire shattered my ear drums.

Jane!

The Sevren never used guns. What was happening? I forced myself to move, but it took long minutes of forcing my mind to stay awake before I was finally able to sit up. I heard Luna yelling at Jane but couldn't make out the words. My eyes finally focused just in time to see Rudy and Jane at my side. Thank God they were alive.

"Aidan?" Jane whispered.

I groaned, trying to ignore the sting that was still running through my veins. I lifted my hand. "I'm all right. I'm not hurt." That wasn't entirely true.

Jane wrapped her arms around me the way she always did, and my muscles instantly started aching.

"Okay," I choked. "Not completely unhurt. Gently, Jane."

"I'm sorry."

"Dorian's dead," Rudy whispered.

I nodded, realizing he must have been. Luna. "I heard the gunfire."

"That was Jane," Rudy said.

"What?" I stuttered. "I told you to run."

"I...didn't listen."

I sighed. "Of course you didn't." That must have been what Luna was yelling at her for. She shouldn't have.

Rudy grasped my arm, and I gripped back tightly, needing it more than I was comfortable with. He helped me stumble to my feet. "Come on," he said.

"Thank you," Jane whispered, pulling herself into my chest again.

"Thank *you*." I smiled. "Rudy will take you home."

"What about you?"

"You'll see me soon. I promise."

Rudy took her hand. She kept her eyes on me. Even as they were walking away, she would turn around to stare at me. I just smiled, loving the way she didn't even hide not being able to leave me.

"I didn't mean to be insensitive," she said as I cut the thread and tied it off.

"I know," I answered.

"I was already so—"

I put my hand up. "Luna, it's all right. No harm, no foul." I smirked at her.

She returned the smile, but it was stripped away when she winced. "Ouch! God, James!"

"I'm sorry," I said, laughing. "Jane is terrible at sewing. You could have waited for me."

"Yeah, well, I wasn't sure I could."

I smiled. "Well, I think you made it worse by trusting Jane with anything that requires coordination."

She laughed quietly. "Thanks."

"For what?"

"Just...everything," she answered, smiling. "I just don't feel like I show my appreciation for you enough."

I chuckled. "I know how you feel."

I knew there were still things Jane needed to know—other things I was not capable of telling her. I wanted to move on. I wanted a life with Jane—to put The Sevren behind me. If that were to happen, she needed to know about *every-thing*—even Daniel.

Chapter Twenty-Three

"IT ISN'T RIGHT," Walter said.

"What *is* right?" I asked. "*Not* telling her?"

He sighed. "Maybe, Clem."

I shook my head and turned away.

"Listen," he started, desperately wanting me not to walk away from him. "I know you love her, boy. I can see that. But none of it is right."

"Is this the whole 'if you love her, let her go' thing?"

He raised his eyebrows. "Well...yes."

"Forget it. I am the only one who can protect her, Walter. I am *not* leaving her for The Sevren to take."

"I know."

"So tell me," I said. "Please. Where is it?"

He sighed. "Top, left-hand drawer of my dresser."

"Thank you."

"Clem?"

I turned back toward him.

"Be careful."

"Always."

I fumbled through his drawer, probably unfolding things, but I took little care or notice. I found the key hidden in the very back of the drawer. It was attached to a dark blue tassel. I slipped it into my pocket, grabbed my brown, leather coat off the back of the couch, and headed out the door.

"I'll be back soon," I called.

I walked as quickly as I could to Jane's house, concentrating on the moist air that was typical of mid-day. I brushed my shaggy hair from my eyes and took a deep breath. I could hear voices inside. I realized Ethan was talking to Jane about what had happened. I thought it best to slip in before she knew I was there. I climbed up the oak tree and brought myself into her room. She never locked her window anymore. I found her school bag and took a piece of paper from a small tablet. I wrote her a note, shaking the entire time, and placed the key under her pillow.

Jane,

I'm sorry I lied to you. There is something you need to know. I couldn't bring myself to tell you before, but now you need to see for yourself. Check under your pillow. I love you.

Yours,

Aidan

I left her room, making sure everything I touched was in the same place as it had been. I left quickly and walked home, truly terrified every second of what she would find in that chest. I wondered what kind of stories the letters and journals held. I wondered how I would tell her about her brother. Should I begin with "it wasn't my fault but…" or maybe "I was doing the right thing when I did this but…" Telling Jane not to blame me or hold me responsible would be almost unethical. It would only hurt her more if she felt I had no regrets. I had regrets—so many.

I couldn't bring myself to walk home. I felt I had to be there when she found out. Perhaps if she didn't have too much time to think about things, she would be more willing to listen to me. I waited for about half an hour then silently crawled into the attic where I saw her reading a leather-bound journal.

"Jane?"

She shrieked and dropped the journal.

"I'm not used to startling you anymore," I said. "I'm sorry."

"Aidan, explain this!" she demanded. "Now!"

I sighed, terrified now that she would turn away from me and never look back. "How angry are you?"

She broke eye contact and hesitated before responding. "I…don't know yet."

"I can't explain everything," I said, trying to stay calm. There was no need for *both* of us to get upset. "All I can tell you is that it was better for you not to know until now." That was at least the truth.

"Why?"

"I didn't want you worrying over any more than you already were. But you had a right to see this."

"How did you know about this?"

I wanted her to know, didn't I? I showed her this for a reason.

"It belonged to a member of The Silver Wing," I started, "who were the ones set up to stop—"

"I know about The Silver Wing!" she interrupted me, angrily. "How did you know about this?"

"It belonged to somebody I knew. It was given to your grandfather."

"My grandfather?"

I couldn't answer, just nodded.

"And Danny?"

Oh God. The question I was dreading. What was I going to say to her?

"Jane—"

"You knew, didn't you? The entire time, you *knew*. Tell me why they killed him!"

"Jane—"

"Tell me, Aidan—James—Clem, whoever the hell you are."

I almost choked from the sting of her words. I saw Vivian in my mind, the day in the woods when she said the same thing to me. It ached just to look at her now. I could see the hatred in her eyes. I tried to hide my anguish and tell her what she had a right to hear directly from me.

"Rudy's great-grandfather Peter knew about The Sevren," I started. "He constructed a group to try to stop them. The group called themselves The Silver Wing. For years, they tried to defeat them but never succeeded. After Peter's death, his son, Rudy's grandfather, took over The Silver Wing. The Sevren was stronger than they ever anticipated. Your grandfather, Jane…he was also a member of The Silver Wing."

"What?"

I swallowed my voice a couple times before forcing myself to continue. "They killed him, and they killed Danny. They lost track of you, your mother, and Ethan when the person instructed to find them disappeared. That's why I was enrolled in school here."

She just stared at me, and my entire body started quaking. The words were in my head, and they repeated over and over until they became meaningless. Again I forced the words from my mouth. "They found me and threatened my life, ordering me to finish the job. I was sent to find you. It was my job…to kill you."

"What?" Her voice sounded throttled.

"I would never hurt you, Jane!" It was the only defense I could come up with fast enough. "I swear it! When I first met you, I didn't know who you were. If I did…"

"If you did, you would have stayed away? You would have left me alone?"

"Yes."

"You lied to me, Aidan, about everything. *Everything!*"

My heart began pounding. She couldn't believe *anything* I had said to her?

"Not everything," I said sadly. "I love you, Jane. That was and always has been the truth."

"Aidan, leave," she whispered.

"What?"

She reached out, handing me a photo. It was an old picture of Walter sitting on his porch beside Rudy.

"I can explain this!"

"You don't need to," she said, weeping. "Just leave me alone like you should have in the first place."

I wanted to argue, but I couldn't have expected anything different. Of course she wanted me gone.

"I'll leave because you're telling me to," I said, "but I'll be back, Jane."

"Don't bother!"

I heard her crying as I left. My entire chest was burning. I couldn't stand hurting her like that. I couldn't stand the look on her face when she realized who I really was. Her eyes that once held that familiar look of love and warmth appeared so cold and hateful. I wondered if she could ever again look at me the way she used to.

I walked all night. I walked until I was completely unaware of the time. It was still dark, not quite morning, but I couldn't wait any longer to see Jane. I was growing more anxious every second. I had to get her to listen no matter what it took.

I brought myself back to her room and stared at her for a moment. She looked just as she looked when things were good between us. I imagined for that moment that things hadn't changed, that things would always be good. I crept closer, admiring her innocence while she slept. I wished I didn't have to wake her up and shatter my illusions. I placed my hand softly on her face, almost wishing she wouldn't stir. She opened her eyes, and I immediately felt that cold stab I felt when she found out who I was.

"I left because you told me to," I whispered. "I thought that maybe now you could stay calm and allow me time to explain."

"Aidan, there's nothing to explain," she murmured, switching on the lamp.

Nothing to explain? If she only knew. If she only knew how much there was that I could never explain even if I wanted to.

"How…can you say that?"

"I know about The Sevren and The Silver Wing. I don't care to know more."

"The Silver Wing no longer exists," I answered, truthfully. "The Sevren killed most of them and most of those connected to them. That's what you need to understand. That is why Rudy was in danger."

"What about Walter?" she snapped. "Were you *ever* planning to tell Rudy his grandfather was alive? That's why you didn't want him there. That's why Dorian wanted him."

I nodded. I had to tell her everything now. No more lies. "Walter left Rudy's life to protect him from The Sevren. It seems Dorian found out who Rudy was after all. Dorian was a sadistic genius, but he's dead now, and as long as Rudy doesn't know about Walter, he will be safe."

She just stared at me with nothing to say.

"That chest belongs to him," I continued. "Your grandfather couldn't stand letting Walter shuffle through all of his old memories. It was making him sick, so your grandfather took it—simply so Walter would stop tormenting himself. The Sevren kill the beautiful and the pure. Those are the ones Abraham taught us were 'made for us.' After the construction of The Silver Wing, it was our job to stop them, to destroy their alliance so we could continue our way of life."

I broke off, replaying the words in my head over and over. I just heaped the truth on her with no warning. The truth is what she thought she wanted. Did she wish now I had let her believe otherwise? She didn't speak for a long time, and the silence was maddening. I had no idea what she was thinking. She finally looked at me. She locked her gaze onto my own, but her face expressed hate.

"You…you killed Danny."

Oh God. My chest started burning again. At least this way I didn't have to tell her. I also now had no way of starting at the beginning like I had planned to tell her what *really* happened. It didn't matter, did it? I was guilty; nothing else would make a difference to her. Either way, I *had* to say *something*.

"I did what I had to do to prevent his suffering," I said. "If Abraham did it, he would have suffered so terribly. I had to."

"I want to tell you it's okay, Aidan, but it isn't." Her voice cracked, but her face remained rock hard. "Danny is dead—by your hands. That's all that matters."

"Jane, my killing of him was mercy. I wish I could help you see that. The Sevren are not who I am, Jane. They are who I *was*."

"You're a killer," she said through her sobs.

The words struck me like a knife through the heart. My breath stopped for a moment, and I blurted out the only thing I could say, hoping to move the direction of her thoughts, possibly derail her hatred. "I love you. Please. We don't have to hurt anymore. We can leave North Bend—together."

"What?"

"In the morning, open the bags I left in the attic."

"Why?"

"Just do it," I said. "I will see you soon."

I remembered only moments after I left that if she were to see what I had stuffed in those duffel bags, it may make her even more angry. Hopefully seeing what I was planning to do to help her couldn't make her hate me any more than she already did.

I was restless that night and found it almost impossible to sleep for more than an hour at a time before waking up again. I couldn't stop thinking about what Jane would think when she looked in those duffel bags. I wanted her to leave with me. I wondered then if it was possible she still wanted me. I couldn't get the look she had given me out of my head. I had never seen her look at me that way. I missed the looks of longing and wonder she used to express. Now, all I saw was coldness and loathsomeness. She would never leave with me, would she? Of course I couldn't expect her to just forgive me for murdering her brother then lying to her about it—and countless other things since the day I met her. It was ending now for us. That I was sure of.

I knew Jane had to leave North Bend, and she knew it too. We didn't even need to talk about it. I would still do whatever it took to keep her save no matter how much she hated me. It wasn't about me anymore. It never really was, but there was still one more thing I had to ask of her.

She was in her room just sitting quietly. She wouldn't look at me. We both knew it was ending. If I tried to keep her here, it wouldn't have been any better than handing her and all of her friends over to The Sevren. I had to let her leave. It's what I wanted in the first place anyway—to get her out of North Bend safely.

"Are you ready?" I asked her, almost afraid of what she was thinking, terrified that she really did despise me.

"Physically or mentally?"

I was surprised at how normal her voice sounded. "Both."

"I'm not packed," she said, "but I'm ready."

"I'm sorry," I murmured. I sat beside her on her bed. She still didn't look at me. "I didn't want it to end this way."

"I know."

I had no words of protest in my mind. This was going to end whether I liked it or not.

"So, this is it then?"

She nodded. "I go home, you go home, and it's all only a memory."

Home. If only I had one.

"Why won't you look at me?" I finally asked, moving closer. Was I really so disgusting to her that she couldn't look at me anymore?

"If I look at you, this will never end."

Never end? So she didn't hate me.

"I don't want it to end," I answered honestly.

"Then don't look at me either."

She stood up, still without turning toward me. She walked toward her window and stared at the falling rain.

"What did you tell Ethan?"

"Honestly…nothing," she answered, her voice finally sounding a little more weak and sad. "He already knows."

"Nobody is going to hurt him," I said. "They won't hurt you either. I won't let them. I can protect you."

"No, Aidan."

She finally made eye contact, and I could see tears in her eyes. Maybe she did still love me.

"You can't protect me," she said. "I won't let you sacrifice yourself for me. If I stay here, everybody I love will be in just as much danger as me."

Everyone I love—including me.

I sighed and bowed my head. "I love you, Jane." It was the only thing I could say.

She broke her gaze almost immediately. "I know. But I can't let that matter anymore."

The pain was eating away at me. She really *did* love me, so why was I letting her go? How could I give up fighting for her? I had to make her safe again, and that meant destroying The Sevren. After that, I would never stop fighting for her.

"What else can I do?" she asked, shattering my thoughts. "Ethan and my mother."

"We, Ethan and I, agreed that we don't want your mother to know about this. I will help your father cover his tracks as I promised. He won't even have to leave North Bend. I will keep The Sevren away from you and your mother. I swear to you, Jane—I will make it safe for you. I will come back to you then."

"I can't look at you that way anymore," she whispered.

I could feel the sting of her words creeping into my chest. "It's too painful."

"Jane—"

"Don't," she snapped. "Please. If you love me, let me go. Let me live my life, and let me forget you so that someday...I can remember you."

I nodded solemnly. I wouldn't stop fighting. I couldn't.

"Can you do just one thing for me?" I asked.

She didn't answer but looked at me with the look I remembered, the look that told me she loved me and wouldn't refuse me anything.

"Help me make things right?"

"How?"

"I know I can't make *everything* right with you. But I want to make things right with Rudy. If that's all I can do, let me redeem myself in one small way."

She nodded. "Of course," she whispered.

Chapter Twenty-Four

HE WAS MOSTLY quiet as I drove. I felt a strange, unexpected respect for Rudy that I never had before. After his concern for me and his "love" for Jane, I realized the kind of person he was. He had a love in him very much like Jane's.

"Why can't you just tell me what this is all about?" he asked.

I smiled. "Well, it's sort of a surprise."

"A surprise?"

I nodded.

He looked to Jane and furrowed his brow.

"It's fine," she said. "It was Aidan's idea, and I promise you'll love it."

"It's a thank you for helping me," I said. "Don't worry."

I tried to ignore Jane and just pretend things were normal for as long as I could. I pulled into the driveway of my house, and Rudy was instantly confused.

"What are we doing here?" he asked.

"You know this is where I live, but you've never been inside." I smiled and unlocked the door.

Rudy looked around the room like he was back somewhere from a past life.

"Are you all right?" I heard Jane whisper.

"Jane..." he choked out, pointing feebly at the horse painting on the wall.

Walter entered the room, and the look on his face was one I had never seen Walter express in all the time I had known him. He had never looked so...happy.

"Ah," Walter said. "I always liked that painting."

Rudy turned to look at him. He was silent, but his eyes widened, and his mouth hung open, slow tears already running down his cheeks.

"You've grown," Walter said. "It's all right. I'm not a ghost."

Rudy stumbled toward him and fell into his arms without a second's delay, without even a fraction of doubt that it was really him.

"I thought you were dead," I heard muffled against Walter's chest.

"Oh, but I had to be," he whispered. "I had to be dead to protect you."

"And now?" Rudy asked, pulling away from him.

"Now it is time for you to know the truth." He touched his face. "We can protect you now. We know so much more about the hunters now than we used to, my boy."

"So you aren't going to leave me again?" he said, sobbing. "You won't disappear?"

He chuckled quietly. "I won't disappear."

"What about Mom?"

"Oh, she'll find out," Walter said with a laugh. "But don't you go telling her just yet."

Rudy nodded. "Okay."

I smiled, unable to stop myself. Walter got his fairy-tale ending.

Rudy turned to me. "Thank you," he whispered.

I gave him a formal bow, still smiling.

Jane wrapped her arms around my shoulders, and I almost jolted out of my skin. It was completely unexpected.

"Thank you for doing this," she whispered in my ear.

I loved the feeling of her breath against my face and the warmth of her pale arms around me. I didn't want to let go.

"I had to," I whispered back.

"I know."

She moved away from me, and instantly, I felt a chill rushing through my veins.

"So after today, you will be all right?" I asked.

"I'll be all right, Aidan. You need to let me go. You need to let me forget everything. That way, I can remember it someday."

"I'll miss you."

She nodded. That was it. Just one, silent, weak nod.

It was Jane's last day in North Bend. I had the nagging urge to drive to her house in the stolen pickup truck, which I never returned, and give her the best send off in the world. I realized that not only would that make things harder for *her*, it would make things *impossible* for me.

I sat down on the couch in Walter's front room. Luna came in as I expected.

"Hey," she breathed.

"Hi, Luna. Don't worry. I'm not going after her."

"I know. I think it was very brave of you, James."

James.

"I mean…with your betrayal and peril and you still wouldn't give up on her."

I almost laughed. "Well, God, Luna. I love her!"

"I know," she retorted. "I'm just saying that I'm not sure I could have stayed that strong. I've never loved anyone like that before. You saved her, James. You *should* be smiling."

I looked at her, and she had a playful smirk on her face and her head slightly cocked to the side.

"I'll let you be," she said, touching my shoulder. She walked toward her bedroom but stopped and continued. "But just remember—even though you can't be with her, she's alive. She can go on living her life…because of you."

I nodded and sighed, resting my chin in my hands. I did save her life. I did exactly what I wanted to do. So why did I feel so awful? There had to be some way I could move on. I wondered if I would ever stop feeling this way for her. At the same time that getting over her sounded like it would make things so much easier—I didn't want to. I enjoyed loving her even if she didn't return it. I didn't want my pain to go away. For the first time in my life, my pain is what made me feel alive again. I wanted to hurt over Jane. That meant she was still in my life somehow. She was in my blood and my bones.

Luna slowly entered the room again. "I'm making you some tea."

I ignored.

"Hello?" she sang.

I looked up at her, and she was leaning toward me with her hands rested on her thighs. "Would you like some tea, Aidan?"

I smiled. "You called me Aidan," I whispered.

She shrugged her shoulders and laughed. "So…does that mean yes?"

"Thanks, Luna. I'd love some tea."

Chapter Twenty-Five

THERE WERE things I had to see to. I wasn't quite finished protecting Jane.

"Luna, I'm going out," I called.

"But...you haven't finished your tea yet," she whined, pointing to the mug on the coffee table.

I chuckled. "It's all right, Luna. I just have one more thing I need to do, all right?"

She narrowed her eyes. "Are you being reckless again?"

I laughed. "No. Stop worrying. I'll be back soon."

I walked out the door without turning to look at her again. I could feel her stare stabbing into my back as I walked quickly to the car, knowing full well I had no time to waste.

I drove the truck instead of the Mustang, thinking it was more inconspicuous. I drove the direction of Jane's house. I turned a corner and parked on the side of the road until I saw Ethan's car. When the Honda came into view, I waited for them to pass the street I was on before moving. I followed a bit behind, trying to stay unnoticed. I had to follow her at least to the airport just to make sure she wasn't being tailed by The Sevren. Once she boarded the plane, there should be no problem.

It was difficult to know she was so close, and I was helping her leave me. This is what I had wanted in the first place—to save her, even from myself. Those old feelings of wanting to hurt her had completely vanished a long time ago, and now I had to protect her even if it meant hurting *myself* instead. It was nothing I didn't deserve. I was never deserving of Jane's love in the first place. I never deserved to feel that happy even for a moment. After everything I had done—I deserved nothing but pain.

Chapter Twenty-Six

"I WAS WAITING for you to tell me," I started, "but you never did."

"What are you talking about, Clem?" he asked. His face looked even more aged when he expressed confusion.

"I heard Rudy's story," I said. "I know about Evelyn."

"Oh," he said under his breath and almost fell onto the couch behind him. I barely heard him when he whispered, "Evey."

I nodded and sat beside him. "Let me help you. She's alive, isn't she?"

He looked at me and nodded.

"Then let me help you."

"No," he cried. "You don't understand. Evey was one of them. She betrayed them the same as you and Luna, only it was worse. In her attempts to send The Sevren away by constructing that treaty, she didn't hold up her end of the deal."

"Which was what?"

He sighed. "If they agreed to leave North Bend, she would see to it that The Silver Wing disbanded. However, when The Sevren left North Bend, Evey didn't leave with them. She joined The Silver Wing."

"My God, Walter. Where is she?"

He shook his head. "I can't. Not until The Sevren are stopped. All of them."

"Walter, she can help us."

"How?"

"If we find her, she can help us bring The Silver Wing back."

He nodded. "Possibly."

"So what do you say?"

"It's logical, but...no." He sighed again. "No. Clem, I'm sorry. It's too risky."

"Walter, listen to me," I coaxed. "Nobody will hurt her, okay? The Sevren are still after me and Luna as well. It's only a matter of time before they find us."

"I know, Clem. I know." His voice had raised an octave, and he sounded like he was going to cry. "Please don't make me do this."

"Walter, it's the only thing we can do. Don't you want to see her again? Didn't you promise her you would come back?"

He nodded, and the unshed tears finally slid down his wrinkled face. "I did."

I nodded and placed my hand on his shoulder. "Then let's do this, Walter. Let us re-establish The Silver Wing with Evelyn's help and change this world. That way you can be with Rudy, Evey, and the rest of your family. Luna can go on living, and I can bring Jane back to me."

He smiled. "Well...we all win that way."

I nodded.

He sighed. "It worries me, Clem."

"I know."

"All right," he muttered.

"Yes?"

He nodded. "Yes."

A huge grin spread across my face, and I lightly embraced him. When I pulled away, he was returning the smile.

"Yes!" he exclaimed louder. "Let's do it!"

Luna came in. "What's the shouting about?"

We both turned and smiled at her.

"Oh no." She cocked her head and crossed her arms. "What are you two brainiacs planning now?"

I wasn't sure exactly where to start. I had point A and point C—where we were and where we needed to be. How to get there was what we were missing.

"Where is she, Walter?" I asked.

He just turned to look at me. "I'm still scared, Clem," he whispered.

"It's just me, Walter. Okay? Nobody else is here."

"She's"—he swallowed and took a deep breath, breaking eye contact—"in... she's in Florida."

Florida? Why Florida?

"Okay, and are there others there as well?"

He nodded. "There is another establishment of the Silver Wing set up in Northern Florida."

"All right. Well, waiting isn't the plan here, Walter."

"I know."

"So let's get ourselves on a plane to Florida tonight."

"Tonight?"

"Yes, tonight."

"You will have to assume a different name, Clem."

"Yes, meaning stop calling me Clem," I answered, smiling.

He chuckled.

I took my wallet out of my back pocket and shuffled through a few credit cards.

"Ah," I said, "how about this one? I have the passport in my dresser drawer."

He took the card and stared at it.

"Are...you sure?"

"It doesn't matter. It's just a name, Walter, and it's not permanent."

"Okay. Then let's get going, Mr. Wright."

I smiled. "Ah, call me Morgan."

We laughed in unison, and Walter called Luna into the room to discuss our plans. She wasn't happy at first. Luna was always one to not trust anything.

"It's not reckless," I told her. "This is something we need to do."

"I don't know," she said. "It doesn't seem right. If we can hide, why don't we do just that?"

"Luna!" I cried, standing up and moving so I was only inches away from her face. "If that was a serious question, you aren't thinking," I said angrily. "Reason one, we can't hide forever. They *will* find us. Reason two, Evelyn. I'm not going to let Walter live out the rest of his days without the woman he loves. Reason three is Jane. I want her back, Luna, and the only way I even have a chance is to stop The Sevren. You also can use this as redemption. Help us so you can go on with your life, Luna—please."

She shook her head. "You really think they will find us?"

"Some of them already have, remember?"

"But Dorian and Mike are dead. They were the only ones who knew where we were."

I shook my head. "David."

She sighed. "Great!"

"So will you help us?"

She huffed and threw her arms up, turning away from me.

"Fine," she said. "But I don't like this plan."

"There's nothing else we can do."

"I know," she murmured. "You're right…as usual."

She left the room, and Walter's expression instantly transformed into worry.

"Don't stress it," I said. "It will all be all right. I promise."

I was never fond of flying. Something about it made me feel unwell in some way. Not to say I had a fear of it, only a dislike. Walter seemed highly entertained and insisted he sit next to the window. Luna sat behind me, murmuring her little remarks the way she usually did. I wasn't listening. I tried resting but was kept alert by all the thoughts of Jane and how all of this was going to help me get her back—if it was going to work at all.

I had several worries I didn't want to bring to Walter's attention. For one, suppose we could kill all the members of The Sevren. What about the ones like Dorian? The ones working behind the scenes, whose names we didn't know, whose faces we wouldn't recognize? What about *them*? I couldn't say anything to Walter because I knew he would never go through with it if he realized that. Would they disband? Or would they regroup? I sighed at these thoughts.

"Clem?"

I turned to Walter. "Peter?"

"Ah." He chuckled. "Morgan."

"Yes."

"Are you all right?"

I nodded. "Fine. Just thinking."

"About?"

I sighed. "Jane."

He looked at me, and his mouth curled up in a false, thin smile. "It's okay. Just focus on what we have to do. We can worry about her afterward."

"Logical thinking," I said. "Thanks."

"No sarcasm?"

A silent laugh shook through me. "No. No sarcasm."

He nodded and patted my shoulder, directing his gaze back out the window.

It was different than I had imagined in my head—the way she looked at him, the way he moved close without a hint of haste in his steps. It was different the way he spoke to her when they were close in a soft embrace. It was different than I had imagined in every way. Maybe Walter was just a bit old fashioned. Maybe it wasn't like him to rush to his love and pull her close into an intimate kiss. Maybe he had a sense of propriety that wouldn't allow that. I wouldn't have been bothered, and I doubt Luna would do anything but coo and get her big blue eyes all bubbly, but still—he held himself together perfectly.

I just stared, transfixed on the look on Evelyn's pretty, aged face. She had small, delicate features that made her look so innocent and fragile. I could see the love and joy in her eyes even though she remained calm. Her eyes were filled with unshed tears, and she just held Walter's face in her hands for what seemed like hours. It was as if she was savoring the vision, engraving it in her memory like she expected him to disappear.

It wasn't until I heard her voice that I realized what she must have been feeling.

"Oh, Walter," she whispered, still holding his face in her wrinkled hands. "What took you so long?" Her voice was sweet but had a slight sound of age in it.

He shed a few slow tears and placed his hand upon hers.

"I was afraid for you," he whispered. "Afraid that perhaps coming back to you would put you in danger."

"I've always been in danger," she answered. "That never stopped you before."

He smiled at her. "It will never stop me again."

I didn't want to interrupt their reunion, but this was not a situation where we had time to waste. I took a step forward.

"Wait," Luna whispered, grabbing ahold of my shirt.

I turned to look at her.

"Just wait."

Evelyn dropped Walter's face and moved away from him, toward me and Luna.

"Who are your lovely friends?"

"Morgan," I said, being sure not to let "Clem" or "Aidan" slip out.

Luna bowed her head. "Mona," she said.

I hadn't realized she had chosen a name yet. Mona—it suited her.

"Let's not drag this out," I said. "We're here for a reason."

Evelyn nodded. "Of course you are," she said sweetly. "What can I help you with?"

"We need The Silver Wing," I said.

She jolted her head toward Walter, and he nodded, moving to stand beside her.

"We have a problem," he said. "See...Clem—eh Morgan here has gotten involved with The Sevren in a way that is irreversible as it usually is. We need to finally put a stop to them."

"How?" she asked. "The Silver Wing has been inactive for years."

"I know," he answered, raising his hand. "That's why we need your help."

"You want me to gather the members?"

Walter nodded. "Yes."

Evelyn narrowed her eyes and locked her gaze onto mine then Luna's. We said nothing.

"This is going to start a battle, am I right?"

"Yes," I said.

She sighed. "I'm more than willing to help regroup The Silver Wing, but this means a lot of proper planning."

"We don't have time for that!" I retorted. "Just get them together and get them to North Bend."

"Mr. Morgan—"

"Just Morgan."

"Morgan," she corrected. "It isn't that easy."

"Why?" I snapped. "Why can't you just get them all to North Bend?"

"It will be chaotic."

"I don't care!" I said. "Really. We just need to intrude on a Sevren gathering."

"Are you crazy?" Luna cried. "Was this your plan from the start?"

I ignored her. "Draw out our weapons and fight them," I said. "To the death."

Luna's mouth dropped open. "Oh, James, I knew you were crazy, but this is going *way* too far!"

"Can't you people just stick to one name?" I yelled, ignoring the rest of what she had said. "It's Morgan. Get used to it."

"Fine," she snapped. "Morgan—you're an idiot!"

"Mona—you're irritating! If you don't want to help us, fine. Don't. But I refuse to stop fighting for Jane...and Walter too. Just look at him, Luna!" I pointed toward Walter without averting my gaze. "Don't you see what he can have? What we all can have if we win?"

"And if we don't win?"

"Then what do we lose?"

She sighed and looked at Walter. She took a deep breath, making eye contact with me again. Slowly, she nodded her head. "Okay," she whispered. Her voice grew louder. "But I still think you're completely crazy!"

I smiled. "I've heard it before."

"Evey?" Walter started. "Can you get the members together?"

She nodded. "We need Ian. We need him to play undercover one more time."

"You want him to call a Sevren meeting, yes?"

"Have him do whatever it takes to get all of them there at the same time."

Walter nodded obediently.

"Take a flight back to North Bend tonight. I will meet you there in a day's time from when you arrive."

"And we will fight then?" I asked.

Evey nodded. "And win."

I had to address my concerns. It wouldn't make sense to get through everything just to have it fall apart because of things I didn't mention.

"What about the others?"

"What do you mean?" Walter questioned.

"I mean…the others," I repeated. "Like Dorian. The ones who work behind the scenes as you put it."

He nodded. "Look…Morgan, when The Sevren are killed, at least a significant number, the rest will flee. If there is no order, then there is nothing to hold them together. The others will flounder and disappear. It won't matter once the leaders are gone and all of the ones who are radical followers. The others take their orders from the upper ranked members. They are the ones who need to be stopped. Once they are, The Sevren will no longer exist."

I nodded. "So…no need to worry?"

He shook his head. "No. No need to worry."

"Okay," Luna announced. "Let's get ourselves prepared."

Back in North Bend, there wasn't much we could do except think positively. Luna stayed locked in her room for hours, clunking and knocking around.

"What's going on in there?" Walter asked, chuckling as usual.

"Luna's fighting an invisible assailant," I teased.

Walter smiled. "It couldn't hurt to practice."

I shook my head. "No. I want to let myself defend as the attacks come. Things never work out as they do in your head. Using my imagination will cause me to imagine things differently and prepare myself for things that won't happen that way."

He nodded. "I understand. Get Luna to help you."

I laughed. "I want to be unscathed *before* I fight."

"Good point." He laughed back.

"I'll talk to her about some practice moves."

"Let me know if you need some more assistance."

I nodded. "Thanks."

Chapter Twenty-Seven

HER FIST CRASHED into my cheek, and I stumbled backward with a groan.

"God damn, Luna!" I yelled. "Didn't I ask you to *not* hit me?"

She laughed. "Sorry. You didn't block the attack. That was on you."

I growled. "You are angering sometimes."

She smiled. "Again?"

"I don't surrender," I said, falling back into my fighting stance.

Walter strutted into the room without knocking.

"You look very concentrated there, Clem," he said, moving my attention to him.

"Morgan."

"Right," he muttered. "Still getting used to it."

"What do you need?"

"Evelyn is here," he said. "She called Ian, and he's on his way. He needs some words with us."

"Ian doesn't trust me an ounce," I said.

Walter nodded. "I know. But he trusts me and Evey. It's all right."

I nodded. "Fine."

I continued taking Luna's blows to my face and stomach until I was able to figure her out a little better and ended up pinning her down a few times.

"Careful," she said as I straddled her, wrenching the fake dagger from her hand.

"I'm not actually going to hurt you," I said.

"Oh, but I want you to."

I instantly got off her. "Good God."

She started laughing as though it were the funniest thing she'd ever heard. "Hey, I'm sorry," she teased. "I'm not being serious. Well...not *entirely* anyway."

"It really isn't funny," I complained.

"If you saw your face, you might have thought it was."

I just shook my head. So typical of her.

Walter knocked on the door then. Perfect timing.

"Come on," he said. "We are having a meeting. We need to discuss how this is going to work."

I sat beside Luna on the couch, and Walter, Evelyn, and Ian stood in front of us. We all looked at each other, not sure where to begin.

"How will this go down?" I asked.

Ian looked at me and shook his head. "I'm not sure. That's why I thought it would be best to discuss it together."

Walter chimed in. "How many are there?"

"A lot," he answered. "Over twice our number."

He sighed loudly.

"We need guns," Ian announced.

"What?" Luna instantly stood to her feet, her blue eyes wide and furious.

"You heard me," Ian snapped. "We are outnumbered, Luna."

"I don't care!" she shouted. "There are enough of us to defeat them."

"No!" Ian answered. "There aren't. There are twenty of us at the most. The Sevren has called together at least fifty. We—need—guns."

"Then you can count me out!" she yelled. "I will not be part of your sickness!"

I wanted to respond, wanted to say something that would calm the tension, but nothing came to mind. I was interested in their debate, unsure of where I stood. I agreed with Luna, but Ian was right. We couldn't win with our strength alone, could we? But guns? I never believed in guns—even before The Sevren, before I was James West. I hated them. I tried to say something, but Luna and Ian were still shouting at each other.

"Hey," I called.

Neither of them heard me.

"HEY!"

Luna turned.

"What, Jame—Morgan?"

"Just relax," I said. "I hate guns just as much as you do. There has to be *something* we can do, some type of compromise."

"There is *no* compromise," she growled. "I refuse to touch a gun unless I have no other choice."

"Ian...is there anything else we can do?"

He shook his head. "I really don't think so."

"Nothing?"

He shook his head again. "No other choice."

Luna just shook her head. "You have talked me into too much already. Guns are not our way."

"Luna, we have no other choice."

"I'm sorry," she said. "I won't be a part of it."

I sighed and stood to my feet. "You have to help us. We can't do this without you."

She shook her head. "No. I won't give in to you this time."

She stormed off to her room, and I heard the click of the lock. Great. She wasn't budging.

Walter sighed. "What do we do now?"

"We don't have a choice," Ian said. "We have to fight without her."

I flopped back on the couch.

"Maybe I can talk to her," Evey said softly.

I shook my head. "She's stubborn."

She smiled. "So am I."

Walter chuckled. "That's the damn truth if there is one."

"Be nice," she teased.

"I'm always nice," he answered back, giving her a quick peck on the cheek.

She smiled and headed toward Luna's door. I ignored her pleads for Luna to let her in and turned my attention back to Walter and Ian.

"When will this happen?" I asked.

"Soon," Ian answered.

Walter let out a sharp sound, expressing his nervousness.

"We are all in this together," Ian continued. "We all need to stay *loyal* to each other." He shifted his eyes to me.

That was it for me. "What do you have against me, Ian?" I demanded.

"I have something against The Sevren," he retorted.

"As do I," I said, standing up again. "Why the hell do you think I'm here? Why do you think I have spent all this time protecting Jane?"

"This isn't the right time to argue this," he said.

"No," I answered. "I think it's the perfect time."

"Morgan," Walter whispered, "please. Not now."

I huffed and sat back down. "Just so you know...I am doing this for Jane... and I don't like you."

Ian nodded. "That's fine."

Chapter Twenty-Eight

THE BATTLE CAME SWIFTLY, sooner than any of us had anticipated. I stood frozen stiff with Walter and Ian at my side. Evelyn stood behind us. She seemed fragile to us, and Walter felt a need to protect her. Fortunately, I knew she was stronger than we were willing to credit her for.

I felt my insides slightly trembling and that familiar burn and yanking on my nerves and a wrenching feeling on the muscles in my chest. Danger was approaching. That was obvious, and I didn't need my annoying radar to be screaming at me right now. I needed to stay focused.

The Sevren were cloaked and hooded in black and dark blue. They didn't even appear human. It was strange not to see Abraham in front of the crowd like I normally would have, and I almost shivered at the memory of killing him. They didn't even seem to notice us yet. My body began to shake, knowing at any moment they would turn around and see us. My knife was already bared, and a gun hid in the waistband of my pants. I shuddered at the thought of using it. Ian had only his muffled pistol raised. I hated him for it.

Going on training alone, I inhaled, telling myself to stay calm. I saw a Sevren member turn around. I remembered him. Dillon—one of Abraham's favorites. He was holding a silver goblet in his hand. My mind began screeching in disgust. I remembered when I had held that same goblet in my hands. I cringed at the memory. I felt Walter touch my shoulder, and I realized I was gnashing my teeth together, practically growling at Dillon like a beast. I inhaled again, trying to regain my control, trying to ignore the blood-filled goblet. The

Sevren stood silent, all of them staring at us. It felt like hours before the maddening stillness was finally broken. Dillon laughed.

"Hand him over," he said, his voice almost sounding feminine in my mind. "No need for a fight. Just hand him over, and we will pretend we never saw you."

"We brought nobody for you," Walter said.

Dillon glared at him. "He's the only one we want," he said with obvious stress in his voice.

"I'm sure he is," Walter answered. "We didn't bring him for you."

Dillon growled, but his words were stolen when the sound of footsteps approached. I tried with every ounce of strength I had to contain the smile spreading its way across my face. They were here. Women and men alike flooded the clearing, surrounding The Sevren with knives and guns bared strong.

"What the hell is going on?" Dillon spat, dropping the goblet, splashing blood onto his cloak.

"Do you need to ask?" I taunted.

"You!" he snarled, stepping closer to me, pointing a bloody finger at my chest. "This is *all* you."

I smiled. "You give me too much credit. But thanks—I'll accept it."

A growl erupted from him, and he pulled out a bone knife still dripping with blood. The others followed, and before I knew it, I was surrounded by a blur of movement. Screams of anger and battle cries filled my ears. It was surreal. I kept myself focused on my knife and Dillon's knife—nothing else.

My anger was boiling, and I instinctively thrust my knife toward him. He simply moved aside, slashing the blade across my torso. That was a mistake on my part. I got ahold of my anger and regulated my breathing. There was no pain yet, but I was certain it was a deep cut—at least four centimeters in length, right between my lower ribs.

He advanced again, coming toward my chest. Relying again on my training, I twisted my wrist and deflected his blade the crucial inch that may very well have saved my life. I swiveled around to his other side and in a series of quick movements, grabbed him by the waist and shoved him face-first into a tree. He groaned and toppled over unconscious. I couldn't take any chances and plunged my blade deep into his chest. I moved away from him, and my eyes flickered to Evelyn moving like a machine, dropping enemies flat in seconds. She was shockingly competent with a blade.

I brought my attention back to the enemy, watching them struggle with the heavy, loose-fitting cloaks obstructing their maneuvers. I caught sight of Walter on the ground, struggling ineffectively to fight off an enemy who was looming over his body. I hurled myself toward them, grabbing the monster by his hair, wrenching his head back and driving my blade across his throat. He crumpled in a heap over Walter's body. I rolled the Sevren member off him, and Walter instantly stood to his feet without help even when I offered him my hand. He nodded at me in thanks and turned away, instantly falling back into his fighting stance, now completely covered in Sevren blood. It even clung to his hair, but he wasn't fazed by it. His mind was focused.

A sharp pain suddenly pierced my back, and I found myself on my knees, groaning in agony. A man quickly approached me, knocking my enemy away and offering me his hand. He was clearly a loyal member of The Silver Wing, judging by the feather tattoo on his bare, upper chest. I took his hand and stumbled to my feet. The shallow stab wound in my back screamed at me. I could feel my heartbeat in my ears.

"I'm all right," I tried to say. I reached out to him again…or I tried to. He caught me as I fell into his chest.

"I'll get you out of here!" he said.

"No!" I protested. "No, I'm all right."

"Are you—?"

I raised my hand. "I'm fine. Go."

He nodded and returned to the battle.

I pushed aside the pain and continued fighting with all the strength I had left. Everything was still a blur. The muffled gunfire and cries were all like something from a nightmare. Another came at me with two knives in hand. My arms were straining to hold off his attacks. My wounds began to throb as I moved, and I could feel the wetness of blood running down the lengths of my limbs. I rammed by knee into his stomach and backed away, drawing out the gun. I shut my eyes and squeezed the trigger. I heard a cry of rage as I shot, but it wasn't from my enemy. It was a female voice. My eyes darted open to see Luna straddling my enemy, pulling her blade from his chest. My eyes grew wide.

"I couldn't let you damage your honor," she said.

I smiled instantly. Somehow I knew she would be there.

"Nice shot." She sounded like she was teasing.

I laughed when I saw the bullet lodged in the tree in front of me.

"I knew you'd come," I said.

"Morgan!" she bellowed.

I spun around and deflected the blade of a young Sevren member and killed him instantly with a jab to his chest.

She smiled at me and nodded in relief.

The moment faded as our minds focused once again on the fight before us. Luna was a mass of hate and rage as she attacked ruthlessly, clawing, biting, scratching, combined successfully with her ability with a long dagger with two serrated edges.

I pulled my attention away from her and back toward another cloaked enemy. He rushed toward me with a huge knife. I heard a muffled gunshot, and the man fell inches from my feet.

"You can thank me for that one later," I heard Ian say.

"I had him!" I spat.

"Sure, sure."

He raced past me, still using that vile gun. I took the knife from the dead Sevren, but it was almost impossible to wield two of different weights. I cast mine behind me and held confidently the longer, serrated blade of the Sevren member.

My rage finally exploded, and my vision went red. I leapt and scrambled, disabling and killing all in my path, feeling the jarring impacts into my back and sides as I fought them off. I realized the trees made great weapons as I smashed my enemies straight into the thick, moss-covered trunks.

I rushed toward another, and my heart began to pound in my chest when I saw him retreating. Fleeing was unheard of for a Sevren. I instantly hurried after him as fast as I could, falling into the deeper woods. I fought mercilessly, moving my blade in quick, blinding movements. I watched my enemy fumbling with his cloak. I rushed around him, waiting for him to turn toward me just to be blinded by the sun. He squinted just long enough for me to advance. I shoved him into a tree and slit open his throat. The blood leaked out like a busted water pipe. I took pleasure in the sight, knowing he got what he deserved.

A familiar name pulled me out of my trance, and suddenly I felt the pain— massive amounts of it all over my body.

"Morgan?" The voices were ghostly in my head as my hearing faded.

I fell to my knees, feeling the cushion of grass. My name echoed in my ears one last time before my eyes went dark.

Chapter Twenty-Nine

I TRIED TO SPEAK, but I couldn't find my voice. I had no idea where I was. My eyes felt like they were glued shut. I tried to pry them open, but they just fluttered closed again before I could focus on anything. I groaned and heard a quiet response.

"Shh."

I tried again to speak and felt the coolness of a wet towel on my forehead.

"You don't need to move." It was Luna's voice. Tending to me like always. "Stay still, love. You've been through quite a bit."

"How"—my voice broke—"long have I been asleep?" I choked out.

"Shh," she answered. "A few days."

Days? Oh my God. What happened? If I could have spoken, I would have been shouting.

"The..." My voice faded again. "The...Sevren?"

"Are dead," Luna answered. "The Sevren are gone, love. We did it."

I tried to smile but wasn't sure if I did.

"How is he?" I heard Walter ask.

"Awake," Luna said. "But weak."

"You gave us quite a scare," he said, his voice closer. "We thought we lost you."

I felt myself smile. "Can't get rid of me that easily," I choked out.

He chuckled as usual. "Luna's making you some lunch. We have you hooked up to an IV, courtesy of Ian, but you should still eat something as soon as you can."

I tried to nod. Food sounded amazing. I pulled the towel off my forehead, feeling cool droplets running down my cheeks.

"I'm not a child," I said. "I'm fine."

Walter just smiled at me.

I was able to open my eyes and sit up enough to eat by the time Luna came back with a tray.

"Thank you," I said, still weak.

"How do you feel?"

I shook my head. "I don't know. Nothing really hurts." I could see I was practically covered in bandages.

"That could be the morphine." She laughed. "You may feel the pain soon."

I nodded. "I'm all right with that. I don't want to be sedated. I have things to do."

"Morgan!"

"You called me Morgan," I said with a struggled laugh.

"Yes," she answered. "There is nothing you need to do except rest."

I shook my head. "I need to get to Jane."

"Why?"

"The radicals."

"Morgan, I told you. The Sevren—"

"I know what you told me," I interrupted. "That doesn't mean there aren't still others that will try at least for a while to reestablish The Sevren. I need to keep Jane safe a while longer."

She sighed.

"Can't you and Walter just take care of the followers while I stay near Jane? That way I can make sure nobody finds her until they are dead."

"You...you don't need to."

"Yes, I do, Luna."

"No," she answered calmly. "I mean...you don't *need* to. We sent Ian."

"What?" I sat up the rest of the way.

"Ian will be near Jane soon, pretending he barely knows me or Walter."

"Jane doesn't need to be lied to. Ian should tell her he knows Walter."

"It's easier if she doesn't know. She doesn't need to feel like she's part of this war."

"But she is," I answered. "And don't think I won't still go after her."

"Morgan, Ian is keeping her safe. You can help us kill the few radicals left, and then you can return to her."

I shook my head. "Fine. But I don't trust Ian to fight like I can. I want to stay close."

She nodded. "All right, but keep your distance. Ian doesn't trust you."

"Still?"

"Still."

I sighed. "Figures."

It didn't make sense that they would send Ian to take Jane somewhere safe. They knew I had made it my job to protect her. I suppose if Ian got killed by The Sevren, Luna wouldn't weep the way she would over losing me. Walter too. I resented Ian for the way he felt the need to protect Jane from me. *Me*, who had done *everything* to keep harm as far from her as possible. He was the one who almost got her killed by Dorian. Who was she going to trust? Of course—him. She would trust *him*.

I couldn't stand staying in North Bend, killing off radicals with Walter and Luna. I knew there were others near Jane. I knew she was being followed. Those were the ones who needed to be stopped at all costs. Ian wasn't clever enough to even know they were being tailed, and Jane was too naïve to realize much of anything pertaining to The Sevren. It was all up to me now as usual.

Chapter Thirty

LUNA DIDN'T EVEN BOTHER to stop me when I got my things together and headed out to California to stay near Jane—and Ian. I knew it was impossible for The Sevren to regroup. We killed almost all of them. A few disbanded, including Alex, I assume, but they weren't my concern. All of the upper ranked members were gone. The few loyal followers left were the only ones to deal with, and some of them were tailing Jane. It didn't take long for me to pinpoint each and every one of them driving down the roads of California. I simply followed behind, sure that they would lead me to Jane. There were at least seven of them. All of them were members I had recognized—men I had seen in the time I had been a member. They could have hidden from Ian—not from me. I knew all of them, not by name, but I never forget a face.

I followed them and noticed they stopped in front of a motel. *Really, Ian? A cheap motel?* I'm sure Jane was just *loving* that. I contained actual laughter, thinking about how she was handling that. Probably driving him crazy. It was one of the things I actually loved about her. She let you know when she wasn't all right with something.

I parked around the back of the hotel, away from the trackers. I had little conception of how long it had been since I last saw Jane. It seemed like years. Three months, maybe four? Finding their room was going to be the hard part. I knocked on every door on the lower floor. Most of them looked at me like I was out of my mind. I wondered for a while if Jane was even there or if The Sevren were just waiting here for some other reason. It was hard to tell with them sometimes.

I climbed the stairs on the upper floor and knocked on about three doors before coming to room 242. When I knocked, I instantly heard Ian's voice, and I felt my breath explode. *Finally!*

"Jane, have you told anyone where we are?"

I couldn't hear Jane's response.

"Then...explain *this*."

He opened the door, and I saw her there with a shocked expression on her face. I had forgotten how beautiful she was. I made eye contact and smiled, waiting for her to say something—anything. She stared back open mouthed. Her eyes bulged, and she fell unconscious at Ian's feet. I sighed. Great. Not exactly the reaction I was hoping for from the woman I loved. How could she really be *that* surprised to see me? She knew me well enough to know that *nothing* would make me give up on her.

"What the hell are you doing here?" Ian demanded.

"Would you like me to leave?" I answered. "Or would you rather live?"

He huffed. "God," he mumbled. His voice rose to a yell. "Look what you've done." He pointed to Jane.

I just smiled.

He picked her up and set her on the bed, whispering her name. It took a few minutes before she opened her eyes.

"Jane?" I whispered.

She put her hand on her forehead and inhaled softly. I sat beside her on the bed.

"Jane, I'm here to help," I said.

Her eyes didn't hold that look of hatred and revulsion I had seen before but instead a look of confusion. She wouldn't look at me.

"Aidan?" she tried to say, but it was hardly a sound at all.

"Yes?"

She just shook her head.

"I'm here to help," I said again.

"Couldn't you have sent someone?" Ian asked.

I broke my attention from Jane.

"You know me." I laughed. "I had to do this myself." I didn't trust anybody else to protect Jane.

"How did you find us?" he asked.

"I followed the man who is tracking you."

"Tracking us?" Jane cried. Her voice was finally strong and terrified.

I nodded. "That's why I'm here."

Her lips curled up in a look of anger, and she almost seemed to be growling at me.

"Please," I said. "I know that look all too well."

"Goddamn wonderful," she muttered.

I sighed and stood up, turning toward Ian.

"We—well...*you* anyway—need to leave."

"Well, if they are tracking us, they'll just follow," he answered.

I nodded. "Of course they will. Do you know how to fight?"

I had to ask him this to make sure Jane didn't know about the battle we were involved in like Walter asked.

Ian nodded. "I can take care of myself for the most part."

"But...what about her?" I asked.

He sighed, and a look of irritation masked his features.

"You can't tell me you didn't know this could happen," I demanded.

He shook his head. "I did know it was a possibility. How many?"

I sighed. "Well, I didn't get that past you." I chuckled.

Ian nodded. "If there were only one, I would believe you'd take care of it."

"I would have, yes. Dorian and Abraham are both dead, which puts my mind at ease, but the radical followers are trying to regroup, which is why Walter and the others are regrouping as well. For now, we have a few more to take care of."

I turned to Jane and saw she looked pale—more than usual.

"Are you all right?" I asked. I didn't want her fainting again.

She still didn't look at me.

"Here," Ian said.

He handed her a bottle of water from the tiny fridge in the corner of the room.

"Thanks," she whispered.

"I'm sorry," I said.

I sat back down beside Jane and placed my hand over hers. I felt electric shocks through my limbs just from being able to touch her again. I felt her muscles tighten, and I moved my hand away.

"I didn't mean to barge in on you like this," I said. My words were cut off when I noticed Ian and Jane ignoring my gaze and looking at each other. Damn it! Had he taken her from me? Of all people, it had to be Ian? What had he told her to turn her against me? He was worse than Rudy.

"Wait," I started. "Are you...?"

I moved my eyes back to Jane.

She gave me a puzzled look.

I looked at Ian again then back at her.

"You're... Are you and Jane...?"

"Oh!" Ian cried. "No, no. It isn't... Jane and I aren't..."

She laughed. "Ian was sent to protect me."

I know that!

"It isn't like that."

I nodded and stuttered an uncertain "okay."

She shook her head, still smiling.

"I'm sorry," I said. "It isn't really my business."

Though I'm more than prepared to make it my business if I must!

"So what do we do?" Jane asked, changing the subject.

"I have some things I need to see to," I said. "People I need some words with."

"When will you be back?" Ian asked. He sounded very calm, yet I could see the obvious distrust he was expressing.

"Soon," I answered. "Today."

"Well, here," Ian started, handing me the room key. "Take this."

I nodded. "Thanks."

I put the key card in my pocket and walked back to the car to call Walter with Abraham's stolen cell phone.

"Morgan?"

"Yeah, it's me."

"Where are you? Did you find them?"

"Yes," I answered. "Easy as pie."

"What's going on?"

"Well, I was right. They were being tailed. I followed The Sevren members, and they led me right to her."

"And Ian?"

"Yes. Ian too."

"So they're all right?"

"Yes. They're fine."

I heard him exhale softly. "All right."

"I promised I'd call, so I am calling. Is there anything else you need me to do?"

"No," he said. "Just go back there and tell Ian what's going on."

"Did that."

"Oh...all right. Well, the rest is up to you. I'm sure you realize running wouldn't make sense. You need to fight them."

Of course!

"Meanwhile, Luna and I will be killing off the other radicals. Sound good?"

"Sounds great," I said. "I'll call later."

"Sure."

I closed the phone and headed back to room 242.

I used the key to open the door and saw Ian moving away from Jane who was lying on the bed. My heart stopped for a moment. Of course. I should have expected it. They didn't even wait twenty minutes before attacking each other. Nice. I tried to push aside the sting of pain and jealousy, but that only brought out anger. It took everything in me not to shove Ian against the wall and scream at him.

You bastard! How could you? After almost getting her killed, you take the liberty of stealing her from me on top of that?

I wanted to tear him apart, but he spoke and broke my focus.

"Um, you're back," he said. He cleared his throat. "Did...did you take care of what you needed?"

Jane sat up and looked away.

"Uh...yeah," I answered. "Yeah, it's taken care of."

"What did you find out?"

"That leaving wouldn't be the best idea," I answered. "That staying here and fighting would be better."

"Fighting?" Jane yelled.

I wasn't in the mood to deal with her. "Yes, Jane, fighting." Even I could hear the irritation in my voice.

Wow, she really got over me easily. I shouldn't have been surprised, but it made me sick to think of somebody else touching her. I tried again to push it aside.

"What—?" Jane started.

"Jane, don't worry about it," I interrupted.

"I hate when you say that," she murmured.

She drew her knees up to her chest.

"Aidan and I will take care of it," Ian started. "You don't need to worry about a thing."

Yeah, Ian, comfort your girlfriend. Good for you.

"You can't leave," she yelled.

She sprang to her feet and nearly clung to Ian.

"He's not," I hissed. "I am."

Chapter Thirty-One

I KNEW I didn't need Ian's help to kill the men after all. I wanted him to help, but I wasn't in the mood to argue with Jane. I walked right up to the black car in front of the motel and tapped on the glass. The driver rolled down the window.

"What the hell...?" He broke off, and a smile spread across his coarse-looking face. "James?"

I nodded.

"What do *you* want?"

I narrowed my eyes. "You know what I want."

"Are you here to help?" he asked. "Or to fight?"

"I'm here to help," I lied. "Meet me back in North Bend. I will bring the Callahan girl with me."

"How can I trust you after your betrayal?" he spat.

I laughed synthetically. "Betrayal? Oh, you have it all wrong. That was an act. I was undercover, gaining information on The Silver Wing."

"And what about the girl?"

"I made her love me," I said. "It will make the kill so much sweeter."

I shuddered and internally cringed at what I was forced to say.

"Didn't you kill Abraham?" he asked.

"Of course not!" I lied. "Stop listening to rumors. Meet me in North Bend."

He nodded. "I'll be there."

Oh, I am sure you will. I'll let Walter take care of you when you get there.

It was so easy to gain his trust. What an idiot!

I called Walter and let him know what was going on.

"He and the others should be there by mid-day tomorrow."

"All right," he said. "We'll be waiting. Thanks, Morgan."

"No," I said. "Thank *you*—for everything!"

Three Months Later

Chapter Thirty-Two

WALTER AND LUNA had sent Jane to a small town in Florida, still unsure all The Sevren were destroyed. I felt it was time to bring myself back to her if ever I wanted her to look at me the way she used to. North Bend was safe if she wanted to come back. She would want to come back, right? All of her friends were there and Ethan—and me. I was the reason she left. I was hoping to be the reason she came back.

I went to her as I was so used to doing, watching her walking through the grocery store, occasionally glancing at a shopping list. She came to the shampoo aisle and glanced at the list again. My memory flashed with the first day I met her at the bookstore. She stood on the lower shelf and reached for the bottle. I watched as she stumbled off the shelf, bringing the entire thing with her.

I rushed over to her as fast as I could and tilted the shelf upright, handing her the purple bottle she was reaching for. She lowered her arms from in front of her face and stared at me for a moment.

I smiled, unable to stop myself. "Hi," I said, lending out my hand. "I'm Morgan Wright."

It was silent for a long time. She didn't even shake my hand. She just stared at me like I was a ghost.

"Aidan?" she whispered.

I dropped my hand, smiling. "You say that like you're unsure."

233

"What are you doing here?"

"I'm here for you. I told you I would come back to you when it was safe. I meant it."

She shook her head. "After everything you have done, Aidan, how can I still let myself love you?"

"Because I saved your life," I said harshly.

"You..." Her voice faded to an even quieter whisper, trying to avoid the spying eyes of the customers in the store. "You killed Danny."

"In an act of mercy, Jane."

She was silent for a moment. "Is that true?"

"Of course it's true."

"Why should I believe you?" she asked. "Please give me a reason, Aidan."

"Because I no longer have any reason to lie to you," I said. "You know everything. You can confirm the entire event with Luna if you wish. She was there."

Jane nodded. "Mercy?"

"Yes."

"I don't need to hear about it from Luna. I don't want to hear about it at all. But I want to believe you, Aidan...so badly."

I took her hand. "Then believe me. It's the truth, Jane. You know who I am. I do not like to hurt anybody."

That was true, wasn't it?

"Except maybe Rudy."

She tried to laugh. "I need some time."

"I know. I am willing to give you that. Are you ever planning on coming back to North Bend?"

"Is it safe?"

I put my hand up. "Completely. I promised you I would make you safe."

She smiled. "Then I assume I would eventually."

I smiled.

"But don't get your hopes up too high, Mr....Wright."

I chuckled. "Understood."

"By the way," she started before walking away. "A few months ago...in California..."

"Yes?"

"You have it all wrong. Ian and I were never like that. It was one time, Aidan, and it was only a kiss."

If you call THAT a kiss.

I nodded, realizing there was no need to argue.

Epilogue

IN JANE CALLAHAN'S Point of View

I always wondered what he would do when he was done being Aidan Summers, who he would become, where he would go. It didn't seem to matter.

The Sevren were dead, and Aidan was alive. *I* was alive. My friends and family were safe, and all of North Bend was safe again. Rudy had his grandparents. Everything worked out. It was always right at times when things seemed perfect that things got messed up. I wasn't sure how it was all going to play out for me. I knew I would return to North Bend someday; I just wasn't sure when. I was weighing the pros and cons for days. I would return either when Aidan would no longer be there or when I was able to let myself love him again. There could be no in between for us.

I wanted to believe what he told me was true, but after so many lies, I couldn't be sure. He killed Danny out of mercy. If that was true, then in some twisted way, he had saved him. It hurt to think about it, to think about Danny's death in a play by play like a horror movie in my head. If I wanted to free myself from the pain, the easiest thing to do would be to believe Aidan, but I had to do what was *right,* not what was easy.

Aidan had been my guardian angel and my sun on the darkest, coldest days of my life. He was my hero, my love, and my enemy all at the same time. I would never have that kind of connection with anyone again. We shared something that only comes around once in a lifetime. I would *always* love him. I knew that. We had something amazing, and then it was over. Maybe it was best to just leave it that way. Maybe it was best to just let all of it go and go on living my life with the other people I loved.

It physically stung to think about leaving Aidan and never seeing him again. At the same time, it sounded so easy in my head. It sounded sweet, like a simple small-town life with my friends, strolling down the aisles of the mall with shopping bags full of clothes I would never wear and laughing at ridiculous things while Becky snapped pictures. All of it without Aidan. Would I really feel as happy as I did in my mind?

I turned to look at Aidan, who was still sitting beside me on the couch in my mother's front room.

"What are you going to do, Jane?" he asked.

I shook my head. "I don't know."

"We should go somewhere."

I smiled. "What?"

"For coffee," he said.

"Are you being serious?"

"I am."

"Why?"

"To hang out," he answered, still with a smile behind his words. "To just be together as friends so I can show you how easy it is to be with me."

I shook my head. "I don't know, Aidan."

"Please."

He had this sad look on his face that was so unfair. He knew I couldn't say no when he looked at me that way.

I nodded, and a huge smile spread across his face.

"I need to take a shower," I told him. "I'll be quick."

"Take your time."

I stepped into the bathroom, admiring the space I didn't have at Ethan's. I turned on the water, just letting it get to the right temperature. I stared at my face in the mirror, trying to figure out who I was to Aidan Summers. How could he love me so completely? Just then, he came storming into the bathroom without so much as a knock.

"Aidan, what are—?"

My question was cut short by a hard, passionate kiss. He pulled me into the shower, still in our clothes. The feeling of his arms around me was like something from a dream. I wasn't sure at first if any of it was real. I returned his touch, and the sopping wet fabric sticking to his body was driving me near mad. I pulled his shirt over his head, and I heard him shudder. I dropped the garment on the floor of the shower and stared at his perfect body—the thin lines of muscle in his stomach and the beautiful build of his chest. I couldn't keep myself from touching him. I ran my fingers across his shimmering skin, and he closed his eyes. He whispered something, but I was unsure what he had said.

"Stop."

"Stop?"

"That isn't nice of you, Jane."

I was trying to think of something to say, but it was too late. His lips found mine again, and he began kissing me almost violently. Before I knew it, we were standing in the shower, wrapped in each other's arms. He pushed me against the tiled wall, and I let out a quiet gasp. His hands touched every part of my body. I had never felt anything like I felt when I was close to him. I stared at his tawny skin as the water slid down between his muscles. The droplets almost made it look like he was sparkling. The water dripped slowly from his dark eyelashes, and I could only imagine what I looked like to him. I hoped I was beautiful to him. I hoped I was making him feel as I was feeling. My entire body was burning for him.

His skin was like satin. I knew his body as if it were my own, as if every movement he made I was making. I knew every inch of his skin against mine—his perfect skin. I felt as if the weight of his body above my own could break me into several pieces, but it didn't matter; I would die in his arms.

Our bodies moved together in a way I had never experienced, in a way I had never even dreamed. His skin, his heat, his beauty, and his love all wrapped into one ball of illumination completely consuming me. I couldn't keep that inside, and I heard myself quietly moan before I could stop it. I wanted him now and forever, only him. And for these moments, close to him when I could feel his love, I had him. I only wondered then how long it would last.

Books in the Hunters Trilogy
Summers' Deceit
Summers' Shadow
Summers' Redemption

Acknowledgments

All of my thanks and appreciation go to my husband, the first person to read this book and my biggest fan. Thank you for always believing in me.

And for Annie-Belle, my Becky. Thank you for all the hours of critique and advice, helping make this book what it is today.

My editor, Kathy Moczerniak, for all her hard work and suggestions that made this as good as it could be. You are truly amazing.

Special thanks to my family who always supported my passion and encouraged me to follow my dreams.

Thank you to all my readers and fans. You help keep me inspired and motivated. I hope reading this brings you as much joy as it brought me writing it.

About the Author

Sara J Bernhardt is an author and poet who has been writing since a very young age and is a winner of several poetry and short story contests. She lives in Southern California with her husband and cat. It is clear that Bernhardt writes in a realistic tone while still creating the enthralling feeling of fantasy. Her writing puts readers in a world that they will truly love to be a part of.

You can follow Sara at these locations:

Facebook: www.facebook.com/Sara-J-Bernhardt
Amazon: www.amazon.com/Sara-J.-Bernhardt
Website: www.sjbernhardt.com

Also by SARA J. BERNHARDT

https://www.amazon.com/Sara-J.-Bernhardt/e/B07DNFCH5J/

Summer's Deceit (Hunters Trilogy – Book 1): Jane Callahan is a reclusive, seventeen-year-old high school student dealing with the death of her beloved brother. Her home in Southern California with her mother is a constant reminder of her loss and pain. In hopes of escaping her past she moves to North Bend Oregon to live with her father, where she meets a beautiful boy named Aidan Summers. Jane is intrigued by his looks as well as his unusual ways of attempting to get her attention. After months of uncommon conversation and frustration, an uncertain romance brews between Jane and Aidan, but Aidan has a ghastly secret that could destroy everything.

Summer's Shadow (Hunters Trilogy – Book 2): Aidan Summers, a seventeen-year-old, stunningly beautiful genius, somehow finds his way into the life of Jane Callahan; a lovely girl trapped in soggy North Bend, Oregon. In this new Tale by Sara J. Bernhardt, Aidan relates his side of the story. All of his dark secrets are revealed and all of his motivations behind his strange ways become known as the story unravels in a captivating narrative of suspense, romance, courage...and murder.

Summer's Redemption (Hunters Trilogy – Book 3): The secret alliance of The Silver Wing and the waging war with their evil rival, The Sevren, come into full view in a new light. The evil that still lurks and stirs behind the supposed destruction of The Sevren steps out of the shadows and spins a new tale of adventure, suspense, romance, mystery and terror.

Behind Blue Eyes Series

A father's desire to save his child presents him with an unthinkable choice that leaves him darker than human, forced to roam through time alone as he searches for the place he belongs.

Adam Gold – Book 1: Fleeing the French invasion of Geneva Switzerland in the 1700s, Adam Gold books passage to America with his family. On the ship, Adam's daughter falls fatally ill. A mysterious man comes to Adam with a way to save his child by turning Adam into something darker than human.

The Medallion – Book 2: Adam Gold, an immortal with sweet eyes of blue, rushes through the centuries on a quest for reason and a thirst for revenge. To cope with his pain and regret, he sleeps away the years and awakes in a new era with a powerful, ancient vampire who sets her sights on him.

Golden Shackles – Book 3: When the ancient queen, Sekhmet snatches up Adam, he is faced with a terrifying decision. To help aid her in her vile plans or dare to stand against her.

Plus 3 more segments!

In Gray

After a near fatal car crash brings Daisy Carmichael the ability to see the future, she is plagued by not only the things she sees, but the deadly secrets of the boy who saved her life.

Also From the Lavish Family

Rosinanti Series
Kevin J. Kessler
http://myBook.to/RosinantiSeries

The Rosinanti Dragons are no more. Since their extinction nearly one thousand years ago these primal powerhouses have fallen into the obscurity of history's forgotten lore. In that time, humans have come to dominate the world of Terra, peacefully ignorant to one horrifying truth: ancient evil stirs around them, waiting to reclaim its lost world.

For Valentean Burai, animus warrior of the kingdom of Kackritta, the details surrounding humanity's victory over the Rosinanti are more than just a history lesson. The long-buried mysteries of this archaic conflict may hold the answers that he has so desperately sought regarding his own past.

As the awful truth of the Rosinanti's supposed demise comes to light, Valentean must stand together with Seraphina, a magically gifted princess, to embark upon a mission to maintain order and light throughout Terra. Only together can these two lifelong friends face down the resurgence of the Rosinanti legacy and combat the greatest threat their world has ever known.

Unexpected Magic Series
Samantha Jacobey
http://myBook.to/UnexpectedMagic

In this series of standalone thrillers, unwitting witches tumble into the dark world of the craft…

The Binding- book 1: One cursed diary will change two strangers forever…

Merideth Monroe was born to a wealthy politician; luxury was her middle name. The happiest childhood, the finest schools, and landing her dream career; her future couldn't have been brighter. She didn't care that her mother wanted a different path for her; but when her mother is murdered and she appears to be next, nothing in her flawless life will matter.

Rider Bradshaw lived a carefree existence. Ex-military, he only wanted out of his family's shaded history and chose to leave the sins of their past behind. However, when a girl he's never heard of is placed in his charge by his father, protecting her becomes his obsession and keeping her safe his only reality.

Can Meri and Rider use her mother's old book to figure out why someone is after them? Or will the guilty party succeed, ripping the tome away before killing them and then slithering back into the darkness…

The Wicked Awakened – book 2: A five-hundred-year-old witch wants to steal Sarah's body

Morcant and Blake Korrigan own a little shop of horrors, where witches congregate and people ending up dead isn't rare. When Karen Hiltzman joins their coven, she has no idea what she's getting into. Drawn in, the group convinces her to recruit her best friend, Sarah Matthews, after discovering that she bears a very special birthmark; one that indicates she's the girl they've been waiting for.

Morcant is eager to reincarnate a witch put to death by an angry mob five-hundred-years prior, and unleashes a spell; a dark and sinister curse. His ritual transforms Sarah's body and will bring Brenna back to life when it's completed.

Blake wants to help Sarah stop him; but will he be strong enough to defeat his elder sibling, and if he does… will he let her go when it's done?

(MA - 18+: contains violence, sexual content, and strong language)